AF579964

WITHDRAWN

I've travelled the world twice over,
Met the famous: saints and sinners,
Poets and artists, kings and queens,
Old stars and hopeful beginners,
I've been where no-one's been before,
Learned secrets from writers and cooks
All with one library ticket
To the wonderful world of books

ENCOUNTER AT DAWN

Lisa Lombard goes down to a deserted beach for an early morning swim and arrives just in time to see a man commit cold-blooded murder. When the man sees her and realises that she has witnessed everything, it becomes a race against time between him and the dedicated police officer Lieutenant Karel Meyer. The Lieutenant, fully aware of the danger to Lisa, finds himself up against a blank wall in a search for clues to identify a victim who has vanished without trace.

Books by Mary Muller in the Ulverscroft Large Print Series:

FLAGDOWN
TREE IN THE WIND
CLOUD ACROSS THE MOON
ENCOUNTER AT DAWN

Dedicated
to
My friends
who held out a helping hand

AUTHOR'S NOTE

All the characters in this novel
are entirely fictitious.

MARY MULLER

Greystones,
Constantia,
Cape Peninsula

1

SOMETHING made her glance at the petrol gauge as the mini crested the hill, and her heart fluttered uncomfortably when she registered that the tank was nearly empty.

What a *fool*! She should have known that the drive last night would have used up most of the fuel. If only she had thought to check before leaving the hotel. But there was no use getting into a tizzy about it now. She shrugged somewhat grimly as she slid the gear into neutral, switched off and let the small car swoop silently down the long slope to the beach. She could only hope that if she free-wheeled whenever she could she might conserve just enough petrol for the return trip to Knysna.

It was light now; but when she had wakened and made the impulsive decision to go down to Roosklip for an early morning swim there had been only a dullish orange glow on the horizon. The sky had lightened to a pale rinsed-out blue and the thin dark clouds that streaked the skyline over to the east had changed into burnished coppery feathers. The sea looked sullen and leaden against the brightening sky.

The air coming through the open window was crisp and cold, having that clean freshness she associated with dew on the grass in the early morning. She could smell the aromatic scent of the *renosterbos* growing in the veld and the salty tang blown up from the sea. She breathed in deeply, filling her lungs, and as she slowly exhaled realised she was beginning to feel a little better. A swim and a run to the end of the beach should restore her further and rid her of this awful stale aftermath of a sleepless night.

She kept her foot well down on the brake to prevent the car from gathering too much speed, keeping it there until the road levelled out at the foot of the hill. She switched on, pushed in the gear and used the engine for the last two miles. The road came to an abrupt dead-end and she turned a trifle sharply into a roughly gravelled clearing near the beach. The mini bucked and bumped uncomfortably over the uneven surface until she slowed down to park in front of a grove of *melk-houts*. The evergreen indigenous trees screened the sand-dunes which lay beyond and hid whatever view one might hope to have of the sea.

She tucked the car-keys above the visor and pushed it firmly against the roof. Bent to loosen her flat-heeled green sandals and kicked them off. Reached for her yellow and white striped bathing-towel and draped it round her neck as she opened the door and got out.

She was half-way to the entrance of the grove when she remembered her handbag and went back to retrieve it from the back seat.

She went through the green archway made by two huge mushroom-shaped *melk-houts* forming a natural entrance to the grove, and walked down the narrow sandy footpath winding through the trees. The gnarled grey-barked tree-trunks in the grove had nothing like the immense girth of the two old trees at the entrance, and leaned at tortured and grotesque angles in a seemingly desperate struggle to reach the light. The interlaced branches overhead formed a deep-green canopy for which she had to stoop a little to avoid catching her hair. Her feet sank ankle-deep into the smooth cupped footprints that had been left in the fine white sand.

Once she was through the grove the footpath ended abruptly on the crest of a high sand-dune overlooking the beach. It was one of a long string stretched out above the curved bay.

The sea breeze blew cool against her face and she pushed her hair back from her shoulders as she felt her spirit rise to the deep roar of the sea and the thunderous crash of the surf.

The tide was rising fast, the heavy swells rolling slowly in. Heightening white-crested as they neared the shore, to thin and become a wavering translucent wall of fiery green water before crashing in a tumbling thunderous fury of white spray and foam.

But for a few black and white gulls, the beach to the right was deserted. They were brilliantly reflected in the hard wet sand at the water's edge where they were optimistically foraging for whatever gifts the sea might have cast up during the night. At the far end of the beach the escarpment of terracotta rock from which the place derived its name glowed warmly pink through a thin ribbon of milky mist. In another five minutes or so the sun would push up out of the sea like a monstrous molten orb.

She lifted a hand to hold back the hair blown across her face and watched a wedge of *duikers* flap across the sky.

She looked to the left and stiffened slightly when she saw that a man was standing with his back to her, ankle-deep in the surf. His body was deeply tanned and well-developed. He was indeed so magnificently proportioned, that as he stood there staring out to sea, he could easily have been a bronze statue of an athlete from Ancient Greece.

The illusion vanished when he moved and waded in, and once knee deep he launched himself face down into the surf and swam strongly out to sea.

It was only then that she noticed a pink bathing cap farther out and realised that a woman must be floating beyond the breakers. The swimmer cleaved his way swiftly towards her and as he reached her dived and disappeared. It was only a matter of seconds before the pink bathing cap vanished too.

She didn't feel alarm at first, thinking it was a game. She even smiled while she waited for them to reappear. But when time lengthened her smile began to fade and she unconsciously held her breath as she continued to stare anxiously out to sea.

He suddenly surfaced, and she expelled her breath in sharp relief and watched him fling his head back to clear the wet hair from his eyes. It was only a matter of seconds before the pink bathing-cap bobbed up like a cork next to him.

He literally pounced upon it, and there was a brief splashing and flurry of churned water. The momentary glimpse of a flailing white arm, before he pushed her under and *kept* her there!

She would often wonder for what length of time she must have stood, eyes riveted on him, unable to move, unable to *think*. Shocked into a state of frozen fascinated horror. How long did it take before he was finally convinced that his victim was well and truly drowned? How much time passed before he rolled over like a seal on to his back and pulled the woman's slack body into his arms and propelled himself back to the shore?

When they were close in, he rose to stand knee-deep in the surf and bent to scoop her up. Her body looked very white against his deep tan. Her head lolled back and a limp arm dangled loosely, swinging rhythmically backwards and forwards as he thrust his powerful legs through the water.

He carried her up the beach to the dry sand above the high-water mark and dumped her as unceremoniously as a sack of flour. He stood over her staring down, drawing deep breaths, his heavily muscled shoulders slightly stooped as if his whole body had suddenly gone slack.

She saw his chest expand as he drew in a deep shuddering breath and he shook his head in a rather dazed fashion and slowly straightened . . . He put up both hands to push his fingers through his hair, and as he lifted his head his eyes came up and looked straight at her.

Time stood still as they stared at each other transfixed. She ceased to breathe and the handle of her handbag slid unnoticed from between her numbed fingers.

He was the first to move. Dropping his hands. Taking a step or two towards her . . . And she still stood watching him, mesmerised like a bird by a snake.

Only when he broke into a run did she give a frightened gasp. Then wheeled and ran for her life up the path. Her feet sinking ankle-deep into the soft dry sand slowed her down, so that she tended to flounder rather than run, using muscles she had never used before. She screamed hysterically when her hair caught in the interlacing branches overhead and jerked her to a standstill. Panting in terror she tore it wildly free and lumbered on again. She could see the sunlight reflected blindingly from the bonnet of her mini parked near the entrance to the path. She exerted every ounce of will to drive herself on, to force her weighted limbs to move faster. Her lungs felt as if they must burst and she was deafened by the thundering of her heart in her ears.

She stumbled through the archway, and once her feet were freed from the soft impeding sand made a wild dash for the car and wrenched the door open.

In, and the door quickly slammed. Hands up, searching frantically for the keys. The visor jerked down too sharply, the keys dropping, but missed as they fall. *Down*, searching for them on the floor. Sweating and scrabbling like a frightened animal. Found at last, and clutched too tightly between slippery shaking fingers. Hands trembling uncontrollably and unable to insert the ignition key the first time. Jaws clenched in an effort of will, fumble again and in this time. Switch on, and sweating relief when the engine roars to life. An awful compulsion to look back. *Don't*! Whatever you do, don't—look—back. The brake released and foot down on the accelerator. The car leaping forward, gravel spurting, tyres skidding and squealing as a U-turn is taken too fast.

A quick frightened glance over her shoulder, and a glimpse of him, huge, menacing, running up the path . . . Foot jammed down in sheer blind panic, and the car hurtling towards the corner. Braking, wheel wrenched round and the tyres shrieking in protest as the car heels over agonisingly in a bucketing turn. A desperate fight with the kicking, spinning wheel as the tyres slither sideways on the loose stuff at the edge of the road. A rock barely missed by inches, and nearly headlong into the

EAD2

veld. The wheel dragged round again and a fearful uncontrolled diagonal swerve across the road. Another desperate wrench at the wheel. A sickening, sliding, slithering lurch and the car under control again and rocketing up the hill.

Several minutes had passed before she unclenched her hand from the wheel and lifted it to wipe away the sweat trickling from her brow into her eyes. Her heart was still thumping heavily, and her shoulders and arms ached from strain and tension. She pushed herself a little back in the driver's seat to ease her body . . . There were at least five miles to go before she would reach the national road. Two miles of scrubby, rocky lonely veld, and then three of pine and gum plantations. No house or dwelling of any sort. No chance of seeing anyone who could help until she reached the national road . . . He must have a car, which he had probably parked on the gravelled strip to the right of the *melk-houts* where she would not have seen it. It would be certain to be bigger and more powerful than hers, and he should have no trouble in overtaking the mini and forcing it off the road.

The engine coughed, and her heart leapt into her mouth as the car momentarily checked.

Oh my God, the fuel! She saw that the needle was now flickering a bare fraction above the empty mark. Sweat broke out on her forehead and her hands automatically tightened on the wheel. Could the petrol last, particularly if she continued to travel at this breakneck speed? There must be at least thirteen miles to go before she would reach Knysna.

She thought of the light she had seen shining from the windows of Mark's fishing-shack when she had gone for a drive after dinner the previous night. He must be down for the weekend. Probably with another couple and a girl, as he had done with her. The light shining from his shack halfway up the hill had gone through her like a knife. Would he know she was back? And if he did, would someone have told him what had happened to her? It would be better that way, then at least he would know what to expect, and would register nothing when they met. In any case, Mark had always been adept at hiding what he felt behind a narrow, inscrutable Van Dyck face.

Her pulse had quietened down and her nerves were now under better control. She was still driving too fast, but with an absence of panic.

She hurtled through the last two miles of pine plantation and slowed down when she saw the national road ahead.

Once she turned into it, she began to feel a little easier . . . With luck the petrol might just last, and even if it lasted only long enough to take her three more miles she would be safe. There were a few scattered houses along the road from that point, and she should be able to stop and ask someone to telephone the police.

The engine missed and the car checked again, hesitating fractionally. Her heart gave a jolt as she got a strong whiff of petrol. She instinctively glanced up into the rear mirror to see if he was in pursuit, and saw the black dot of a car in the distance. She might have missed it if there had not been a bright flash as the sun's rays caught the windscreen.

She knew that the track leading to Mark's shack lay roughly three hundred yards ahead and watched out for it. As soon as she saw it on the right she swung the mini sharply across the road and drove straight up it. Fifty yards from the shack the engine cut off without warning.

For a second she was immobilised, frozen, and then quickly jerked up the handbrake. She searched for her handbag, realised it was missing, but wasted no more time, scrambled out and ran bare-footed up the path.

"Mark!" she screamed.

By the time she reached the wooden steps leading up to the stoep her legs had nearly seized up, and her lungs were pumping agonisingly. She stumbled and fell to her knees when she was half-way up, somehow dragged herself to her feet, crossed the narrow wooden stoep and flung herself at the front door. It was locked.

She lifted both hands and hammered on it. "Mark!"

The wind had come up during the last half hour and blew her hair across her face. She could hear a dog barking far down in the valley.

"Mark." This time it was no more than a hoarse whisper.

The silence ultimately defeated her. The fight went out of her and she closed her eyes and slumped against the door, her breathing deep and painful.

The door opened suddenly and she lost her balance and staggered forward, nearly falling headlong into the passage. "Blast this bloody door, it always tends to stick . . . *Lisa—*" And it was then as she had always dreaded it would be. His face tightening, staring at her in shocked incredulity. "*God*. What happened to you?"

Blood drummed in her ears. Knees turned to water, ice cold sweat broke out on her brow.

She swayed. "I think I'm going to faint."

He caught her as her knees buckled. She was dimly aware of him supporting, half carrying her over to the couch under the window. She shoved him away as he tried to persuade her to lie down, and sat crouched, head well down between her knees. She heard him force the warped window open, and felt the cool air waft on her damp skin.

He said: "Wouldn't it be better if you lay down?"

She shook her head, keeping it down and sat crouched in the same position until the heavy slamming of her heart slowly eased and her head cleared.

When she straightened at length he was standing beside her and handed her a half tumbler of neat brandy. She nodded her thanks and took the glass with a shaky hand, without looking up at him, raised it to her lips and swallowed a mouthful. The raw liquid went down her throat like liquid fire, made her cough and brought tears to her eyes.

"Drink some more," he said after a minute.

She tried, but shuddered convulsively at the next mouthful and quickly put the glass on the table beside the couch. "I *can't*. It will make me sick." She lifted an arm to draw it across her brow.

"Lisa—"

"Yes, Mark?" She looked up at him pale-lipped, a sheen of sweat glistening on her face.

"What happened?" he asked quietly.

She instinctively lifted a hand to cover the left side of her face. "D' you mean about my face?'' she asked with an attempt at lightness.

He remained silent looking down at her.

"... It happened while I was in England—''

"What did?''

"I had an accident. It was entirely my fault. I—stepped off the pavement before first looking to the left and a car hit me. I stepped right in front of it and there was nothing the driver could do to avoid me. I was lucky, really.'' She was speaking in a flat overcontrolled voice. "It could have been much worse. No important b-bones were broken.'' She had drawn her hair forward to cover her left cheek. "As you saw, the left side of my face took most of the punishment. The cheekbone was smashed and most of the flesh gouged out. They thought for a time that I might lose the sight of my left eye, but fortunately it responded to treatment. It's not as good as it was, but the vision isn't too badly impaired.''

His face had thinned. "When did this happen?''

She swallowed but didn't speak.

"*When* did this happen?'' he repeated more loudly. "Which month last year?''

She wrung her hands in a sudden gesture of distress. "Mark, there isn't *time* to talk about this now! I only came here because I'd run out of petrol, and was certain I was being followed."

His brows rose. "*Followed*?" he said sharply. "By whom?"

"I was down at Roosklip for an early morning swim and saw a man d-drown a woman. He *murdered* her."

"*What*!" He saw she had gone white and quickly reached for the tumbler of brandy and gave it to her. "Here, have some more of this before you pass out."

She took the tumbler and brought it to her lips and obediently swallowed another mouthful, concentrating hard on trying not to gag. She watched over the rim of the glass as he reached for a chair, faced it round and sat down opposite her. His black hair was a little longer. He was wearing roped-soled shoes, khaki shorts and a shabby old jersey badly in need of darning. She guessed he must have been on the verge of setting out to fish.

He waited for her to put the tumbler on the table before he spoke. "Right. Now take it easy and take your time. Tell me exactly what happened, and start at the beginning."

This she did, and while she told him kept the left side of her face cupped in a long-fingered slender hand. Once or twice she had to stop, swallow and clear her throat before she could go on.

He listened intently and without interruption, his direct deep set blue-grey eyes fixed upon her face.

When she finally faltered to a stop his first comment was not entirely unexpected.

"My God, you must be crazy!" he said angrily. "Surely you know by now, what a risk you run to go down to a lonely spot like that by yourself."

She smiled slightly. "The same old Mark—"

"And the same old Lisa, it seems," but he said it without smiling.

He saw her smile quickly fade as she turned her head to look through the window . . . No, Mark. Not the same old Lisa. She's gone forever . . .

"Where are you staying?" he asked abruptly.

"At the Royal, in Knysna." She clasped her hands. "Mark, I must have dropped my bag. I think it happened when he saw me—while we were staring at each other—"

"In that case it will still be there. It's unlikely that anyone would go down to the beach at this ungodly hour."

"*They*—the man and woman did—"

"What we must do now is to inform the police, so we'd better get moving. I've often thought of installing a phone in the shack in case of an emergency, but have never got so far as doing anything about it. I'll fetch my car and bring it to the door."

"You may have difficulty getting past my mini. It died on me in the middle of the track."

"I'll have a look and move it if necessary. All I can say is, thank God you came when you did. If you'd been five minutes later I wouldn't have been here."

He saw her repress a shiver and went into the bedroom and came back a moment later with a thick hand-knitted navy blue jersey and handed it to her. "Put this on while I fetch the car."

She waited until he went out before she took off her flowered bathing wrap and pulled the chunky jersey over her green and white bikini. She remembered borrowing it the last time they had gone fishing off the rocks.

Her eyes traversed the small room, taking in his fishing rods stacked in the corner where he always kept them. His disreputable old fishing hat which he had told her belonged to his father, tossed as usual on to the teak table by the door. The room still had that shabby unlived-in look of a place seldom used. The cretonne-covered couch looked a little more faded and the blue striped curtains were now bleached almost to white.

She went into the tiny cabin where there was barely room for the two bunks and found his comb where he always kept it on the narrow shelf below the cracked mirror. She picked it up, dragged it through her hair and peered into the mirror which always divided one's face. The plastic surgeon had told her that the two purple scars curving across her left cheek would fade in time and become less noticeable. She knew that this side of her face remained pale whenever she flushed. She stared into her long, dark-lashed green eyes and thought that at least they were still the same, though her left eye had less resistance to light and tended to become bloodshot at times . . . And her hair, which she knew Mark had always liked, was still long, fair and silky with the same platinum streak springing from the centre of her forehead. She remembered how he had always suspected her of cultivating it, and for some reason this made her want to cry. She felt tears prick her lid . . . If only he hadn't looked at her like that. It was even worse than she had imagined it might be. She clenched her jaws, willing herself to stop feeling emotional.

She heard him come in at the front door and put the comb back and after a minute or so went through to join him in the other room.

He looked at her as she came in. "I managed to push your car off the track, and if you're ready we'd better go." He noticed that she looked strained and rather pale. "Are you sure you're all right? You wouldn't like to lie down for a few minutes?"

"No, I'm quite all right."

"How about another slug of that brandy before we go?"

She smiled a trifle stiffly and shook

her head. "I think I've had enough. It wouldn't do to create a bad impression at the police station."

"Well, as long as you don't pass out on me," he said a shade doubtfully. "You certainly look as if you've taken a beating." As the *double entendre* struck him he flushed to the temples.

Her lips barely moved. "I won't pass out on you, Mark. Let's go, shall we?"

2

THEY hardly spoke on the way to Knysna. When they did, it was with the stiff formality of mere acquaintances. Mark enquired how long she had been back in South Africa, and where she was living in Cape Town. She told him that she had been back just over six weeks, and had been lucky enough to find a flat in Rondebosch. Added, after a moment or two, that she had been pleased to see the announcement in the paper of his appointment as Senior Counsel—the youngest in the Republic. He grunted at this, but made no comment. She cleared her throat and enquired politely after his mother, and he replied shortly that she was in good health.

For the first ten minutes she had been as taut as a bowstring, expecting him to ask her more questions about the accident, or worse still, to question her about things for which it would be more difficult to find convincing answers. But when he relapsed into a preoccupied silence she realised with relief that he had no immediate intention of questioning her. She slowly relaxed and stared unseeingly through the window, thinking of his betraying flush. It was like a bleeding internal wound deep inside her. Though she kept her face averted she was aware of him glancing at her once or twice, and was thankful that he was sitting on her right.

The sun was well up by now, but there was still not enough heat in its rays to evaporate the mist swathed like a grey shawl about the wooded flanks of the hills, and wreathing thin and vaporous from the still, shining waters of the lagoon.

As they neared the town they passed the coloured people on their way to work. Most of them walking in cheerful groups along the sides of the road, but here and there one or two hurried on alone.

In the town the shops were still closed, and though a few coloureds were loitering about the streets, it was mainly deserted. Only the café at the corner was open and a man stood in the doorway scanning the morning paper.

A small boy carrying a carton of milk ran past the police station as Mark drew up at the kerb. Lisa made a move to get out, but he suggested she wait in the car while he made enquiries.

He was gone about five minutes and then came back to tell her that a bit of a flap was on. The duty officer had suffered a heart attack that morning and there hadn't been time to replace him, but the sergeant in charge had put through a call to Lieutenant Meyer of the Peninsula Murder and Robbery Squad, who was down from Cape Town for the weekend, and he had promised to be at the police station within ten minutes.

Mark suggested that if she would like to change, it should give them just enough time.

He drove her to the Royal and waited in the car while she hurriedly changed into a green linen frock.

When they walked into the police station ten minutes later the Lieutenant had already arrived. The sergeant said good-morning to Lisa and ushered them out of the charge office into a small bare featureless room where the Lieutenant was waiting for them.

He knew Mark and rose from behind his

desk and reached across to shake hands, and greeted him by his christian name. Mark introduced him to Lisa, and they all sat down.

The Lieutenant wasted no time and began questioning her at once.

He was a man in his early thirties who had allowed himself to put on too much weight, but despite this there was no hint of flabbiness about his heavy muscular frame. His manner was smooth and he smiled easily. He had good teeth, even and very white against his sallow skin.

Lisa sat a little stiffly in the straight-backed uncomfortable chair, shielding the left side of her face while he questioned her . . . The benign look on his smooth sallow face was belied for her by the disconcerting coldness of his pale blue discerning eyes.

His questions were brief and to the point, fired in crisp staccato sentences . . . At the same time he appraised her, cold blue eyes fixed on her face, speculating on what could have happened. Looking at her hands, her legs. Assessing the quality of her frock, the cost of the white cashmere jersey draped over her shoulders . . . Questioning her and summing her up at the same time.

Finally he sat back and pressed the bell and looked at the door until it opened. "Tell Sergeant Jooste I want him," he said in Afrikaans.

He stared absently at the pencil he was twisting between his fingers until the sergeant came in.

"Ah, Sergeant . . . Miss Lombard, this is Sergeant Jooste."

She glanced up and smiled. "We've already met."

The sergeant's goodnatured homely face flushed to the roots of his cropped red hair. It reminded her sickeningly of how Mark had flushed, and she wondered miserably if the Sergeant had just noticed the injury to her face.

"Miss Lombard, I must be on my way. It shouldn't take us much more than ten minutes in the police car to get down to Roosklip, but in the meantime I'd like a signed statement from you. The sergeant will take it down and read through it with you before you sign." He put his hands on the arms of his chair and levered himself up.

She said, "Lieutenant Meyer, you may remember that I mentioned I must have dropped my handbag. My cheque book's in it, and all my money of course. I'd be quite lost—"

"Don't worry, Miss Lombard, I haven't forgotten. If your bag's there, we'll find it. And Sergeant—"

"Yes, sir?"

"Take Miss Lombard's fingerprints while you're about it."

"Yes, sir."

"I take it the car's waiting."

"Yes, sir, it's at the door."

"How about Jannie? Did they manage to get hold of him?"

"Yes, sir. He's waiting at the car with the others."

"Good. Well, I must be on my way."

He glanced at Lisa as he came round his desk and saw how strained and dark-eyed she looked.

"Miss Lombard, I'd suggest that when you've finished making your statement you go back to the hotel and have a rest. I'll naturally want to see you again but I'll give you a chance to rest first. I'll ring you later and send the car round." He gave Mark a brief nod as he went out. Quick, despite his weight, and light on his feet.

She glanced at Mark who had been sitting silently in the chair beside her for the last ten minutes. "Why don't you go, Mark? There's nothing more you can do, and —"

"I'd prefer to stay," he said abruptly.

He borrowed the morning paper from the sergeant and pushed his chair further back, but he was still close enough for her to hear him turn a page, and the flare of a match once when he lit a cigarette.

By the time Lisa had finished making her statement and read through it with the sergeant she felt exhausted, and strangely lethargic and heavy-eyed. The cumulative effect of shock, a sleepless night, and the strain of meeting Mark, had taken a heavy toll of her reserves.

She got up and shook hands with Sergeant Jooste and said goodbye, and then she and Mark went through the charge office and out on to the pavement.

She turned to him as he opened the car door for her. "I think I'll take Lieutenant Meyer's advice and lie down for a while—if you wouldn't mind driving me back to the hotel."

"That's what I'm here for."

She waited until he slid in beside her, switched on and eased the car on to the road before she spoke again. "I'm sorry I brought you into all this—if the petrol hadn't run out, I would never have bothered you. It hasn't been very pleasant for you, and it's also meant that you've missed half your morning fishing." She cleared her throat. "I want you to know how very grateful I am, Mark, for all you've—"

"Lisa," he cut in abruptly. "You never answered my question."

She looked at him silently.

"When did you have your accident? Which month was it?"

"Oh God, you surely don't expect me to discuss this with you now!" she cried hysterically. She quickly turned her face to the window as she felt tears sting her lids. She stared blindly out until he swung the car through the gates and parked to the left of the steps.

She opened the door and scrambled out before he could come round, but he took the steps two at a time and joined her as she reached the stoep.

She stopped at the front door and didn't speak for a second or two.

"Sorry about that," she said at last, back to the cool controlled voice she had employed all morning. "I'm not usually so hysterical. I suppose it's a result of everything that's happened this morning."

He put a hand to the doorframe and straightened his arm to lean across the entrance and look down at her. "You don't have to apologise, I'm the one who should be doing that. The question was ill timed and should never have been asked . . . But you do realise, Lisa, don't you, that you won't be able to evade the question for ever? Sometime or other you'll have to answer me."

Her eyes flickered briefly up to his, and then she quickly ducked under his arm and went in.

Mark waited for an hour before he went to the police station to find out if the Lieutenant was back. When he went in he found him leaning on the counter in the charge office, talking to Sergeant Jooste.

He turned as Mark came in. "Ah, Mark, the very man I wanted to see! I was just about to try and contact you. Sergeant, see we're not disturbed for the next half hour, and tell Jannie to wait when he comes. Come in, Mark—" He waved him into the room they had previously occupied and banged the door as he followed, then went over to the desk and sat down with a grunt.

"Sit, man, and have a cigarette." He nudged the packet of Lucky Strike across the desk. Mark helped himself though it was not the brand he usually smoked, and they both lit up.

Lieutenant Meyer undid his jacket and eased himself back in his chair, surreptitiously slackening his waistband which tended to become too tight whenever he sat. He brought the cigarette to his lips, drew on it and let his eyes rest on Mark's tight introspective face.

He disliked everything Mark Standish stood for. He considered him to be the typical product of an affluent English-speaking background. He had been born and bred in the Constantia valley which everyone knew housed the moneyed set of the Cape Peninsula. Though Mark was as fluent in Afrikaans as he was, he refused to regard him as a true South African. He disliked the clipped way in which he spoke

English, and the modest arrogant manner he affected. If his father had still been alive he would have been on the Court of Appeal or Judge President by now, and he had heard that Mark's mother was a woman of considerable means. Mark had never known insecurity or poverty. Everything he had ever wanted had been handed to him on a platter. He had never known what it was like to be hungry nine days out of ten, or to trudge barefoot three miles to school every day on an empty belly. If reports were true, his parents' marriage had been a happy one. Mark didn't know what it was like to have a drunken father who beat up his mother, and who never held down a job. He had never had to listen to the never ending stream of bitterness pouring from his mother's lips; or the sounds of her screams when his father hit her. No, the only knowledge Mark Standish had of what life was about, he had learned in court, not from what he had personally experienced. His father had died a loved and respected citizen of Cape Town. He hadn't gone off with another woman and left his wife and child destitute . . . Mark had ability, no one would dispute that. On several occasions when he had been witness for the prosecution, he had been subjected to Mark's searching cross-examinations and occasional scathing sarcasm, and knew just how good he was. He wouldn't be the youngest S.C. in the Republic for nothing.

Karel Meyer and Mark had come to know each other through their work, and through a mutual love of fishing off the rocks at Knysna. They felt for each other a reciprocal distaste and respect. Their relationship could best be described as one of friendly animosity.

"We found nothing of course," Karel Meyer said bluntly, flicking the ash off the end of his cigarette into the glass ashtray on his desk. "No corpse, and no sign that anyone had been on the beach. The tide was full, so there were no footprints. Nothing."

"Surely there were tracks coming up the sand-dune from the beach? That was the way he would have run up after her."

"Oh! Use your kop, man!" he said impatiently. At times he tended to adopt an over-familiar manner towards Mark to make up for the deference he had to show him in court. "Of course there were footprints going up the sand-dune. *Hundreds* of them! Have you forgotten that the school holidays ended only two days ago? That's the way the whole bunch went up and down to the beach."

"Did you find where he had parked his car?" Mark enquired coolly. "It would seem obvious he'd have one."

"No, nothing. Nothing. The ground was baked as hard as a rock. The only evidence we found were the skidmarks on the gravel where she must have taken off from the carpark like a rocket, and also those at the corner where she said she nearly turned her car over." He leaned forward to put his elbows on the desk and clasped his hands, keeping the cigarette smouldering between his fingers. "You were present while Miss Lombard was making her statement, so you know it all. I finished reading it just before you came in, and found it makes very precise and—er—unemotional reading. The sergeant said she made an excellent witness." He looked down to brush away the ash that had fallen off the tip of his cigarette on the desk . . . "A great pity about her face."

"Yes, Karel. A bloody great pity."

The *bastard*. Staring at him down his long well-bred nose as if he smelt. He hid his anger beneath a bland enquiring smile. "Have you any idea what happened to her?"

After a longish pause Mark replied. "Yes. She told me she was knocked down by a car."

"I guessed it must have been something like that . . . She must have been a beautiful girl." It was said with a faint note of enquiry.

Mark drew at his cigarette but didn't speak.

"D'you know each other well?"

"Come off it, Karel. You must know we were engaged."

Meyer smiled smoothly. "I admit Jannie Barnard supplied that information, but I couldn't be sure if it was correct." He pushed the telephone further away from his elbow. "Quite a character, Jannie. He's barely turned twenty-three, yet he's already a mine of information. He's got a mind like a sponge—it absorbs everything. And once something's docketed he never forgets. He's also got a nose like a bloodhound for clues. A born detective if ever there was one. But even Jannie couldn't find any clues this morning." He took his elbows off the desk and sat back. "One thing puzzles me about all this, Mark."

"What puzzles you?"

"If a man drowned a woman, tell me why he'd bring her body back to the beach? Surely he'd let her float out to sea and make it look as if she had got into difficulties and drowned. He could get away with that. But once he brings her body back to the shore, he's got to dispose of it somehow, not so? This simply doesn't make sense to me."

Mark continued to look at him silently, his face expressionless.

Meyer lifted a hand to stroke his cheek with two fingers. "One must recognise, of course, the psychological effect it might have on a girl—having her face smashed up, I mean. Particularly if she happened to be a very pretty one."

"Just what the hell are you getting at, Karel?"

"I'm getting at *this*." He slapped his hand palm down on the desk for emphasis. "In a case such as this, there would have to be a considerable amount of readjustment on the girl's part, wouldn't there? Her prospects of marriage could no longer be considered so good, and she'd be sure to find this out pretty soon." He looked down and fingered the ashtray. "One could hardly condemn a man for breaking off his engagement if he found his girl's face had been smashed up."

Mark's face tightened. "Is that what you would have done?"

Meyer had deliberately laid himself open for the insult, nonetheless the contempt with which the remark was made offended him. He managed to hide this behind his usual bland smile. "I haven't as yet been tempted to ask a woman to marry me, so I'm in no position to tell you how I would react . . . But don't get me wrong, Mark. I'm not casting aspersions on the man who'd walk out."

"And that, I take it, is what you think I did?"

Karel Meyer half shrugged. "Well, since you ask—"

"Christ! And you're supposed to be such a bloody good detective! I wonder how many times you get hold of the wrong end of the stick when you're engaged in your sordid little investigations. Because you've got hold of the wrong end this time, Karel. *Lisa* broke off our engagement, not me."

". . . Ah, so?" His cold blue eyes were fixed unwinking on Mark's face. "May I ask what reason she gave?"

"The oldest reason in the world, Karel. She met someone else."

"I see . . . Did she say if she was going to marry this man?"

"I assumed as much."

He continued to stroke his cheek and stared reflectively at the nails of his other hand. "It seems your assumption was incorrect."

"So you're not such a lousy detective after all," Mark sneered. His narrow aquiline-nosed face lent itself to a particularly offensive sneer. "No, she's not wearing a wedding ring, Karel. Even *I* could see that."

Karel Meyer imperturbably ignored the gibe. "So this is the first time you've met since she's back? Jannie mentioned that she's been back about six weeks."

"But he couldn't tell you whether we've met? Maybe your nasty little bloodhound isn't the bright boy you think he is."

"Keep your shirt on, Mark."

Mark stretched across the desk to grind out the stub of his cigarette in the ashtray, and then sat back and looked Karel Meyer over. "I'm asking you again. What are you getting at, Karel? What are all these questions in aid of? And what have they got to do with the fact that Lisa saw a man drown a woman at Roosklip?"

Meyer ground out the stub of his cigarette as well, but did so with studied deliberation. "*That* is the point I'm trying to make. That is the very thing I'm getting at . . . How do we know that she saw him do it?"

Mark stared at him for a long moment. "Are you trying to tell me that you think she's lying?" he asked slowly. "Are you saying that she's fabricated the whole story?"

"Don't try and put words in my mouth, Mark. I didn't say that."

"But you've implied it," Mark rapped back. "Where's the bloody difference?"

Meyer shifted impatiently in his chair. "Look, man, use your nous! You're a first class cross-examiner. I've listened to you often enough in court, and you've cross-examined me on occasions so I know what I'm talking about . . . I'm a good detective. And for all your offensive remarks to the contrary, you know it. And there's something else we both know, Mark. Neither of us can afford to take a witness' evidence at face value."

"Oh, for God's sake! What possible motive could she have for fabricating a story like this?"

Meyer leaned forward and jabbed a stubby finger at him. "*You* could be her motive, Mark. *You!* This could be a very clever manoeuvre on her part to get you involved."

"I'm beginning to wonder if you're the right man for this job, Karel."

"So that's what you think, hey?" He was beginning to lose his smooth urbanity. He fumbled for his handkerchief and dabbed at his brow. "Why don't you listen to what I'm saying for a change, instead of getting so het up." He thrust the handkerchief back into his pocket. "Take this man—this fellow you thought she was going to marry. It's obvious he walked out on her, isn't it?"

Mark looked at him with cold distaste.

"Carry on and say what you want to say, but don't sit there expecting me to agree with your twisted thinking."

"OK, Mark, OK. Maybe my thinking isn't quite as twisted as you think it is . . . Look at it from this angle. After this fellow walks out on her she comes back to South Africa and naturally starts thinking about you—the man to whom she had been engaged." He lifted a protesting hand as Mark was about to speak. "Listen to me first—let me finish what I want to say, and then you can talk . . . She knows you often come down here to fish and stay in your shack, and she finds out you're coming down this weekend. Any bloody fool could have found that out. So she thinks up this idea." He smiled slightly. "You see, Mark, you're just the type who might have stuck to her. She may have cottoned on to that and—"

"Christ, Karel, you make me want to puke!"

"*Listen*, man, that's only one point of view. Now this is the other: everything Miss Lombard told us may be true, and this is the way I intend handling things. But with my eyes open, Mark. Not like a damned ostrich with its head buried in the sand. She said she would have no difficulty in recognising the man. And this would obviously go for him too. In which case, as the only witness to what he'd done, her life would be in danger, and I intend giving her full police protection."

"Bloody generous of you." Mark said with cold sarcasm and pushed back his chair and got up.

"Wait, man. I haven't finished yet."

"I think I've stomached all I can take."

"There's a point that should interest you."

"I doubt it. Our minds don't seem to work the same way, Karel."

"Sit down, man, and at least listen to what I have to say."

Mark didn't move.

Meyer's sallow face suddenly reddened in anger. "OK. So you don't want to listen. Well, go on, clear off!"

Mark hesitated.

"What are you waiting for? Beat it!"

Mark sat down slowly. "Well, what is it you want to say?"

Meyer reached for the pencil and sat back twisting it between his short strong fingers, waiting for his anger to subside. He didn't speak or look up for a whole minute. This was done partly for effect—one of the few weaknesses he had.

He eventually looked up. "We found Miss Lombard's handbag where she said she might have dropped it—on top of the sand-dune—"

When it seemed he had nothing further to add, Mark flung himself back. "Go on, get on with it!" he said impatiently.

"Don't rush me, Mark." He dropped the pencil and stopped it from rolling off the desk. "When we got back I had someone check her bag and everything in it for fingerprints. We have hers, as you know, and I wanted to see if there were any others."

"And were there?"

"No . . . But this is the point that will interest you. *Her* fingerprints were missing."

Mark stiffened. "What?"

"Her bag and everything in it had been wiped as clean as a slate."

"He must have gone through her bag!" His face tightened. "Was there anything in it which would make it easy for him to identify her?"

"Yes, the works! Her driving licence and her engagement book in which she had written down her name, where she works and the number of her flat. She had even made a note of what time she intends leaving for Cape Town tomorrow morning."

"You tell me this! And only a few minutes ago you were implying she had fabricated the whole story."

The chair creaked under Karel Meyer's weight as he pushed himself back. "Not so fast, Mark. It's a good thing you don't leap to such hasty and hot-headed conclusions in court. It would prove fatal in your profession, and if you'd made a habit of doing it you certainly wouldn't be the youngest S.C. we have in the Republic today. Let's take things a little more slowly. As I said, this case can be looked at from two angles. Firstly, if her story's true, the man opened her bag—we won't argue about that—and she's in big trouble . . . And so am I, Mark, let's make no mistake about that. Not only must I find out who he is, but I've got to do so damned quickly before she comes to any harm." He lifted a hand to rub his indented chin and waited just long enough to make the pause heavily significant . . . "Miss Lombard struck me as being a highly intelligent girl. I'd say a very bright girl indeed—"

Mark looked at him steadily. "Well, so you think she's bright. Go on don't stop."

"If she were clever enough to have everything planned, then I reckon she would also be bright enough to have thought of doing just that very thing about her bag."

The chair screeched on the bare boards as Mark thrust it violently back. "I've taken about all I can stomach of your crooked thinking Karel. You're no longer capable of seeing things straight. None of the lines run straight for you anymore, do they? Maybe you should have yourself psycho-analysed. Or change your profession and take up something more suited to your intellect."

"Now, look here, man—"

Mark crossed the floor, threw the door open and went out.

3

WARRANT Officer Jannie Barnard had been leaning indolently against the counter in the charge office for the last ten minutes. He had made one or two attempts to start up a conversation with Sergeant Jooste but had met with little success. The sergeant had either stonily ignored him, or had given him a curt discouraging reply.

Jannie glanced round as the door opened and repressed a grin when he saw Mark's face as he stalked past. He wondered what the chief had said to make this character so angry. He caught Sergeant Jooste's eye, winked and gave him a grin.

The sergeant stared at him stony-faced . . . Cocky little twerp. Just because he was Lieutenant Meyer's blue-eyed boy he thought he was Christmas. It was high time someone took him down a peg or two.

He nodded coolly. "OK, you may go in now."

Jannie half saluted and grinned cheekily. "Thanks, sarge."

He sauntered over to the door Mark had left open, and tapped twice before entering.

The lieutenant had just finished lighting a cigarette and looked up as he shook out the match. "Oh, it's you. Come in and shut the door," he said in Afrikaans.

Jannie gave him a quick look and immediately gauged his mood. He would have to watch his step. He shut the door carefully and crossed over to the desk and stood at attention.

"How long have you been here?"

"Half an hour, sir."

"Humph." The discerning pale blue eyes looked him over as if he didn't believe him. "I want you to take someone along with you and see about Miss Lombard's car. She said she left it at Mr. Standish's fishing shack. D'you know where it is?"

"Yes, sir."

"You think you know everything, don't you?"

Jannie stared straight ahead . . . It seemed that not only Mr. Standish's feathers had been ruffled.

"Her car's out of petrol, so see about

picking up two gallons at the garage before you go. I want you to check on the tank before you put anything in and make certain if it's dry."

"Yes, sir."

"Bring the car back to the garage and have them fill it up and tell them to give it a thorough overhaul. We'll charge her for it."

"Yes, sir."

"Park it at the Royal, but keep the keys. You're to fetch the car before eight tomorrow morning, and drive it back to Cape Town. I'll arrange for Miss Lombard to go back with Mr. Standish."

"Yes, sir."

"And when I say before eight, I mean before eight. It's a small car and I don't want it pushed. It will be in your charge, and any damage done to it, or any fines incurred for exceeding the speed limit will be paid for out of your own pocket. Understood?"

"Yes, sir." Jees, the old boy was sure spoiling for a fight.

Karel Meyer watched him as he drew on his cigarette. "I regard this as a precaution we should take. It would be irresponsible if we allowed her to drive back alone . . . D'you agree?"

"Yes, sir." He relaxed with an inward smile. This was better. Man to man. The old so-and-so was showing signs of easing up.

Karel Meyer looked at him through slightly narrowed lids. "What time did you get to bed last night?"

"Me, sir?"

"Yes, you."

Jannie gave an engaging grin, hoping to disarm him. "It was pretty late, sir."

"How late?"

"I dunno, sir. I didn't look at my watch."

"I thought as much. Look at you! Anyone can see you've been on the tiles . . . Is this the reason why you were so keen to come down with me—to have a good time?"

Jannie shifted his feet and dropped his long-lashed brown eyes.

"Who was that girl with you last night?"

"Sannie . . . Suzanna Nel, sir."

"You certainly seemed to be very well acquainted. Was she the reason why you cadged a lift from me when you heard I was coming down here for the weekend?''

Jannie, well aware of his charm, gave a wide candid smile.

''Yes, sir.''

''Humph.'' His lips twitched as he tapped the ash off the end of his cigarette.

Jannie's body stiffened slightly as he steeled himself to speak. He had promised Sannie to break the ice. It would have to be done sooner or later, so it might as well be now. ''Sannie and I are thinking of getting married sir.''

Karel Meyer thrust himself back in his chair. ''You must be crazy! What does a youngster like you want to get himself tied up for? If you must have your fun, take it, but don't get yourself hooked.'' It was the way he conducted his own affairs.

Jannie's eyes went past him to something out of range.

Karel Meyer looked at him half frowning. ''You're on a good wicket. You could have a great future in your profession, d'you realise that? But not if you're going to saddle yourself with a wife and kids while you're still wet behind the ears. For God's sake, use your kop, man! That's the trouble with all you youngsters today, you think you know everything. You never want to listen or take advice from anyone. You've got to smack your heads up against a brick wall to find things out for yourselves, and usually by then it's too late to do anything about it.'' He had been watching Jannie's poker face and gave a heavy sigh. ''OK, so I'm wasting my time.''

Jannie continued to stare past him.

Karel Meyer looked down at his lapel and flicked off a speck of ash. ''Your watch still keeping good time?''

Jannie's posture visibly relaxed. ''Yes, sir, it hasn't lost a second in weeks.'' He was off the hook, and had better leave things that way; but he would have to broach the subject again. Better butter him up now. He turned his wrist to glance at his watch. ''It gives me a kick every time I look at it, sir. I never dreamed I'd ever own a watch like this.''

Karel Meyer looked down and ground out his half smoked cigarette. He had erred in giving the watch to the boy. He had given way to a foolish weakness, and considering his position, it had been an extremely unwise move. Jannie wasn't one to keep his mouth shut, and there must have been talk.

"Well, you only turn twenty-one once," he said gruffly, grimacing inwardly at the hackneyed phrase. He sat back, his fingers automatically seeking the pencil. "Now, about tomorrow. I want you to leave Miss Lombard's car at her flat, Oakapple Crescent, below the line at Rondebosch. Do you know where it is?"

"Yes, sir."

"If you've carried out my instructions and haven't pushed the car, she should have arrived before you get there. Let her have the keys. She's in No. 6. If by any chance you find she's not there, leave the car, and see she gets the keys first thing in the morning."

"Yes, sir."

"And give me a ring when you get home."

"Yes, sir."

"Have something done about that cold of yours. You've been coughing and sniffling all day. See a chemist, and get him to fix you up."

"Yes, sir."

"And see you have an early night."

Jannie didn't speak.

"Before I see you on Monday morning, get your hair cut. You should know the regulation length by now. I suppose your girlfriend likes it long?"

"No, sir."

"OK, get moving . . . And Jannie—"

He turned back. "Yes, Sir?"

"I meant what I said about an early night." His eyes looked just about as cold as ice. "It's an order. Understood?"

Jannie smiled slightly. "Yes, sir."

He went out and shut the door, and Karel Meyer reached for a pad and scribbled a brief note to Mark. When he had signed it, he searched in the top drawer, found an envelope, addressed it and then rang the bell and asked for Sergeant Jooste. He directed him to see that the note was delivered at once. He mentioned one or two of the fishing spots along the coast where Mark might be found in the event of his not being at the shack.

At one o'clock he went back to have lunch with his mother. She was expecting him, and brought in the serving dish as soon as she heard him come in, and put it in front of her place at the head of the small oblong dining-table. He saw that she had baked a small portion of his catch from last night. It had been a twenty-five pound Kabeljauw in good condition, which had given him a fight lasting over ten minutes. If he knew his mother she would pickle what was left, and live off a diet of pickled fish for the next ten days.

The fish looked dried out and over-cooked, and he watched her help him to a larger portion than he wanted. He took the plate when she handed it to him, and reached for the small earthenware dish which contained three plain boiled potatoes, two for him and one for her. No parsley and butter sauce. No sliced lemon. No salad. He proceeded to eat without much relish, thinking how much better his cook, Maggie, prepared his food.

He was preoccupied, and listened with only half an ear to his mother's endless list of complaints. He had heard them all a hundred times before and knew them off by heart. Even though she was more comfortably off than she had ever been, nothing satisfied her. She grumbled about the inefficiency and stupidity of the little daily help, the high cost of living in Knysna, the exorbitant price of meat and the poor quality of the fruit and vegetables, the unfriendliness of the neighbours and the bad service in the shops.

But her chief complaint was his adamant refusal to allow her to live with him. This not only offended her, but cut her to the heart and she never failed to refer to it whenever he came to stay with her . . . One would think a son would be only too pleased to have a mother run his home and look after him until such time as he should marry. But oh, no, not her son! He didn't want to be bothered with his mother. He had to go and buy her a house here in Knysna, and force her to live hundreds of miles away from him, among a lot of English-speaking strangers who looked down their noses at her. He might think, because he was a policeman, that that coloured cook of his was too frightened to steal from him, but she could tell him he was making a big mistake. Unless there was someone to watch, they always stole, especially when it came to food. She had hardly been able to credit her ears when he had told her the size of his household bills. With the amount he spent, she could feed *four* people, let alone two. She didn't spend even a quarter of that amount on herself, and no one could accuse her of not keeping a good table. If anyone knew how to economise, she did. Look how she had managed all those years after his father went off, and left them destitute. She had taken in sewing, skimped and scraped, working her fingers to the bone to provide for him and give him a home. She had insisted on his staying at school and completing his education, so that he would be able to hold down a good job when he became a man.

Karel Meyer glanced at her across the table, though he was paying scant attention to what she was saying. He thought her down-turned mouth looked as if it had forgotten how to smile. He couldn't remember that she had ever kissed him spontaneously when he was a child, or that she made one gesture of affection towards him. Maybe the frightening struggle for their survival had left her too drained and exhausted to leave any room for love. He sometimes found himself wondering cynically whether she had become embittered and impossible to live with because of his father's treatment of her. Or whether his father had beaten her, taken to drink, and finally gone off with another woman because of her incessant nagging and complaining.

He knew he owed everything to her, and would repay her for this by seeing that she was well provided for until her death. The cottage he had bought in her name was already valued at twice the price he had paid for it. The two P.G.s she took in paid her well and set his mind at rest that she was not living alone. With the money she earned from the sewing she took in, plus what he gave her monthly, she was now well set up.

He too was well set up. Old Maggie was a good cook and manager and ran things the way he wanted them, and if she helped herself here and there, provided he didn't catch her at it, good luck to her! His flat in Three Anchor Bay was ideally situated, and the other tenants in the block were far too occupied with their own affairs to take any interest in his. If he chose to entertain the odd girlfriend for most of the night, no one knew or cared. He had no intentions whatsoever of allowing his mother to change his mode of life.

As soon as he returned to the police

station he telephoned Lisa and sent Jannie Barnard round by car to fetch her.

When she came in he thought she looked better than when last he had seen her. She seemed less tense, and the colour had come back into her face.

However, when he told her that he had arranged for Mark Standish to drive her back to Cape Town the next morning, she flushed and became visibly upset. He noticed that the left side of her face had remained pale.

He smoothly overruled her objections, and also her suggestion that she should drive back in her own car with Jannie Bernard.

He could see she was angry, smiled and said: "Miss Lombard, you must appreciate that we have to take every possible precaution as far as you're concerned. I'd be failing in my duty as a police officer if I didn't do so. It isn't my intention to alarm you in any way, but you must realise that you could be in danger. Until the man has been apprehended, I want to stress that on no account must you place yourself in a vulnerable position. In other words, go off anywhere on your own. We'll have you tailed, of course, but it would be of great assistance to us if you'd co-operate and keep us fully informed of all your movements. It is for this reason that I've asked Mr. Standish to drive you back tomorrow. He telephoned just before you came, and has asked me to let you know that he'll pick you up at ten past nine. I'll be following you."

She said nothing to this. Her manner had been cool and she barely smiled when she left.

The south-westerly wind blew up during the afternoon, and by the evening a great black canopy of cloud had settled above the hills and from beneath this the sun flung its last rays across the town.

Karel Meyer had arranged to play snooker with Sergeant Jooste after dinner, and it was close on eleven o'clock before he left the hotel and made his way home. The wind had dropped, and it was still heavily overcast with not a star glittering in the sky.

He stopped to cup his hands and light a cigarette and then made a slight detour and saw that Jannie Barnard's room was in darkness. This could mean Jannie was either in bed or on the tiles . . . He half frowned as if he grimly suspected it of being the latter.

When he turned the corner he saw his mother had left the light on for him in the porch. It was just as well because the rain suddenly came pelting down and he had to sprint the last twenty yards for cover.

4

FROM every point of view it had been a nightmare day for Lisa, leaving her with this dread feeling of being both entrapped and pursued . . . And by tomorrow nothing would have changed. *Nothing*. There would still be the frightening knowledge that her life might be in danger, and Mark must be faced in the morning with the additional ordeal of having to share his car for about six hours.

Damn Lieutenant Meyer for his dictatorial managing of her affairs! Damn him for his smooth overruling of her objections. And damn him for not trusting her and confiscating the keys of her car . . . Something else had added fuel to her burning resentment and dislike of him. Despite his apparent concern for her welfare, and all the precautions he said he was taking on her behalf, she had nonetheless got the impression that he hadn't entirely accepted her story.

Her whole body felt stiff and sore. Sometime during her terrifying flight to the car she must have wrenched her back. It could have happened when her hair caught and jerked her to a stop. Or maybe it was her desperate floundering up the sandy footpath that had done it.

She went up to her room shortly after dinner and slowly undressed and crawled into bed. She had brought several books with her and one, a thriller which she had started before tea, promised to be good and should keep her occupied for several hours. But she soon found her mind too deeply disturbed to assimilate anything, and eventually gave up, closed her book and put it on the bedside table.

She could hear the rain coming down, and the cold night air blowing through the window which she had left slightly ajar smelt of the sea and damp earth. She could see glittering drops of water streaking down the panes against a black starless sky. The eiderdown had slipped off and she winced as she leaned forward to pull it up. She lay back and drew it up to her chin and stared at the ceiling thinking of Mark. For months she had schooled herself not to think of him at all.

She had met Mark shortly after her father's death.

It still made her stir uneasily to remember the way her father had died. They had spent Christmas together in Grahamstown, and when she left to return to Cape Town he had been cheerful and seemed in his usual good health. The sudden news of his death four months later, had been shocking and unbelievable. She learned that he had known for some time that he was going to die, and she was overwhelmed by grief and remorse when told that he had spent the last few weeks of his life in hospital.

The undated letter which was posted to her after his death, though it explained everything, had done nothing to allay her deep sense of guilt.

He wrote: When you were twelve and Robert seventeen, for over a year you had to watch your mother die, and I saw what this did to you. When the doctor told me I had only a few more months to live, I won't deny that it took some getting used to at first. But once I had accepted the fact, I found death held no fears for me. I became philosophical, and felt quite calm and ready to face it. But what I found I *couldn't* face was the thought of you and Robert having to go through it all again. The more I thought of this, the more I realised that the one thing I could not endure was seeing you and Robert suffering on my behalf. Call it cowardice if you will, or a false kind of pride. When you read this I'll be gone, but you must remember that this was the way I chose to go. You and Robert must never reproach yourselves that you were not with me at the end. I've written to him and expressed the hope that you will continue to keep contact with each other. As you know, I've always regretted that he chose to make his life in England, but it was what he wanted, and I've never stood in his way. You're both strong willed and independent, and I know you haven't always got on. But if you should ever need him, don't fail to turn to him. He's a shade pontifical, and will doubtless lecture you, but he has sterling qualities and I know he would always help you if it were in his power to do so . . .

Despite what he wrote, she *had* reproached herself. When looking back she saw the signs had all been there, but she had failed to recognise them. There had been the unusual brevity and falling off of his letters. The shakiness of his handwriting towards the end. The momentary twinges of uneasiness experienced while reading his last few letters, which she had shrugged off and dismissed. She would always reproach herself that she had not had the intuition to sense that he was ill.

This period was probably the lowest ebb of her life and she even contemplated giving up her job and settling in England, with some unformed idea that it might have pleased her father if she lived near Robert.

Mark succeeded in talking her out of this.

She had told him her vague plans and gave him her father's letter, which he read and handed back without comment. But after a moment's thought he said: "You've allowed yourself to get a guilt complex about your father, which was the very thing he didn't want."

"You don't understand."

"I think I do. Maybe I understand your reactions better than you do yourself. Running away to England, Lisa, isn't going to solve anything."

"I'm *not* running away," she said angrily.

"Aren't you? Then what is your reason for doing so? You can't really believe your father would agree that this is a good idea."

She looked at him silently.

"*This* is your country. You were born and bred here and you're a South African through and through. This is where you belong and where you should make your life."

"Robert is also a South African and yet he chose to make his life in England."

"Granted. But his position is somewhat different to yours. I've never met your brother, but from what you've told me of him I'd say he's dedicated, and that medicine's probably the biggest thing in his life. He specialised in London, and was offered a highly flattering appointment which would set him on his feet for life. Furthermore he had fallen in love with an English girl, whom he has subsequently married."

"I know all that," she muttered.

"Your brother had every incentive to stay in England. This does not apply in your case. In fact it would be sheer madness. You have admitted that you never got on with him, and you'll find he hasn't changed—people rarely do. It seems unlikely that a doting wife would improve him."

"Why should you assume that his wife is doting?"

"Those dedicated types invariably attract the worshipping female."

"Stop criticising Robert, you don't even know him! . . . What type of female do you imagine *you'll* attract?" she added childishly.

He smiled. "That remains to be seen. Seriously, Lisa, don't be an ass. All your friends are here, and you've told me that you find your job creative and stimulating. Didn't you mention that they're sending you over to London in six months for further training?"

". . . Yes," she said unwillingly.

"Well, wait until then. See how you find the set-up in London before you rush into things."

"Is this the way you bully the witness in court?"

He gave the ghost of a smile. "If need be."

He was different to the other men she knew. Older and more self-contained. A hardness of purpose in him, as though he knew where he was going, and what it was he sought in life. He was different too in his approach to her. Though he kissed her and made love to her, he always kept within the bounds she set . . . She had become accustomed to kissing being a prelude to an ensuing breathless and embarrassing struggle to fend off more urgent demands. It never failed to anger her that men should take it for granted that if she went out with them, it would be their privilege to paw her with sweaty hands and use every means to persuade her to be intimate with them . . . Mark, though ardent, never became too pressing, nor had he ever suggested they should go to bed.

On several occasions he took her home. It was usually to lunch on a Sunday. He lived with his mother in the gabled double-storied red-roofed house his parents had built shortly before he was born. The house stood at the upper end of the Constantia valley and overlooked the vineyards of the neighbouring farm. Beyond lay False Bay, and way out to the east the long pale blue range of the Hottentots-Holland ending with the hump of Hangklip rising from the sea.

Mark's mother, Mrs. Standish, was a tall handsome woman with greying hair and a well bred rather horsey look. Whenever she smiled her brown eyes half closed in amusement. They usually found her wandering in the garden, casually dressed in well cut expensive looking slacks and her wide-brimmed gardening hat. Toby, her little black Pomeranian, was invariably at her heels, and the lilac-pointed Siamese, Ming, somewhere in the offing, ready to scale a tree if Toby jealously pursued her.

Mark's relationship with his mother was an easy one. Lisa had often thought they appeared more like brother and sister than mother and son.

Twice he invited her to spend a weekend at his fishing shack near Knysna. Both times they went there with another couple, Peter Simpson, a colleague of Mark's at the Bar, and Peter's girlfriend, Sue Brown. She and Sue had slept on the bunks in the cabin and Mark and Peter had dossed down in the living-room. Peter slept on the couch under the window, and Mark on a camp stretcher near the door. She suspected that Peter and Sue spent most of their time on the couch while she and Mark were fishing off the rocks . . . Mark had barely kissed her half a dozen times during the weekend.

She was well aware that Mark took out other girls and she hadn't minded this at first, feeling she was hardly in the position to do so as she herself went out with a varied assortment of men. But one night she was taken to a play and saw him in the foyer during the interval with an older, more sophisticated girl. She recognised instantly that this slim, elegant, dark-eyed beauty smiling up at him would set no limits to his love-making. She was surprised by an awful plunging stab of jealousy which corkscrewed through her and left her badly shaken. Mark looked across at that moment and saw her, half raised his hand and smiled. She nodded faintly and smiled coolly back.

He had gone on circuit two days later, thus she hadn't seen him for three weeks. He wrote once while he was away, a short impersonal note asking her to dine with him on his first evening back.

She knew by now that she was deeply

involved but was uncertain of the state of his feelings. Consequently her manner was a little distant and haughty when they met. If he noticed this, he gave no indication of it.

After the show he suggested they should go home for a nightcap. His mother had already gone to bed and he took her through to his father's study and left her there while he fetched two glasses and the whisky decanter.

It was the first time she had been in his father's book-lined study, where Mark told her, he worked most nights. The portrait of Judge Standish, which hung above the fireplace, showed from whom Mark had inherited his penetrating deep set grey-blue eyes. The wavy greying hair must once have been as black as Mark's, but his was a more open benign face, the cheekbones broader, and the jaw squarer . . . The narrow cast of Mark's face was his mother's, but the dark closed look was peculiarly his own.

He came in with the drink tray and set it on the desk. When he saw she was looking at the china pieces on the mantelshelf he went over to join her.

"You're looking at these. I'm always telling my mother what a risk she takes leaving them here. Collecting china was one of my father's hobbies—a weakness I seem to have inherited from him." He picked up the fluted blue and white cup she had been examining and lifted the saucer to show her the raised ridge in the centre. "This is what is known as a *trembleuse*, because however shaky you may be, you'd still be unlikely to dislodge the cup. You may think because it's decorated in underglaze blue, and the pattern being Oriental, that it's Chinese, but it's French in fact, dating from 1690."

"Oh, I would never have guessed, I could have sworn it was Eastern . . . How about this?" touching a flat dish with a tiger and bamboo design. "Is this also French?"

"No, English. Made in Chelsea." He turned the dish over. "There's the anchor—the recognised mark." He put the dish back on the mantelpiece. "I'll show you something else."

She watched him go over to a light mahogany French display cabinet which stood between the desk and the window and switch on an interior light which immediately revealed an array of china pieces set out on the shelves.

. . . She found she could still remember a few. A pair of deep blue Sèvres vases. A yellow parrot. A rather abandoned-looking sleeping shepherdess with one rounded white breast uncovered, and a jade green coffee pot with a white dragon handle . . .

He half knelt to reach in, lifted a piece carefully, rose and came back and held it out, cupped in the palm of his hand.

"And where d'you think this was made?"

She stared down at the dark blue heart-shaped toilet box. The opulent blue was overlaid with a delicate tracery of minute gold leaves and flowers, and two cupids garlanding a white lamb formed a knop in the centre.

"France," she said promptly.

He smiled, looking pleased. "Wrong again. It was made in Chelsea." He turned the box between his long fingers and showed her the anchor.

"Oh, I could have sworn it was French. That dark blue—"

"It's known as mazarine blue and was in imitation of the Sèvres *gros* blue," indicating the two vases. "This piece is certainly

French in conception, and it's one of the few worthwhile contributions I've made to my father's collection. I found it one day while I was prowling around an antique shop in Long Street, and fell in love with it on sight. I knew what it was worth and hoped I might have found a bargain, but I should have known better. The old boy was very knowledgeable: my father had often dealt with him and though his price was fair, I baulked at it." He smiled, rubbing his chin, "Collecting china is like a disease. Once you've seen a piece you covet, it never lets you alone, but haunts and takes possession of you. I often saw the same thing happen to my father . . . And as you see, I paid up in the end."

"You don't sound very pleased about it. Did you regret buying it?"

He lifted the lid and turned it over. "Look."

She saw the thin threadlike line of a crack. "Oh *Mark*. How did it happen?"

"It's pretty certain old Lizzie must have broken the lid when she was dusting my desk, though she denied this, of course. I can really only blame myself for what happened. Instead of putting this away with the other pieces in the cabinet I couldn't resist leaving it on my desk for the first few days, where I could see it. I did this despite always warning my mother of the risk she takes in putting things of such value on the mantelshelf." He glanced down at the little china box, a slight frown creasing his brows. "I must get rid of this sometime."

"Get rid of it!" she cried, outraged. "But *why*?"

"It has lost its value and no longer belongs in the collection. There seems no point in keeping it."

"But it's still exquisite, and no one would even know the crack was there unless you pointed it out."

"But *I* know it's there, and every time I see this, it depresses me. I'm better rid of it."

She looked at him uneasily. "Are all collectors so ruthless?"

He smiled slightly. "I can't speak for the others, but I know my father and I felt the same way. He was utterly without sentiment, and never hesitated to get rid of a piece once it was damaged."

She looked down at the brilliant little

toilet box gleaming like a jewel in the palm of his hand. "I don't know how you can bear to part with it."

He suddenly smiled and held it out. "Would you like to have it?"

She withdrew slightly as she felt a hot flush burn her cheeks. "I couldn't possibly accept it . . . Mark, how can you think of just—giving this away, when you told me a moment ago you'd fallen in love with it?"

He smiled down into her eyes. "Did I say that?" and lifted his hand to put the toilet box on the mantelshelf. He took her face in his hands and studied it seriously, ran his cool fingers along the delicate moulding of her cheekbones and along the fine clean line of temple and jaw. "Fall in love with a piece of china? When there's warm flesh and blood to fall in love with, as perfect as any one of my father's pieces. Do you think I'm crazy?" He bent to kiss her on the mouth and then put his arms about her and drew her to him.

Later she said a little sulkily "You hardly kissed me when we stayed at Knysna."

"I was playing a waiting game. A wise fisherman never pulls in his line until he knows his fish is hooked."

"Oh," she said, not altogether pleased. "When did you know I was—hooked?"

He brushed her hair back from her brow. "My dear Lisa, you were tied up in a hundred different knots after your father died. My chief concern then was to prevent your leaving. The idea of wooing you by correspondence held no appeal for me—with the added possibility that I might have to fly over to England to clinch matters." He smiled. "And you were in a blue funk I might try to seduce you. I decided to wait until you might find the idea more attractive."

She dropped her lashes and didn't speak.

"You began warming up a little more each time we kissed. And when we saw each other in the foyer and I saw you looking Cornelia over as if she were the scarlet woman, and going cold on me, I decided you were hooked."

"Cornelia," she said coolly. "So that's her name. She's very pretty . . . She looks as if she might be fast."

He smiled easily. "She's that all right."

She struggled to free herself. "Mark—"

But he tightened his arms and covered her mouth with his.

After a time he said: "We could go up to my room, but my mother is a light sleeper and somewhat Victorian in outlook. I wouldn't like to upset her. And old Lizzie would know for sure we'd been there and would be suitably shocked, not withstanding the fact that she's got three illegitimate children, each fathered by a different man. I've noticed that the servants have a different standard of morals for their employers . . . You're sharing a flat with someone, so that's out. I don't want this in the back of a car or in some room in a motel . . . When shall we get married?"

"You haven't asked me yet," she mumbled against his face.

"I'm asking you now. Do you *have* to go on this trip? Can't they send someone else?"

"Mark, they've had me on designing children's clothes for the last year and they've now made special arrangements for me to work for four months with someone in London. How can I let them down and walk out on them three weeks before I'm due to leave? You must see I can't do it."

. . . Four months, she had said. But in the end she had stayed away for over a year . . .

"We'll marry then, when you get back."

"But I'll have to work for them for a time when I get back. I mean I can't—"

"We'll get married nonetheless, and you can work for them for six months, no more."

"I'm beginning to wonder if you aren't one of those bossy, unattractive, domineering men."

"I know what I want."

. . . He took her down to his fishing shack the weekend before she flew to England. They arrived as usual before Peter and Sue, and Mark carried in their things and opened all the windows and doors to let in the sea air and rid the shack of the stale sweetish smell which always filled it after it had been closed up for some time. She sorted out the provisions meanwhile and stacked the groceries in the kitchen cupboard. Mark came in and lit the gas for the fridge and she put in the meat and butter. Later she unpacked and hung up the few things she had brought.

When she went into the tiny living-room

Mark had lit the lamps and poured out two drinks. At half past seven he suggested it was time they cooked themselves something to eat.

"Don't you think we should wait for them?" she asked.

"No, they'll be late."

He found he had forgotten to bring cigarettes and after they had finished their meal they drove down to Knysna and he bought a carton of two hundred at the café on the corner. It was well after nine when they got back.

He had been different all evening, taut, restless. Usually he spent the first night fixing his fishing tackle but now he sat smoking and talking.

He got up and paced the room once or twice and went to stand at the open door to stare out into the night.

"Do you think something could have happened to them?" she asked.

"No," he said abruptly.

With an air of decision he flicked his cigarette through the doorway. He shut the door, came over to her, took both her hands and pulled her to her feet and kissed her.

He released her and said "Let's make up our beds."

"But what about—"

"Don't argue."

She went into the cabin to fetch the bedding which he had dumped on to one of the bunks. When she came back he had pulled the couch away from the wall.

"Will you be sleeping on the couch tonight?"

"Yes."

"What about the camp stretcher for Peter? Don't you think we should—"

"For God's sake stop fussing," he said testily.

He moved to the other side of the couch and helped her make it up.

"It's not cold," he said. "Two blankets will do," and when he had tucked them in on his side, joined her and kneed the couch back against the wall.

As she straightened he gave her a shove which sent her sprawling across the couch and within seconds, flung himself beside her, pulled her into his arms and began kissing her with absorbed passion.

Her dress buttoned down the front and

he undid it clumsily, his fingers uncertain.

"Mark," she said breathlessly. "Peter and Sue—they'll be here any second—"

"They're not coming," he said.

5

THE sky was still threatening when Jannie Barnard strolled through the hotel entrance the next morning and made his way to the pale green mini which he had left parked under the trees opposite the steps.

The bonnet of the car was wet from an early morning shower and crystal clear drops of water still freckled the windscreen. When he opened the door he found a pool of water on the driver's seat, there because he had forgotten to close the window when he parked the car. He opened the cubby-hole and pushed aside a green and yellow scarf and found a cloth at the back, mopped up the water and pushed the cloth back into the cubby-hole and slammed it shut. He got in, switched on and revved up the engine, and once satisfied it was sufficiently warmed up, he reversed, straightened the car and drove out into the main street. There was no other traffic on the road and in seconds he was out of town.

Jannie handled the little car competently, and he was likewise a courteous and considerate driver, a fact which never failed to come as a surprise to those who knew him, or to those who had previously had the misfortune to be driven by him. There had been a time when Jannie was the worst possible speed-fiend, with the obsessive ambition to pass everything on the road, to swerve in and seize a gap at all costs, to accelerate if a car tried to pass. He blared the horn compulsively and snarled at pedestrians if they kept him waiting. But since becoming Lieutenant Meyer's official driver this had all changed—the Lieutenant had seen to that. Now Jannie always kept well within the speed limit and never failed to give way. Tardy pedestrians were waved on with a smiling urbanity to rival the Lieutenant's.

The time was now a quarter to eight, and it had required a real effort on his part to crawl out of bed, shave and drag on his clothes so that he could be at the car early enough to satisfy the Lieutenant . . . He had ignored one or two of the chief's orders, but had been wise enough not to ignore this one. He knew the chief would find out for sure if he were late, and this would spell nothing but trouble.

Once he was on the national road he settled himself comfortably behind the wheel and kept at an even pace. This was another of the chief's orders he intended carrying out. The old so-and-so would probably take his time and leave shortly after nine. If he knew him, he had probably worked out to a T when he could expect to pass the mini, and where. He could remember the chief doing this to him once before, and he had turned real nasty when he found out his orders had been disobeyed. He had even threatened to demote him and suspend his licence.

He lifted a hand to pass it gingerly over his head and round the back of his neck. Jees, he certainly wasn't feeling his best. His head was feeling about the size of a soccer ball. He hadn't gone to the chemist about his cold as the chief had told him to, and it had now settled mostly in his head which made him feel thoroughly stuffed-up and muzzy. And it didn't improve matters that he had only had a few hours' sleep. It must have been well after two when he got back to his room. He had taken the precaution of getting undressed in the dark, just in case someone was snooping around outside. He wouldn't put it past the chief to have someone check on what time he'd gone to bed. He was a martinet all right, and hot on discipline.

It was still overcast and unseasonably cold. Jannie had not thought to bring any warm clothing with him for the weekend and now found he was shivering slightly. He hunched his shoulders against the cold and wondered miserably if he might be running a temperature. The chilly draught coming through the open window, blowing directly on to the right side of his face, didn't make him feel any better. He pulled up his collar and then tried to close the window and cursed bitterly when he found it had stuck. He drove on until he reached a green verge on the side of the road and turned the car on to it and switched off. He tried again and snarled angrily when he found he couldn't budge it. If that wasn't typical of a woman! They never bothered to have anything fixed, but always waited until some sucker of a man came along and did it for them. He remembered the scarf, opened the cubby-hole and took it out. He fingered the heavy silk, lifted it to his nose to sniff at it delicately, and raised his brows eloquently when he found it was faintly perfumed. The silk was patterned with intertwined deep gold and pale yellow chrysanthemums and ragged pale green blue-tipped leaves. "Jacqmar" boldly written in black along the edge. He whistled silently. It was pretty and looked real classy. He wouldn't mind taking it for Sannie, but he'd better not risk it. It must have cost a packet and the scent smelt expensive. She must be loaded. He draped the scarf round his head and knotted it under his chin and then reached up to tilt the mirror. He lengthened himself to peer into it and grinned as he freed a lock of brown hair and let it fall over his forehead. He didn't make a bad-looking bird. Sannie was always telling him that he had the biggest eyes and the longest lashes she had ever seen. She often said that most girls would give their back teeth to have eyes half as beautiful as his. He set the mirror again, switched on and edged the mini back on to the road.

. . . He had promised Sannie that he would speak to the chief soon. Sannie and

Jannie, they had often laughed at this. It almost looked as if they were meant to be teamed up. He had at least broken the ice when he told the chief they were thinking of getting married. But let's face it—this was no longer a case of *thinking* about it, they *had* to get married, and soon! The chief was going to blow his top all right when he heard about the baby. He lifted his chin and eased the knot. He had now worked out exactly how this must be handled. He had found if the chief was handled the right way, he could be as soft as butter. It always made him laugh that the others were so scared of him. And they were jealous, of course, because he was the chief's blue-eyed boy. Some of them had made pretty snooty and sneering remarks that time he had flashed his watch around and casually mentioned that the chief had given it to him for his birthday. One or two of them had openly accused him of toadying and sucking up. He grinned to himself. Well, maybe he did play it up, but if you knew you were on a good wicket you'd be a sucker not to play the game the right way. There were several things he and the chief didn't see eye to eye on, but he certainly hadn't been a big enough fool to let on. Take the way the chief felt about the police force, for instance. He was always yakking on about it. That dedicated outlook was a lot of crap as far as he was concerned. And this bribery thing was something else they looked at from different angles. If you could make something on the side, why shouldn't you accept the dough and keep your mouth shut. Who'd know, anyway? . . .

He tapped the horn at a dog which looked as if it might cross the road.

. . . He hadn't been so pleased when Sannie suddenly sprang this baby business on him. What with her mother always at her about this respectability thing, Sannie had been the most straight-laced girl he had ever taken out, and it was only after he had asked her to marry him that she had finally consented to go to bed with him, and even then it had taken a great deal of persuasion on his part. Once she had found out what sex was all about she had proved to be no different to the others and he'd had no more trouble. They had planned to get married next year, so if they did it then or now, what was the dif? He loved her, and she was the best-dressed classiest girl he knew. She was different to the other girls he had taken out. Quiet, and acted like a lady, without being snooty. He knew the chief would approve of her once they met, and he'd spoken to her. But he and Sannie would have to get things fixed before her mother started getting suspicious. He was more scared of the old bitch than he was of the chief. She was a martinet too, strict with Sannie and snooty with him, as if she suspected he were up to no good. She had this bee in her bonnet about respectability. He had never known anyone so worried and obsessed by what the neighbours might think. For himself he couldn't care less what they thought, as long as they left him alone. There'd be one hell of a fuss when the baby came, and the old girl started doing her arithmetic. But they would be married by then and he'd be prepared to lay a hundred rand that she would lie to the neighbours about the date . . .

The little car was running sweetly, and he noticed that the leaden clouds seemed to be thinning and lightening over to the south. With any luck he might run into good weather within an hour.

As he passed Fairy Knowe he glanced at the speedometer and automatically slowed down when he saw he was travelling a fraction above the speed limit. He bowled past the deserted car park and failed to notice the dark grey Mercedes parked at the back of the clearing half hidden in the shade of a clump of wattle. As the little car disappeared round the bend the Mercedes glided from beneath the trees, increased its speed across the car park and nosed its way on to the road.

. . . One thing was sure. He must break the news to the chief at the very next chance he got. He'd have plenty to say. He could guess the lot! But he must take his medicine and let the chief say his piece. Once the gassing was over he would butter him up. He would tell him that he and Sannie had been talking things over and that they would be greatly honoured if he would consent to be godfather to their baby. He would also tell him that they had decided to call the baby Karel after him—and Carol if it was a girl. That would get him all right. The others didn't know how mushy the chief could be. On several occasions he had seen him close to blubbing when he had been compelled to break the news of violent death to the nearest relative . . .

He slowed down for a lonely fisherman at the edge of the road, waiting to cross. He eased his foot off the accelerator in case the man decided to make a sudden dash for it. This was one of the things the chief had taught him. "Use your imagination and try to anticipate some other fool's stupidity. Learn not to trust stop streets, yield signs or traffic lights. The same applies to children and dogs. Watch out for a man on a bicycle and give him a wide berth. If he's coloured, ten to one he'll be drunk and swerve out just as you're passing him."

As he drew level, the fisherman, who was young and goodlooking, stared and gave him the eye. Jannie was momentarily nonplussed and then remembered the scarf knotted under his chin and slowed down, smiled brilliantly and winked as he went slowly past.

He was still grinning in amusement as he cruised along the edge of the tidal river towards the pass. He must remember to tell this to the chief. It was just the sort of thing that made him laugh.

The tide was full. The smooth shining

water duplicated the cottages ranged along the edge of the bank on the opposite side of the river. The cottages were well spaced, many screened by trees and the thick indigenous bush. It had often puzzled him how the owners managed to reach them. He had always meant to ask the chief if he knew. Would they ferry themselves across the river? Or was there a road he didn't know of, hidden by the vegetation?

The little car soared up the incline, but began to slow down imperceptibly as the road steepened. He changed down to save the engine. It was a plucky little bus and a joy to handle. The ideal car for a girl who wouldn't push it and tear its guts apart like a youngster would. He glanced into the rear mirror and saw that a car had appeared in the road about quarter of a mile back.

He turned on to the wide bridge curving over the confluence of the two streams. The chief had told him that this was one of the few curved bridges in the Republic. He was always a mine of information about that sort of thing. By now he was probably sitting down to breakfast with his mother. Jees, she was an old sour puss if ever there was one! The only time he'd met her she had looked him up and down as if he'd been something the cat had brought in. He didn't envy the chief staying with her. That probably explained why he spent most of his time fishing off the rocks.

Once over the bridge his eyes traversed the great ramparts of rock looming above. The immense grandeur of the scenery in these parts always had the effect of slightly chilling his spine. It was not only the ascent carved and hacked up the escarpment with the bastion of rock poised above it, but also the view from the summit once one had rounded the final bend. The chasm on the left, a sheer drop of hundreds of feet into the cool-looking wooded gorge, carpeted by the lush deep green virginal forest, with here and there, a paler green-bearded yellow-wood pushing its way up through the others trees. These giants of the forest reduced by the height to the size of match-sticks, and the still dark waters of Donker-gat, gleaming black as ink between the trees.

As he took the final bend to reach the summit some instinct made him glance into the rear mirror and he saw the dark grey

Mercedes coming up behind him like a rocket. The unexpectedness of it sent a shock through his body which spread out to finally tingle in his fingertips.

He gave way, and as he moved closer to the stones at the cliff's edge, felt a sudden premonition of danger. In that split second it suddenly dawned on him whom the driver of the car might be, and he immediately jammed his foot down on the accelerator and felt the little car respond gamely. A second later the Mercedes torpedoed into the right side of the mini and stove it in like tin.

The explosive deafening sound of the crash rolled and reverberated through the high peaks, and echoed and re-echoed down in the gorge. The force of the impact killed Jannie on the spot and catapulted the mini over the whitewashed stones at the edge of the precipice and into space.

The little car rolled over and over, glinting as brightly as a new toy in the early morning sun. It fell slowly down into the silent gorge where the deep, dark waters of Donkergat lay waiting to receive it.

6

WHEN Karel Meyer reached Cape Town shortly after four that afternoon he had become a very worried man indeed.

He had sent a message instructing Jannie Barnard to do two things on the way back, only to find that in both cases his order had been flagrantly disobeyed.

Firstly, Jannie had been instructed as to which garage in Mossel Bay he must fill up, and he had been told to have the petrol put down to his, Karel Meyer's, account. There would be no trouble on that score as the owner of the garage knew him well, and had often seen Jannie with him. Jannie had also been told to make a note of the cost of the petrol so that they could settle with Miss Lombard later . . . When he reached Mossel Bay and stopped at the same garage to have his own tank filled, it was to find that his instructions had been ignored.

At this stage his reaction had been more one of annoyance than concern. Jannie knew as well as the next man that petrol cost just that bit less at Mossel Bay. But he guessed this would be unlikely to influence him unless he had to dip into his own pocket. The distance from Knysna to Mossel Bay would have left the tank fairly full and if he felt so inclined Jannie was capable of breaking orders and filling up where it suited him best. Karel Meyer knew there were times when he was guilty of allowing him too much latitude. He set his jaw grimly. Jannie would find it not to be the case this time. He would see to it that he was made to pay the difference from his own pocket.

Secondly, Jannie had been ordered to stop for lunch at the Outspan Café outside Swellendam. He was to tell the proprietress that Lieutenant Meyer would also be stopping there for lunch and would square the bill with her when he came. He knew Jannie was usually short of cash and it would be unlikely that he would have enough to pay for a square meal. It had never ceased to surprise him that a slim stripling like Jannie could tuck away a meal twice the size of anything he could manage.

Mark and Lisa had turned in at the Outspan Café ahead of him and were sitting at a table near the window when he went in. Mark looked up and signalled to him to come over and join them. Though he would infinitely have preferred to lunch alone he acknowledged the signal, crossed over and pulled out a vacant chair from the next table and sat down next to Mark. He had to admit, Mark had been civil enough, despite their differences of yesterday. He was possibly embarrassed by the girl making it so plain that she disliked him. She had barely raised her eyes to greet him and had remained silent throughout the meal. He had thought she looked rather pale and dark under the eyes, as if she hadn't had much sleep.

They left first, and he sat on and had a second cup of coffee and finished his cigarette before he got up and went over to the counter to settle for his lunch. It was only then, when the proprietress stared at him in surprise and said Jannie hadn't been in, that he felt his first twinges of doubt and alarm.

He paid with a note, frowning slightly while he waited for the change. Alarm had brushed his nerves and he looked thoughtful and worried as he went out and walked over to his car. He got in, slammed the door and switched on. He battled with an overwhelming urge to swing the car round and head back, but in the end commonsense prevailed. Good Lord, Jannie didn't need a wet nurse! He was a man now. Old enough to look after himself. His first duty as a police officer lay in keeping an eye on Mark and the girl.

Nonetheless worry gnawed at him all the way. Despite what he had said to Mark, he believed Lisa Lombard's story. He had protected himself and chosen to be cautious, never having forgotten how a seemingly reliable witness had made a fool of him once. And if he were completely honest with himself, he would also admit that Mark always got under his skin, and he had wanted to rile him . . . He should never have risked letting Jannie drive the mini back. He hadn't even warned him to be on the alert.

Once he reached the outskirts of the city and saw Mark turn off to the southern suburbs he felt he could safely leave them and drove on to Caledon Square police station.

It took him ten minutes to arrange for someone to keep an eye on Miss Lombard's flat during the night and when this was done he left and drove to his flat in Three Anchor Bay. He found the air stale when he went in, and opened the windows wide. He thought again how cold and unwelcoming the room was. It lacked something, but he couldn't say what. He grinned wryly to himself—the feminine touch no doubt.

His shirt was sticking to his back and he felt unkempt and sweaty after the long drive, but decided to telephone Lisa Lombard before having a shower.

He had kept a note of her number and looked it up before he lifted the receiver and dialled. He lit a cigarette and drew at it while he waited.

When she answered, he told her who he was, and enquired courteously whether her car had arrived and if Jannie had left the keys.

She replied coolly in the negative.

When he hung up he found he was sweating thinly and his hand shook as he stubbed out his cigarette.

He immediately put a call through to Sergeant Jooste in Knysna. His manner when he spoke to the Sergeant gave nothing away. It was as abrupt and peremptory as usual . . . It looked as if there was a possibility that something could have happened to Jannie Barnard and he wanted them to check if there had been any report of an accident between Knysna and Mossel Bay that morning. They were to make the fullest enquiries and ring him back.

There was nothing more he could do at this stage so he went through to the bedroom, stripped and had his shower.

He felt refreshed and less tired by the time he had finished dressing but he was still taut and on edge. He went through to the living-room and paced it uneasily, pausing only to light one cigarette from another. Occasionally he stopped at the window to stare unseeingly out, hands clasped behind his back.

The telephone rang and he almost leapt at it and snatched off the receiver. His heart sank when he recognised Jannie's mother's voice. Mrs Barnard was usually breathlessly in awe of him, but now she sounded agitated and upset. Was Jannie with him?

He explained why Jannie hadn't come back with him, but this in no way allayed her alarm. Surely he should be back by now. Jannie knew how she worried, and he always phoned if he knew he was going to be late. Why hadn't he done so? Had anything happened to Jannie? Was he trying to hide something from her?

He told her that the car Jannie was driving had received rough treatment the day before, and it was on the cards it had broken down.

But if this was the case Jannie would have *phoned*.

It had required all his smooth urbanity to calm her down.

Sergeant Jooste telephoned half an hour later. Only one accident had been reported in the district. It had been a collision between a lorry and a light delivery van which had taken place at ten o'clock that morning a mile from George, and the drivers of both vehicles had been coloured.

Karel Meyer came to a sudden decision. "Sergeant, I'll be on my way within ten minutes." He consulted his watch, reckoning the time it would take. "I should be there round about one a.m. Who will be on duty?"

"I'll make a point of being here myself, sir."

"Thanks, sergeant. I appreciate that." He said goodnight somewhat abruptly and rang off.

He threw a few things into a suitcase. Shirts, socks, underwear, shaving kit. There were six loose packets of Lucky Strike on his chest-of-drawers and he stuffed two into his pocket and tossed the rest into his suitcase. Within quarter of an hour he was on his way.

He drove through the night hunched over the wheel, staring grimly ahead while thoughts revolved in endless procession through his mind . . . Lisa Lombard had mentioned that she had seen the man running up the path after her, which meant that he would have seen her drive off in the mini. He had probably taken the number, and would recognise the car anytime he saw it. If he had gone through her engagement book, he would also have known at what time she intended leaving the next morning.

He lit another cigarette though his throat

felt parched and burned from incessant smoking . . . If the man wanted to get rid of her, he could have lain in wait, followed and forced the mini off the road. But then the mini would have been found by now. Someone would have seen it. He narrowed his eyes against the smoke, thinking round this. Where could he do it? Where could it be possible along the route to force a car off the road and leave no trace? Where would *he* do it, if he were bent on murder? . . . There was only one place, if you had the nerve, and by God, it would require that all right. Ice cold nerve. And split second timing. The smallest error in judgment, and you'd plunge to certain death over the edge.

One of the reasons for Karel Meyer's rapid promotion in the Force was his almost uncanny ability to project himself into the criminal's mind and guess how he would think and react under a given set of circumstances. He knew that he was dealing with a man who had already committed one premeditated murder. This must make him a much more dangerous, cunning and desperate animal.

It was well after midnight when he

reached the summit above Donkergat. He resisted an impulse to start his investigations *now*; to stop the car, keep the headlamps on and search the road.

He reached the police station in Knysna in under an hour. Sergeant Jooste must have heard him slam the door as he got out, and came to the entrance to meet him. Karel Meyer nodded at him, muttered good-evening and went through into the charge office, lifting a hand to shade his eyes against the light. He sank into a chair behind the counter, suddenly overcome by deadly fatigue.

"The wife made some sandwiches, sir," the sergeant said diffidently. "She thought you might be hungry after the long drive."

He realised that he hadn't eaten since lunch, but the thought of food almost turned his stomach.

He forced a smile. "Thanks, sergeant. It was good of your wife to go to so much trouble, but I'm not hungry."

"How about coffee, sir?"

He glanced at the tray on which were a small thermos, two thick white cups, a cracked sugar bowl. He passed a hand over his face, fighting the stupor of weariness that had overtaken him.

"Coffee might be a good idea. Would you pour it, sergeant."

He watched the sergeant open the thermos, pour out the coffee and took the cup when he handed it to him and helped himself liberally to sugar. "How is Colonel Venter?" he asked. "Has a specialist been in to see him yet?"

"Yes, sir, the doctor says he's had a coronary, and they've taken him off to hospital. He said it would be some time before Colonel Venter will be up and about again." He cleared his throat. "If you'll excuse me, sir, I think I'd better telephone Major Theron, our District Criminal Investigation Officer, who has taken over. I mentioned to him that you were coming, and he particularly asked me to let him know when you arrive."

"OK. Phone him and tell him I'm here."

"Would you like to speak to him, sir?"

"No. Just tell him I've come."

He sat slumped in his chair, sipping gingerly at the scalding coffee, and didn't speak again until the Major walked in half an hour later.

Major Theron knew Karel Meyer well by reputation and saw at once that he was dealing with a man under great stress. He had read through Miss Lombard's statement, and sat back listening and nodding while Karel Meyer picked out the main points, and tersely gave his theory of what he thought might have happened to Jannie Barnard.

Like Karel Meyer, the bluff Major was a dedicated police officer. He was endowed with less intelligence, but with a more tolerant, easy-going disposition. There was not an ounce of pettiness or jealousy in his make-up. Karel Meyer had handled this case from the start and despite the Major's rank and this being his district, he made it clear that he expected the lieutenant to take charge.

Karel Meyer nodded briefly in acknowledgement, grimvisaged, unshaven, gaunt and grey with fatigue.

They were up at the summit shortly before dawn and saw the splintered glass scattered all over the road. The deep scours of heavy tyre marks cutting diagonally across the road—and other lighter tracks dangerously close to the edge, ceasing abruptly at a recently decapitated white-washed stone . . . Everything they saw bore out Karel Meyer's theory.

A frustrating period of inactivity followed while they waited for a block and tackle to come from George, and for a diver to be flown up by helicopter from Port Elizabeth.

The news soon got around that there had been an accident at Donkergat and once operations started down in the gorge it was plain for anyone to see that something was afoot. Despite the rocky terrain and the lush undergrowth in the virginal forest, and a river which had to be crossed, unwanted spectators began arriving on the scene . . . The ghouls, the jackals, the vultures, Karel Meyer called them in a moment of savage anger.

It took two days before they found Jannie Barnard. The little group of people clustered on the bank stood watching in silence as the diver surfaced with his body. And when he began paddling somewhat laboriously towards the shore Karel Meyer quickly stripped and waded out chest-deep into the icy water to help him.

Between them they carried Jannie's body

up the bank and laid him out on the grass, partly shaded by the overhanging trees.

Karel Meyer shivered and shook, teeth clenched to stop them from chattering, his sallow face taut and ashen as he stood staring down at what was left of Jannie Barnard. He was wracked by grief and terrible remorse. He knew that *he*, and only he, must take the blame. When he had ordered Jannie to drive Lisa Lombard's mini back to Cape Town, he had virtually sent him to his death.

Sick and oppressed he turned away and walked slowly over to the clothes he had cast off in such haste near the bank. As he bent to pick up his shirt someone handed him a towel and he took it without glancing round and dried himself and then pulled his clothes over his shivering body.

He was attempting to button his shirt with trembling fingers when he saw one of the ghouls watching him, and recognised Sam Walker, a crime reporter belonging to the Argus group.

He stiffened slightly. He had no time for newspaper men, and least of all for Sam.

He left his shirt partly unbuttoned and

felt for his cigarettes as Sam Walker came over.

"He was one of your boys, not so, Lieutenant Meyer?"

"Yes." He was on the brusque side. Struck a match and bent to cupped hands to light a cigarette.

"Got any idea what happened?" Walker asked.

Karel Meyer looked him over. Thin mottled face, prominent bad teeth, a suspicious reddened nose, eyes blinking at him from behind thick-lensed spectacles.

"That's why we're here, Walker—to find out."

Lisa Lombard would be safe for as long as the murderer was under the impression that it was she whom he had sent over the cliff's edge. Karel Meyer wanted him kept under that impression for as long as possible.

He said smoothly: "Look, Walker, for the present we would prefer to have this kept out of the Press."

Walker blinked quickly and his thin nose sharpened. There were several things about this case which puzzled and intrigued him. Take Lieutenant Meyer for instance. Why was he handling the case? . . . He had been up to the summit and had noticed one or two things which he would very much liked to have explained.

He said: "I was up at the top yesterday and had a good look around. Some of those tyre marks puzzled me, and that glass lying all over the road. It makes one wonder—" He gave a thin smile which was meant to be ingratiating. "Any theories, lieutenant?"

Karel Meyer bared his even white teeth, but his eyes remained cold. "When we have the facts, Walker, we'll give them to the Press."

He turned on his heel and went over to join Major Theron who was standing in shirt sleeves supervising the block and tackle.

"How are things going?" he asked.

The District Investigation Officer looked round when he spoke. "They tell me another hour should do it, if there are no snags." He thought the Lieutenant looked ready to drop. He was still shivering and his face looked gaunt and tight, his eyes sunken.

"I'd like to have this place cleared," Karel Meyer said harshly. "I don't want any vultures flapping around when they bring in the mini.''

"I'll see to it.'' The Major beckoned to one of his men and when he came over said: "Clear the place. Tell all these people to move off.''

Karel Meyer's hand shook as he raised the cigarette to his lips. He drew on it deeply before he spoke. "Christ, Major, I've never known a case with so few clues. The girl described the man as being tall, blond and handsome. She also mentioned that he had an exceptional physique. Surely you'd expect that *someone* would have seen a man adding up to that description by now—but so far no-one apparently has. We've been in touch with every garage within a radius of two hundred miles, trying to find if anyone has seen a car with the left front fender smashed in. It stands to reason he would have damaged his car when he crashed into the mini, and it also stands to reason that wherever he comes from he would sooner or later have had to stop for petrol, yet all we've drawn to date is a blank.'' He rubbed his cheek with two fingers. "We can only hope that he's left some of his paint on the mini, then we'd at least know the colour of his car."

"Well, if he's left any we should know within the next hour . . . By the way, lieutenant, one of my men mentioned that a visitor from up-country, who is staying at the Wilderness Hotel, said he saw a pale green mini early in the morning the day before yesterday, but he says a pretty girl was driving it."

"A *girl*?" Karel Meyer said sharply, staring at him with raised brows.

"Yes. She was apparently wearing a green and yellow scarf tied round her head."

". . . Ah, so?" He said slowly and thoughtfully. "It could be Jannie wore the girl's scarf. He had a bad cold, and it would explain something which has been worrying me all along."

"And what would that be, lieutenant?" the Major enquired, lifting his bushy brows.

"It has puzzled me why it wasn't immediately apparent to the murderer that a man was sitting at the wheel."

"Since you've mentioned it, I must confess that same point worried me."

A discreet cough at his shoulder made Karel Meyer glance round quickly. "Yes, Walker?"

Walker's spectacles glinted in the sun. "Lieutenant Meyer, they've told everyone to leave. As you know, I represent the Press—"

"I know quite well what you represent," he said offensively, making it sound like an insult.

The mottled face reddened. "As a member of the Press I think I'm entitled to—"

"Mr. Walker, you're entitled to nothing!" No smooth urbanity now. "It was my decision to have this place cleared, so will you kindly get moving."

Sam Walker stared at him angrily.

"And I repeat what I said before. We want this kept out of the Press."

Sam Walker opened his mouth to make a retort but then thought better of it and shut it like a trap.

When he was out of range he muttered to himself: "Who in hell does he think he is, telling *me* what I must do? Thinks he's a bloody little Poohbah ordering everybody around. Like hell I'll keep it out of the

Press." He swore as he tripped over a root and nearly fell.

There were a few hitches before the wreck of the mini was raised from the bottom and brought ashore. Karel Meyer and Major Theron were the first to examine it, and found the traces of paint the former had been hoping for. It was dark grey paint on the right side of the mini, where it had been stove in.

They also found a knotted flowered green and yellow scarf caught in the handle of the door.

7

MRS. STANDISH tapped twice on the study door before she opened it and went in.

Mark was sitting at his desk and looked up with a slight frown. He disliked being disturbed and seldom took the trouble to hide it.

She smiled with her eyes. "Sorry to disturb you, darling, I know how much you hate it, but a Lieutenant Meyer is here to see you . . . He said it was something important."

No one else could read his face as she could, and the smile faded from her eyes when she saw the almost imperceptible tightening of his features.

"Mark, is something wrong?"

"No."

"He's a policeman, isn't he?"

"A detective would be a more accurate description. In actual fact, he's head of the Peninsula Murder and Robbery Squad." He smiled, albeit a trifle grimly, at the change in her expression. "Don't worry, I haven't been breaking the law."

He pushed back his chair and got up, and waited at the door for her to pass.

They found Karel Meyer standing with his hands behind his back, studying the titles of the books in the bookcase at the end of the long sitting-room. He turned and greeted Mark as he came in.

Mark noted his gaunt strained appearance, but hid this behind a polite smile.

"Have you met my mother?" he asked.

"We introduced ourselves a few minutes ago," she said before Karel Meyer could speak.

"Mark, could I have a word with you?" Karel Meyer asked brusquely. "I know you're busy, but I promise I won't keep you long."

"Yes, certainly. Come through to the study." He glanced at his mother. "Will you excuse us?"

She regarded him somewhat anxiously and he tried to reassure her by giving her a conspiratorial grin as he went out.

He ushered Karel Meyer into the study and shut the door.

"My God, Karel, what's happened? Have you been ill?"

"No, Mark, not ill—I'm dead beat, that's all. I haven't slept for three nights and can't remember when last I ate."

"How about something to eat now? I could easily fix it."

"No thanks, I'll have something when I get home."

"A drink?"

He smiled faintly. "I daren't risk it. I haven't got much of a head at the best of times. If I had a drink now it would probably knock me for a six."

"How about a beer?" Mark suggested. "That could hardly knock you for a six."

He half shrugged. "OK. Maybe a beer isn't such a bad idea."

Mark went out and Karel Meyer let his eyes traverse the room, taking in the rich Persian carpets, the china pieces in the display cabinet, the cream figured brocade curtains drawn across the windows, the embossed leather-bound books in the bookcases on either side of the fireplace. The buffed pomegranates in a chased silver bowl reflected in the patina of the wood. He picked up one, turning it between his strong stubby fingers, and thought that it looked as if it could have been fashioned from red leather. He looked up and saw the portrait of Mark's father above the mantelpiece and went over to stand beneath it. He studied the square serene face, with its thoughtful deepset eyes and noble domelike brow. He reckoned it must have been painted a year or two before he died.

"I remember your father well," he said as Mark came in. "It's a good likeness."

"I agree. I'm glad my mother persuaded him to sit for it."

He put the tray on the desk and while he was pouring out the beer Karel Meyer sank into one of the easy chairs drawn up in front of the fireplace and let his head fall back.

He almost fell asleep and sat up with a jerk when Mark spoke and handed him his glass.

Mark put his own glass on the mantelshelf between two china pieces, offered Karel a cigarette and helped himself, and they both lit up.

He leaned back against the mantelpiece and studied the other from beneath his lashes and thought he looked not only ill, but also tense and on edge. There was no longer any sign of the smooth urbanity which never failed to make his hackles rise.

"Anything wrong?" he asked quietly.

"*Plenty.*" He gulped down a mouthful of beer.

Mark watched him and waited.

Karel Meyer stared down at the glass in his hand. "Jannie Barnard's dead," he said abruptly.

"*What*?"

"Yes, Mark, he's dead . . . I killed him."

"What in hell are you talking about? What are you trying to tell me, Karel?"

"I'm telling you that I killed him," he said harshly, looking up at Mark with haunted eyes, sunken in deep dark bruises. "When I told Jannie Barnard to drive Miss Lombard's car back to Cape Town. I wrote him off."

Mark stiffened. "What d'you mean?"

"Do you remember Miss Lombard had written down in her engagement book what time she intended leaving for Cape Town the next morning?"

Mark nodded, but didn't speak.

"Jannie left at the same time." He dropped his eyes and tapped the ash off the end of his cigarette. "He left then on my orders—"

Mark watched him tensely. "And?—" he prompted when he didn't go on.

"We now know that Jannie was wearing Miss Lombard's scarf. It was knotted when we found it, and we've assumed he must have worn it round his head, which would explain why anyone following the mini would think a woman was at the wheel."

Mark put a hand to the mantelshelf. "*Was* someone following?"

". . . Yes, Mark. We have all the evidence to prove that Miss Lombard's car was rammed by another bigger car and sent over the precipice above Donkergat."

"My God!" Mark exploded.

Karel Meyer glanced at his tight face. "We don't know much more. But we know the car's dark grey—we found some of the paint where it hit the mini."

"Well, Karel, are you satisfied that Lisa's story was true?" Mark asked savagely. "Or do you still believe she was telling you a pack of lies?"

Karel Meyer's features contracted in a spasm as if Mark had struck him across the face . . . "I never doubted her story," he said heavily.

"Christ Almighty, you have the gall to say this to me! Listen, Karel—"

He lifted a protesting hand. "Rather, you listen to me, Mark." He felt for his handkerchief, wiped the sweat from his brow and dabbed at his upper lip. "I know how this looked to you . . . I bluffed myself I was playing things the way I did because a witness made a bloody fool of me once, and I was going to make sure that it didn't happen to me again." He rubbed his cheek with two fingers. "Nor was that all. I—we've never liked each other, Mark. Ever since I've known you, you've succeeded in getting under my skin and I wanted to give myself the satisfaction of getting under yours for a change." He ground out his cigarette, twisting and turning it between his fingers. "This—this pettiness of mine blinded me to other things. It blinded me to the danger of allowing Jannie to drive the mini back." He smashed his fist down on the arm of his chair. "Christ, Mark, I didn't even warn him!"

Mark didn't speak.

"I'll pay for this in remorse for the rest of my life."

"Look, Karel, it's senseless to reproach yourself like this. You took all the necessary steps to protect Lisa. No one could have done more. And you'll find that no one will criticise your decision to let Jannie Barnard drive her car back—"

"It's no good, Mark. I, more than anyone, should have known that a man who had already committed one premeditated murder wouldn't stop at committing another to silence the only witness who could identify him."

Mark moved involuntarily as he felt his stomach muscles knot.

Karel Meyer glanced at him. "She's off the hook—for the time being anyway," he said quietly.

"Yes, but for how long? How long do you think it's going to take before he finds out that he killed the wrong person? *God.*"

"The first thing we must hope for, is that Sam Walker keeps his trap shut."

"Who?"

"Sam Walker. You must know him. He's one of the crime reporters for the Argus Group."

"I don't know him personally . . . What about him?"

"Unfortunately Sam got wind that there'd been an accident at Donkergat—as quite a few other people did. He was ferreting around the scene with his long nose this morning."

"Didn't you tell him that you wanted this kept quiet?"

"Yes, I told him we didn't want a report in the papers and I also told him to push off . . . I didn't handle him as tactfully as I should have done. I—had just seen Jannie and I—" He broke off as the horror of the memory came flooding back.

Mark took his eyes from his ravaged face and reached for his glass.

". . . How does one handle a rat like that anyway? He feeds on sensationalism—"

Mark took a sip of beer and put his glass back on the mantelshelf. "Do you think he suspected it might have been something more than an accident?" he asked.

Karel Meyer hunched his shoulders, still half submerged in the nightmare. "Walker's nobody's fool. He's shrewd—not much gets past him. He's good at his job, one must grant him that." He smiled without humour. "He'd make a first class detective."

"How about the murderer? Have you any inkling who he is? I thought Lisa gave a good description of him. Have you found anyone who might have seen him?"

"No one." He shifted his weight as if he felt confined. "We've had a network of men questioning people throughout the district and so far not a soul has come forward who has seen him. He could just as well have disappeared into a hole in the ground. Nor have we succeeded in finding a motorist who noticed a dark grey car with a broken fender—the left front fender, it would be, if he came up from behind. Nor have we located a garage where he might have stopped for petrol—" He stopped and fingered his jaw. "Except for one, maybe—"

Even now, when he was under enormous stress and tense almost to breaking point, the habit did not desert him and he paused for effect.

Mark made a slight movement but didn't speak.

"We received a report from a garage at Riversdale and I stopped there on the way back this afternoon to check. A night attendant said that a car had stopped for petrol at about nine p.m. on the day Jannie was killed. He noticed when it drew up that the left front fender was badly damaged . . . The attendant proved to be a young Xhosa, new on the job and as dumb as you make them. He was naturally in a highly nervous state because I was a police officer, and this didn't make it any easier to get sense out of him. I asked him about the car and he could only tell me that it was big—a four-door and darkish in colour. He wasn't prepared to commit himself to its being dark grey. Despite working in a garage, he knew feathers about cars, and could give me no idea of its make or vintage . . . But he did notice that the number plate was missing—"

"Which means you don't even know from which district it came?"

"No, not a clue. But the boy said the car drove off in the direction of Cape Town. He had just enough savvy to notice that—" He spread his hands. "Not that this helps much—he could have been heading for a hundred different places."

"How about the driver?" Mark asked. "What did he have to say about him?"

Karel Meyer stroked his cheek. "Not much. He said though the man didn't get out while he was filling up, he could still see he was a big baas. I asked if he'd recognise him if he saw him again but he shook his head."

"Surely he must have got some impression of the man," Mark said impatiently. "His hair, for instance. Couldn't he tell if it was dark or fair?"

"He said the driver was wearing a hat which he'd pulled well down and also mentioned that he was wearing sunglasses which rather puzzled the boy, but he saw him take them off and slide them into his pocket as he drove off."

He lifted his glass, downed the beer in one long draught, put the glass back on the occasional table beside his chair and felt for his cigarettes. "And that, Mark, is the sum total of any clues we have to date." He struck a match and drew at his cigarette. "And I'm not even sure if this is a clue. Jannie was killed some time between half past eight and nine in the morning, and this man stopped for petrol twelve hours later, at a distance of not more than a hundred miles from Donkergat."

"Maybe he thought there might be less chance of a damaged car being noticed at night—or that *he* would be noticed. He must know that Lisa would have given a pretty accurate description of him to the police."

Karel Meyer looked at him with a gleam of approval. "Could be. He may have holed up somewhere until it was dark." He leaned back in his chair. "Despite what you said to the contrary, it seems our minds do sometimes work the same way," he added with heavy irony.

Mark, unsmiling, ignored his remark. "It seems your chief hope lies in a report of a missing woman."

Karel Meyer thrust himself further back in his chair. "Use your kop, man!" he said angrily, reverting to form. "You should know as well as I do, that a woman could be missing for six months and no one any the wiser that something had happened to her! She could ostensibly have gone off on a holiday. Gone to stay with friends. Gone overseas. *Anywhere*," He dragged at his cigarette. "It could take a long time before anyone would start becoming suspicious. And I can't afford to wait that long,

Mark . . . How long do you think it's going to take before the murderer finds out Miss Lombard is still alive?''

Mark felt the same sensation of cramp in his stomach. ''Have you told her about Jannie Barnard?'' he asked.

''No, but I'll have to. Up to now she's been under the impression that he damaged her car, and that this is the reason why she hasn't got it back. One of my men drives her to work every day and fetches and takes her home in the evening. I've also got someone keeping an eye on her flat at night. Fortunately we found it burglar-proofed and I intend having a chain attached to her door tomorrow and fixing her with a spy hole. She must be able to identify anyone who wants to come in.''

''She shouldn't really be living alone.''

''I couldn't agree with you more. Maybe you could talk her out of it. I tried, but she wouldn't hear of it. She said that as it's a bachelor flat, it would be too inconvenient and an invasion of her privacy.'' He gave a pale rendering of his smooth smile. ''She strikes me as a strong-minded rather independent young woman.''

He glanced at Mark when he didn't

speak, and wondered if by any chance he was still in love with her.

He put his hands on the arms of his chair and heaved himself up. "Well, I've kept you long enough. I must be on my way. I thought I'd just drop in to keep you in the picture."

Mark cleared his throat. "Thanks, Karel, I hope you'll continue to do so."

"If anything of importance crops up, I'll let you know."

Mark accompanied him to his car and remained standing at the end of the drive until his rear lamp disappeared round the bend and then strolled through the archway on to the lawned terrace in front of the house.

It was a clear cold night and the shimmering coastal lights fringing the bay glittered as coldly and brilliantly as diamonds and sapphires. Here and there a warmer mellower light gleamed from a homestead in the velvety blackness of the valley. The starlit sky was faintly luminous, and the thin sliver of a new moon was tilted above the looming profile of Table Mountain. The peace and quietness of the night was all embracing.

He looked down as he felt Ming rub herself sensuously against his legs. His mother's lilac-pointed Siamese had a thick coat as soft and white as ermine. She was full of character, perverse, passionate and bad-tempered. Her pale blue squinting eyes reminded him of Karel Meyer's. He bent and stroked her.

The light was on in the sitting-room which meant his mother was still reading. She would have heard Karel Meyer's car leave, and he knew she was worried. Though he still had several hours of work ahead, he felt he owed her some explanation.

She glanced up as he came in through the french doors and laid her book face down on her lap. Toby, the black Pomeranian, was lying stretched out on the window-sill where he could keep half an eye on what was going on in the garden. He cocked an eye at Mark without raising his head, and the plumed brush of his tail moved once in recognition.

Mrs. Standish was sitting by the fire in the wing chair beneath the standard lamp, and Mark seated himself in the chair beside her.

"Your policeman's gone?" she asked.

"Yes. I've just seen him off."

"Why did he come, Mark? Was it something to do with one of your cases?"

"No: he came because of something that happened in Knysna while I was there."

"Oh." She looked surprised and slightly anxious. "Were you involved in it?"

"Partially."

"If it was only partially, why did this policeman—"

"Detective."

"Detective then—go to all the trouble of coming to see you,"

She was as direct as he was, and at times this irritated him.

"Lisa was the one who was involved," he said somewhat stiffly.

"Lisa?" Her face froze.

"Yes, she's back."

This explained something that had puzzled her ever since Mark had returned from the weekend. He had been more withdrawn, and she had assumed that the embezzlement case must be worrying him. Unlike his father, Mark never discussed his cases with her. But from the report in the *Cape Times*, and reading between the lines, she had gathered that one of his chief witnesses had broken down badly under the prosecutor's cross-examination . . . But all along she had felt it must be something deeper and more personal than this.

She said: "Was she staying there—in Knysna, I mean?"

"Yes, at the Royal."

She avoided his eyes, looked down and picked an imaginary speck of fluff off her cuff. "Was her fiancé with her? Or is she married now?"

"She was alone, and she's not married."

She felt anger against Lisa welling up within her. She was probably the only person who knew just what the broken engagement had cost Mark. He had only spoken of it once, and then it had been to tell her unemotionally that the wedding was off as Lisa had fallen in love with someone else . . . Mark was a romantic by nature, though he would hotly deny it. The occasional cynical comments she had overheard him make on love and marriage, demonstrated for her the depth of his disillusion and hurt.

Lisa had done this to him, and she wondered bitterly what had made the girl come back. She had understood from Mark that she intended settling in England.

Ming announced her arrival with a harsh discordant miauw as she leapt through the open window and a second later sprang into Mark's lap. He absently ran the palm of his hand over her back. "Lisa had an accident while she was in England," he said quietly.

"Oh, what happened?" She was trying to read his face.

"She told me she stepped off the pavement and was knocked down by a car."

She put up a hand to finger the pearls about her throat. "Was she badly hurt?"

Ming had caught the ball of his thumb between her teeth. He smacked her rump sharply and she quickly released him. "Her face was injured."

She felt her heart turn over, as much for him as for the girl. "Has she been badly—disfigured?" Her voice was not completely steady.

"The left side of her face seems to have taken all the punishment. The scars are there—across her cheek. Deep purple at present, but I was told by a surgeon that they will fade in two or three years. As it is, they are nothing like as bad as she imagines them to be. She had developed a complex. I've noticed that she always tries to keep that side of her face covered."

She murmured something incoherent, feeling a tightness in her throat despite everything

"I'm afraid I've contributed to this hypersensitivity of hers." He shifted his weight. "When I met her so unexpectedly and saw what had happened to her, I was unable to hide that I was shocked. It was the *unexpectedness* of it," he said half angrily. "To be suddenly confronted by her, with no idea that this had happened." He could not bring himself to add that he had also flushed like a callow schoolboy.

"When did she have the accident, Mark?" she asked, trying to make her voice matter-of-fact.

"That's just what I don't know," he said slowly, stroking Ming under the chin with his index finger. She stared up at him, eyes narrowed to slits.

"What about this man you told me she had fallen in love with? Is she—are they getting married?"

"I know no more than you about him or her plans," he said tersely.

". . . Is she over here on holiday?" Her voice had gone unconsciously cold.

"No, she's back with the same firm she was with before. I drove her back to Cape Town and she opened up a little, not much. Apparently the firm was very good to her and she continued designing children's clothes for them in between the plastic surgery she had to undergo." He stroked the curve of Ming's back as she tucked in her head and curled herself into a ball. "She feels she owes them something, and this is the only reason why she's come back."

"Where does Lieutenant Meyer come into things?"

He told her.

Mrs. Standish had been well trained by Mark's father and listened in silence until he had finished speaking.

Then she said after a moment or so: "Mark, I don't want to advise you. As you know, I gave up trying to do that years ago. But I would like to say just this . . . It's only natural that you should be worried. To say the least, Lisa's situation is an extremely ugly one, and I can understand that you must feel concerned for her. On the other hand, from what you've just told me, I've gathered that the police have taken every possible precaution to protect her. There is really nothing further you can do to help. Try, if possible, not to—" She broke off, seeking the right words.

"Not to get involved?" he queried with a slight smile.

She nodded, not quite meeting his eyes.

He cupped Ming in one hand as he eased his legs and laughed shortly. "You can forget about that. I have no intention whatsoever of getting involved."

"If that is the case, then it would be better for you to steer well clear of her."

"Which is precisely what I intend doing. But I want her to answer a couple of questions first."

"If she answered your questions, would it solve anything?"

"No, it would solve nothing at all. But I feel I have the right to know . . . And I'll have the answers soon."

She looked at him a little sharply. "Do you mean you intend pressing her? Do you think you should, darling? Everyone is entitled to their privacy, and if there are things she'd rather not discuss with you—"

"You've got me wrong."

"What do you mean?"

"I'll get the answers, but not from her—"

"From whom, then?"

"She has a brother living in England—Dr. Robert Lombard. We've never met, but I have a hunch that he'll be able to give me the answers I want . . . I wrote to him three days ago."

8

THE following evening Sam Walker's account of the accident appeared in the third column on the front page of the *Cape Argus*.

It was headed: Young police officer from Cape Town killed in accident near the Wilderness.

Sam went on to say: Warrant Officer J. B. Barnard, aged twenty-three and a member of the Peninsula Murder and Robbery Squad, fell to his death when his car left the road above Donkergat, three miles from the Wilderness, and plunged over the edge of the precipice, to fall hundreds of feet into the wooded gorge.

He was alone in the car, and the accident must have occurred some time between eight and nine a.m. on Sunday.

A block and tackle was used to bring the car to the surface of the deep pool into which it had plunged, and a diver was flown from Port Elizabeth to assist with the operations. The head of the Peninsula

Murder and Robbery Squad, Lieutenant K. J. Meyer, was in charge, assisted by Major J. C. Theron, the District Criminal Investigation Officer. Shortly before the car was brought to the surface Lieutenant Meyer ordered the place to be cleared of all onlookers, including members of the Press.

The next paragraph was headed. Foul play suspected?

. . . Our correspondent noted several puzzling features connected with the case. It has been verified that Warrant Officer Barnard was driving a mini minor. One speculates on what could have happened to send it over the edge. Imagination boggles when trying to conceive how it could be possible for so small a car to hurtle over the precipice despite the large white-washed rocks placed along the edge. The splintered glass scattered all over the road also gave cause to pause and reflect. Tyre marks scoured out dangerously close to the edge seemed, even to a layman's eye, to belong to a bigger, heavier make of car. Not the least intriguing mystery was the presence of the head of the Peninsula Murder and Robbery Squad on the scene. Lieutenant Meyer, known for his geniality, was unusually grimvisaged and tight-lipped. All enquiries from the Press were met with an uncompromising "No comment"

For three days Alan Lincoln had combed through the morning and evening papers. It was worrying him more and more that there had been no report of an accident at Donkergat, nor any reference to a girl being missing. It stood to reason that someone would have reported this to the police by now.

He had sent the farm foreman down to the village to fetch the *Cape Argus*, and was waiting for him on the stoep when he came back. He took the paper with a brief nod and went straight into his study and sank into the nearest chair.

He saw the headlines the moment he unfolded the paper and felt his body stiffen. As he read through the report he became pale and there was a noticeable tightening of the facial muscles. Sweat broke out on his forehead and the paper crackled as his fingers tightened and clenched.

It was a trap! They were *lying*! Nobody could tell him she wasn't dead. It hadn't been a police officer at the wheel, it had been *her*. He had seen her with his own eyes. She couldn't still be alive. God, it didn't bear thinking of!

He flung the paper from him and leapt compulsively to his feet. It *had* to be her. It was her car, the right colour, the right number, and he'd seen her wearing a green and yellow scarf. The *bitch*, she *must* be dead.

He paced the room like a caged panther . . . Could it be a trap? A police officer driving her car? She would obviously have gone straight to the police. Would they have arranged for someone else to drive her car back? Would he have worn her scarf? *No*, he refused to believe it!

He bent to pick up the paper and sank down into the chair and read through the report again. Dropped the paper on the carpet and put his hands to his throbbing temples. He felt as if someone had hit him over the head—half stunned, unable to think coherently, as if part of his brain had seized up . . . His reaction had been the same when he had looked up and found the girl staring at him from the top of the sand-dune. The confrontation then had also momentarily paralysed him.

Everything had been so perfectly planned. Drowning Maisie had proved surprisingly easy. Diving and taking her unawares had done the trick. She must have swallowed gallons of water. And filling his lungs to capacity before he dived had enabled him to keep her under for a considerable length of time. She had virtually been half drowned when she surfaced, and it had been child's play to push her under and keep her there . . .

He pushed a blond lock of hair off his forehead with an unsteady hand . . . The way he had planned things, no one would have suspected that it could be anything but a tragic drowning . . . Tell the police that he and Maisie had decided to go down to Roosklip for an early morning swim; she had gone down to the beach ahead, while he had remained in the car to listen to the early morning news. When he followed, it was to see her floating face down, far out to sea. He had swum out, brought her back and had applied artifical respiration for twenty minutes, but had been unable to resuscitate her. No one would have suspected a thing. To all intents and purposes he and Maisie had always got on. There had been a lot of talk when they got married, but after five years it was generally accepted that their marriage was working. Once the police started making enquiries they would naturally find out that Maisie had been stinking rich, and quite a bit older than he was; and that he stood to gain not only a tidy fortune, but also the farm L'Horizon. This might possibly arouse their suspicions, but what if it did? They could prove *nothing*. And then that girl, that *bitch*, had to see him do it!

The initial shock of seeing her had had this paralysing effect on him, and then, as his brain cleared, his first instinct had been to *get* her before she could reach her car—but his reaction had been too slow. Even when he reached the end of the path and saw her careering off in her small mini, he had contemplated giving chase in the Mercedes and forcing her off the road. But as he stood there panting, cursing her, wanting nothing more than to be able to put his hands around her throat, he knew it was out of the question. *Two* bodies to be accounted for, Maisie and an inexplicable accident, with possible evidence that the car had been forced off the road. Both events taking place at dawn. The police would undoubtedly connect him with both deaths . . . So he had let her go, and there was now no longer any question of telling the police that Maisie had drowned. He must remove her body from the scene as quickly as possible. . . . Spotting the girl's handbag as he ran back, had been a stroke of luck. By this time he had calmed down, and his brain was once more functioning normally. Every instinct had urged him to hurry, but he disciplined himself to be coolly methodical. Even at that stage his mind had digested the important fact that she intended returning to Cape Town at 7.45 the next morning. And he had also had the presence of mind to fetch his towel and wipe the bag, and everything else he had touched. He was now in complete command of himself, and had at no stage allowed himself to panic. He reasoned that it would take at least three quarters of an hour before the police could possibly arrive. This should allow him more than enough time to save his skin, if he kept his head . . . Maisie was a big woman, and at any time she would have been a heavy burden; but dead weight, it had required every ounce of his strength to carry her up the sand-dune and along the sandy path to the gravelled strip behind the *melkhouts*, where he had parked his car. Not many men could have managed it. Only someone of his physique and in his condition. And even he had felt his legs beginning to fail. By the time he reached his car his arms had ached agonisingly, as if they were being torn out by the sockets. The final effort of bundling Maisie into the boot had left him panting, buckling at the knees, sweat dripping off him like water. Once he was in the car he couldn't get away from the place quickly enough. It was the only time he had been close to panic, and he'd had to compel himself to take it easy, to slow down at the corner, remembering how close the girl had come to turning her car over. But when he rounded the bend he had pressed his foot flat down on the accelerator and must have touched a hundred most of the way until he saw the dark green blanket of the pine plantations a mile ahead on the left. He had slowed down and taken the first track going up through the trees, driving on until he reached a subsidiary track into which he could turn; where he had been screened by the trees, but could still watch the road. It had been imperative that he must hide at that stage. The one thing he dared not risk was a meeting with the police-car along the road. He could still remember how he had tensed and sweated slightly when he saw it streaking past to the sea. He had allowed himself five minutes before he drove out of the trees and back on to the road. It had taken him less than five minutes to reach the national road, swing into it and turn right, towards Plettenberg Bay. He drove several miles before he reached the pine plantations which stretched for miles on either side of the road. He made sure no car was in sight before he turned into one of the rough roads going through the trees, and must have driven well over a mile before he stopped. He had remained there all day, hidden in the deep resinous silence of the forest. He had made himself wait until dark before he drove out and made his way to Maisie's holiday cottage, where they had spent the previous night. He had never been more grateful that it stood on a lonely stretch of coast, with no other house in sight for miles, which made it unlikely that anyone would notice a light burning late at night. He had toyed with the idea of burying Maisie there, but in the end decided against it. If her body were ever found, it would be remembered that they had spent the night there, prior to her flying to Europe from Port Elizabeth the next day. That had been another stroke of luck. It would take some time before there would be any suspicion that Maisie was missing. Everyone would assume that she had prolonged her trip overseas, as she had often done before.

He had left as dawn was breaking the next morning. First tossing her overnight things into a suitcase, and stashing it with her air luggage and his things on the back seat of the Mercedes. When he went through Knysna he had slowed down as he passed the Royal Hotel, and had spotted the green mini parked near the steps . . . The hour which followed in the car park while he sat waiting in the Mercedes for the mini, had been the longest in his life. Tension escalating. Scalp tightening. The palms of his hands sweating. The growing fear that she might change her mind and decide to leave later. Then the little car had suddenly appeared and he had switched on and followed. Even though he had felt each hammer-stroke of his heart, he had still remained clear-headed and quite calm . . . He had timed everything to the last second, and had at no stage lost his grip. Not even when the bone-jarring crash hurtling the mini over the edge, had sent the Mercedes momentarily out of control. He had resisted an impulse to drag the wheel round, and kept the big car along the very edge, even as it heeled over agonisingly at the brink, and smashed jarringly against a rock—for a heart-stopping second he had thought he was going to follow the mini over the edge . . .

He stirred as he felt his stomach muscles bunch at the recollection of those long drawn-out seconds when he had been certain he was done for . . . Luck had remained with him, and there had been no traffic on the road before he swung the Mercedes into a rough unmade track cutting up the incline through the indigenous bush. The Mercedes had bumped and lurched drunkenly up the rutted road for nearly a quarter of a mile before he found a green verge among low-growing trees into which he could turn and park. The second he switched off, reaction hit him and he had slumped across the wheel, clinging to it with both hands as his body suddenly began to shudder and shake uncontrollably. Sweat had broken out and streamed down his face, and he'd had to clench his jaws to stop his teeth from chattering . . . Reaction had had a somewhat similar effect when he dumped Maisie on to the beach. He had found his knees suddenly weakening, and had felt light-headed, queer, thinking for a second that he might faint.

He had felt curiously drained and exhausted once the shivering stopped, and leaned his head back and fell into a heavy drugged sleep; only to awaken from it in a muck sweat, his heart slamming because he had dreamed he was hurtling into space. He had dozed on and off during the day, and at some stage forced himself to eat the sandwiches he had made early that morning. He was tormented throughout the day by an unslakeable thirst which must have been an aftermath of shock and tension. At some stage he got out to examine the left front fender, and found it badly damaged, and it had taken him quite a time to remove the two number plates. Again he had waited until it was dark before he switched on, turned the car and drove down the rutted path. Once back on the road, he set out on the long drive through the night which would bring him to Somerset West and L'Horizon. He stopped only once, at Riversdale, to fill up the tank, and it was after one o'clock when he passed through Somerset West, and it took a further ten minutes before he turned in at the L'Horizon gates and drove through the farm up to the old homestead.

The next two hours had all the qualities of a nightmare. First unlocking and thrusting open the heavy doors of the shed where the farming equipment was kept, and searching by torchlight for a spade. Tossing it at the back with the luggage, and then starting up the car and taking the road to the southern end of the farm, well away from the coloured cottages. Cutting across the veld and down to the irrigation dam, past it and on to the poplar wood which lay beyond. Weaving his way through the white-boled trees until he reached the gully which lay at the edge of the wood, where he knew the dark sour soil was deep and easily dug. Facing the car so that the head-lamps would give him all the light he required. No moon, the stars glittering brilliantly in a black sky. Shrugging off his jacket and stripping off his shirt despite the cold . . . It had taken all of an hour to dig a grave wide and deep enough to accommodate Maisie and her luggage. Digging with the sweat dripping off him, vulnerable and nakedly visible for anyone to see in the bright glare of the head-lamps. Feeling that a hundred eyes were watching from the darkness. Stopping occasionally to rest and draw an arm across his forehead to wipe away the salty sweat trickling into his eyes, and seeing the movement duplicated by the long grotesque shadow flung out by the lights . . . The awful struggle of heaving and pulling Maisie's rigid jack-knifed body from the boot. The sickly sweet smell that had arisen from the boot, catching at his throat. A feeling of vertigo had assailed him and there had been a moment when he'd thought he might lose his senses. Horror had beaten through him as he carried her over to the grave. Dropped her in, then back to the car for her luggage. Shovelling sand into the grave like a maniac: and the unutterable relief when he could no longer see her. Treading and tamping down the earth. Carefully flattening and smoothing it once the grave was filled, and then covering it with twigs, and with the tall reeds that grew abundantly in that area. Breaking off a branch and sweeping away his footprints. He had taken the precaution of parking the Mercedes higher up, where he knew the ground was hard and if any imprints had been left by the tyres they would be washed away by the next winter showers . . . Then the drive back to the homestead. Dragging open the doors of the old shed which had stood empty for years. Driving the Mercedes in and parking it well back. Padlocking the doors . . . The old house had stood silent and in darkness. When he unlocked the front door he had heard an owl hoot once. The familiar musky smell that greeted him when he entered the hall had been like a benediction to his fevered spirit. Down the long cold passage to his room. First brushing the sand off his shoes and trousers. Washing his socks, caked with black soil. Then under the hot shower, letting the water wash through his hair, soaping and scrubbing his body, cleansing it of his last horrifying contact with

Maisie . . . The sky was brightening above the peaks and over to the east when he finally switched off the light and fell onto the bed.

Five years back, when Alan Lincoln first drove out to L'Horizon to meet Maisie van Stalen, he had just turned twenty-six.

He would often be ironically amused to think that if it had not been for Linda Freyer, it was unlikely that he would even have known of Maisie's existence. Linda had commanded him to look up Maisie as soon as he reached Cape Town. Linda had never been one to request or suggest. Whatever she wanted, was couched as an order. "Pour me another drink . . . Turn down that damned radio . . . For God's sake, Alan, get a move on! . . . Put more wood on the fire . . . You must phone Maisie van Stalen and look her up as soon as you get to Cape Town."

. . . Maybe Linda felt entitled to order him around as she had more or less supported him since he had become her lover. It had been at her command that he had flown down from Johannesburg at his own expense to spend a fortnight at the Cape.

He had been showing signs of baulking and becoming sulky under her high-handed treatment, and she had decided that a change of air, and having to put a hand into his own pocket for a change, should bring him to heel . . .

He would wonder later what had made Linda so insistent that he should visit Maisie. She had mentioned that they had been at school together, but it was difficult to imagine what they could have in common.

Linda was a divorcée. A slim, expensively gowned, impeccably groomed woman in her late thirties; sophisticated, highly sexed and as hard as nails. Maisie on the other hand was a big, plain, good-natured woman, who had allowed herself to go to seed. She was naïve, and astonishingly innocent and easily shocked. As far as he could see, the only thing they could possibly have in common was their age and their wealth.

. . . For a sophisticated intelligent woman, who was under no illusions regarding her young lover, Linda made two stupid mistakes. Not for one second had she imagined there would be any risk of competition from fat, good-natured, untidy old Maisie. Even in the unlikely event of Maisie's attracting a man, she would still be far too straight-laced to take a lover. But Linda had underestimated the fact of Maisie being a widow of considerable means. And she had also discounted what effect L'Horizon might have upon Alan.

Almost from the second he turned through the imposing gateway and drove along the winding road through the farm, something within him stirred and quickened. He drove at a snail's pace, taking in everything. Stopped to stare at the peach orchards heavily burgeoned with blossom. A sudden gust of wind shook the branches and sent a shower of pink petals floating down. He stopped again when he reached the narrow white-washed bridge spanning the stream and leaned out to peer down into the clear golden water and saw a brown trout flash across the smooth round stones on the river bed. White and pink blossoming orchards seemed to stretch for miles along the right side of the road. He passed the cow byres, backed by a single row of immensely tall Lombardy poplars; and the

Jersey cows in the wide green pastures stopped their placid chewing to watch as he went past. He came to a fork in the road and took the turning to the left which Mrs. van Stalen had told him over the telephone would take him to the homestead. He drove slowly up the shaded road twisting through the stately oaks, and knew that all this was something he wanted, more than he had ever wanted anything in his life. He tried to remember what Linda had told him about Maisie van Stalen, and cursed himself for not having paid more attention at the time. She had mentioned something about their having been at school together, which would make them much of an age. She was a widow, he knew that. Had Linda also said something about her husband having been much older? And something else about her being fat? Christ, he could remember nothing.

He parked the car which he had reluctantly hired, under one of the old oaks in front of the house. Got out and paused to look over the gracious old homestead before going up the steps. The upper half of the front door was open, and a whitecoated African houseboy who must have been loitering in the hall, waiting for him, greeted him with flashing white teeth, opened the lower half of the door and led him across the long hall running the breadth of the house and out through the door at the other end into the garden.

Maisie was talking to one of the gardeners in the shade of a camphor tree at the end of the lawn and was somewhat taken aback when she turned and saw this tall, tanned, good-looking young man coming across the lawn towards her. She had formed an entirely different picture of Linda's friend when she had spoken to him over the telephone, envisaging a much older man. Certainly not this almost overpoweringly handsome young man, with long grey eyes and cold clean-cut classical features. His searching look and brilliant smile when he greeted her brought a faint flush to her cheeks.

Within an hour Alan had made up his mind. Maisie was fat and blowsy but by no means unprepossessing. She had an unaffected wholesome charm and a warm candid smile which lit up her face. Fortunately her teeth were good and if she could be persuaded to lose weight, take more trouble over her appearance and dress more stylishly she wouldn't be too bad looking. The main thing was she was good-natured and easy-going, and should be pliable and easy to handle . . . Living with her in a place such as this would offer him everything he wanted most in life. Wealth, background, security, and his self-respect back. A landowner and a farmer. No longer a lap dog at the beck and call of a demanding wealthy mistress who could order him around at will.

Unless he intended prolonging his stay, which would cost a fortune and could result in arousing Linda's suspicions, he would have less than a fortnight in which to pressurise Maisie into marrying him.

He achieved his object with two days to spare. His whirlwind courtship, combined with his physical beauty and the devastating effect of his charm which he turned on full blast, swept Maisie off her feet.

Once she made up her mind to marry him, she refused to listen to advice from anyone. *Nothing* and *no one* would stop her from marrying him. She turned a deaf ear when she was warned that he was nothing but a fortune hunter and, when told that he had never done a day's work in his life but had been kept by older wealthy women practically since the day he left school, angrily and contemptuously refused to believe it. For the first time in her life she was in love. Her first husband, Jan van Stalen, had been a prosperous widower nearly twenty years her senior. He had hoped that this big, cheerful, strapping, healthy girl would provide him with the heirs that had been denied him by his first marriage. Even though these hopes were not fulfilled their marriage had nonetheless been a successful and happy one. She had been devoted to Jan, but realised now that she had never been in love with him.

Alan was the only one whom she believed and listened to. She finally became convinced, that incredible and miraculous as it may seem, this god-like young man nearly twelve years her junior had fallen as deeply in love with her as she had with him.

Linda's letter to Alan when she got wind of the marriage was a masterpiece of bitchiness. If Alan had had a sense of humour, or if it had been Mark for instance, he would have grinned in acknowledgement of the artistry with which she had expressed herself. But Alan whitened with rage before he viciously tore the letter into small pieces. He never forgave Linda, nor did he forget what she had written. He was inordinately self-centred, and vain, and Linda better than anyone knew the chinks in his armour and where she could hit him that it would hurt most.

Despite what everyone had predicted to the contrary, it soon became evident that the marriage was working. Maisie's appearance alone gave proof. Being happy and in love lent her face a becoming glow. At Alan's insistence she fined down, and under his guidance acquired a casual elegance. It was easy too to see that he was happy and that he had taken to farm life like a duck to water. He took his new role very seriously and soon made it clear that he intended learning all he could about farming. He picked the brains of the white manager who had run the farm since Jan van Stalen's death. He and Klaas Colliers regarded each other with mutual suspicion and dislike, and the manager parted with the information he was asked for both reluctantly and grudgingly, recognising in Alan a threat to his future.

Alan also cultivated the neighbouring

farmers and asked them endlessly for advice. He studied until late at night, working tirelessly to acquire all the knowledge he would need to run the farm.

At the end of eighteen months he summarily dismissed Klaas Colliers whom he had suspected for some time of lining his own pockets, and took over the management of the farm himself. This led to his first quarrel with Maisie, who had been angered by his high-handed act, done without her having been consulted. She considered that he had been grossly unfair, and stood up to him with a surprising amount of spirit, and furiously and flatly refused to believe that Klaas Colliers was dishonest. She had known the manager for over fifteen years and considered herself to be in a better position to judge his character. Unbeknown to Alan, she recompensed him handsomely for his abrupt dismissal.

After two years had passed and Maisie still showed no signs of becoming pregnant, Alan hinted that as her first marriage had been childless, the chances were they would have no children. She held her tongue and didn't tell him, as most women would have done, that it had been found that the fault lay with Jan van Stalen and not with her. She knew it would be inconceivable for Alan to believe that a man of his physique could possibly be sterile.

Though she was still deeply in love, she was no longer blinded; and recognised and accepted his faults. She knew he was vain and self-centred, and that he lacked bigness and warmth. She was gently amused that he was unable to pass a mirror without furtively glancing at himself, and once or twice she had caught him smiling brilliantly. She knew how aware he was of the impact his blond handsome looks made on women, and how carefully he cultivated his deep tan and kept his body in trim.

She found he could be mean in petty penny-piching ways, alien to her nature, and though he constantly tried to curb what he termed her slapdash disregard of the value of money and her wild extravagance, she merely laughed and took no notice. Alan was a taker in life. He had an inability to give, either of himself or materially. His meanness was part and parcel of his cold nature, just as Maisie's casualness and generosity was part of her warmth.

After Jan van Stalen's death, she had

formed a habit of leaving the Cape in the winter months to enjoy the warmer climes of Europe. When she first suggested to Alan that they should take a holiday each winter, he had refused even to consider it, being far too wrapped up in the farm. But in the fourth year of their marriage she managed to persuade him, albeit unwillingly, to accompany her on a trip to Europe. She knew he had never been overseas and she was as excited as someone arranging a treat for a child, and went to great lengths to arrange a trip which would be memorable for him in every way. Only the best was good enough for him, and she booked at the most luxurious hotels and they dined in the most exclusive and famous restaurants. She hired a car and driver to take them down the Rhone valley to the South of France. They spent a few days at Rapallo and Portofino. Visited Naples and Capri. She rounded off the trip with a brief stay with wealthy friends who lived in an Elizabethan house in Surrey, and arrived opportunely at the height of the spring.

The trip was an unqualified failure. Alan had not wanted to go, and from the start became a disinterested and critical traveller. He went with a closed mind, finding little to enthuse about, but much to condemn. He was appalled at the vast amount of money they were spending. It became almost physically painful for him and he could barely bring himself to eat the food when he knew what it was costing them. He angrily accused her of wantonly pouring good money down the drain. It irked him to be away from L'Horizon which had by now become the hub of his life. It worried him that Corneels, the coloured foreman, might be letting things slide while he was away. He became sulky and made no effort to pretend that he was anything else but thoroughly bored.

So the following year Maisie went alone. He grumbled at what this must cost, but was agreeable she should go, provided she didn't expect him to accompany her. And it was while she was away that he met Lorne Sellars and fell in love for the first time in his life.

9

HE saw Lorne Sellars for the first time the week after Maisie left on her annual trip to Europe. It was at a party given by their immediate neighbours, the van Eedens, who lived on the farm Welgemoed. It was a mixed party of the young, the middle-aged and the old, to celebrate the engagement of their eldest son Adam, and Lorne had been among the slim young girls present.

He had noticed her almost at once, a tall golden girl standing in a group of young people clustered beneath the brass chandelier hanging from the yellow-wood rafters in the centre of the room. She was by far the tallest girl present and also the most poised. He was half amused to see that she was as aware of the effect she had on men as he was conscious of the impact he made on women.

His dealings with the opposite sex had been only with older women, yet he found himself studying this girl with undue interest. The light from the chandelier shone on her smooth thick wheat-coloured hair which hung like a curtain nearly to her waist. Her eyes were slightly tilted and her mouth in repose looked full and a little sulky but curved warmly and sensuously when she smiled.

The first long look they exchanged across the room had been both challenging and half in recognition, the attraction between them immediate and electrifying.

Alan stiffened as he recognised its danger. His methods had always been devious and up to now, any approach made to a woman had been calculated, with the definite object in mind of improving his status.

He had virtually had no contact with a girl younger than himself. He had just turned eighteen when he had his first affair with a woman of twenty-five, who made a dead set at him while her husband was away. This was not only his initiation into sex, but also his first taste of good living and the comforts that went with money. Their liaison from necessity had been of short duration, ending with the husband's return to the connubial nest. Alan's mistress found she did not have to exert undue pressure to persuade him to accept a handsome monetary gift before they parted.

His father, John Lincoln, a clerk in a small business and a humourless, intensely religious man, got wind of the affair. Someone must have talked, and after a flaming row he threw Alan out of the house. Before he left, his mother tearfully pressed three hundred pounds on him which represented her entire life's savings, and armed with this, and with the money his mistress had given him, plus the addresses of two wealthy friends of hers in Johannesburg, Alan set out for the Golden City.

He knew what he wanted and he also knew that his best hope of leading the life he had in mind lay in women; older, wealthier women who could afford the luxury of supporting a young lover. He became a kicker away of ladders, each mistress he acquired a little richer than the last, a little higher up the social scale . . . Linda had been his last. She had stolen him from his current mistress by blatantly pursuing him and more or less bribing him to become her lover. Of all his mistresses she had been the most demanding, the bitchiest and the most generous.

He knew people had talked and sneered at him behind his back. There had been occasions when he had intercepted a wink or a quickly suppressed smile which had filled him with white-hot rage. Linda in particular had diminished his self respect by ordering him around like a lackey in front of her friends. He had told her once that she would drive him too far, but she had laughed in his face and then made one of her typical bitchy remarks.

That was all over now, and people could no longer point a finger or sneer at him. As a conscientious hard-working farmer, up every day shortly after dawn, he would earn the respect of everyone; and no one could possibly accuse him of living off Maisie. L'Horizon had given him back his pride and his manhood. He had found that Maisie took little interest in the workings of the farm and had been content to leave the management of it entirely to him, once Klaas Colliers left. But in other ways she had proved less predictable and tractable. Though basically easy-going and even-tempered, she had become surprisingly stubborn on occasions and he had found that if a moral issue were at stake nothing could budge her. He privately thought she was much too straight-laced—verging on being old-maidish. Since he had married her, he had not looked at another woman for this very reason. If he were honest with himself, he must admit that he had never experienced this tremendous sexual urge one always read about. Except maybe that first time, when he had been half in love. For him sex had always been a means of climbing another rung up the social ladder.

But this sudden flare-up of mutual attraction between the girl and himself he instantly recognised as something different, and every instinct in his being warned him against the danger of making any move towards her. It would be sheer insanity to jeopardise his whole future by risking an entanglement with this tawny-eyed young beauty. He knew Maisie's views well enough by now to be certain of what her reactions would be if he were to have an involvement with another woman.

So he steered well clear of Lorne, content to merely watch from the sidelines. He didn't speak to her, nor did he ask her to dance. Only once, when he caught her looking at him, did he smile brilliantly. At midnight he took leave of his host and hostess and drove home.

The next morning being Sunday he slept late. While he was shaving he noticed that the sky had become heavily overcast, and by the time he went in to breakfast the rain was pelting down. It still showed no signs of abating by the time he had finished his coffee, and faced with a day indoors, he decided upon fetching the *Argus* and the *Sunday Times* from the little Greek who owned the corner shop in the village.

If he had made this decision an hour earlier, or an hour later, he would have missed Lorne and it was doubtful if he would have seen her again. They moved in different circles and belonged in different age groups. He lived in the country, and she led an active social life in Cape Town. It is possible that she may have remained somewhat regretfully in his memory as a lovely, vital, desirable girl who had stirred him unduly, and maybe if circumstances had been different—

As it was he clapped on a hat, shrugged into his raincoat and left the house shortly before ten. The driving rain was sweeping across the farm like an undulating veil and he took the winding gravelled road very slowly, knowing how treacherous and slippery it could become in bad weather. When he crossed the white-washed bridge he saw that the rains had swelled the stream to a swirling, muddied torrent.

He drove through the pillared gateway and turned into the main road. The rain showed no signs of letting up and he drove slowly, keeping well behind a blue Volkswagen travelling in the same direction. He listened absently to the hissing of the tyres on the wet road and found himself thinking of the girl. He wondered how old she was? What she did for a living? All the young girls worked these days. Would she have a steady boyfriend? There had been no one in whom she had shown any interest, but a girl with her looks would certainly have some man tagging along.

The Volkswagen veered sharply to the right and left the road. He instinctively braked and immediately felt the back tyres slither uncomfortably on the wet tarred surface. He quickly released the brake, checked the skid and once he had straightened the car, he let it come slowly to a halt, turning at the last minute on to the grass at the edge of the road. He switched off, jerked up the hand-brake and leapt out.

He pulled down the brim of his hat to protect his face from the driving rain and sprinted over to the Volkswagen which lay at a steep angle with the right front and rear wheels embedded in a deep ditch running along the fence.

He caught the handle of the door, wrenched it open and peered in.

She had managed to half lift herself to reach up and clutch the steering-wheel with one hand, and was attempting to drag herself from where she had been flung, sprawled against the door.

"Are you all right?" he asked anxiously.

She caught the wheel with her other hand and heaved herself up. "Yes."

Her thick mane of hair had fallen like a curtain across her face and it was only when she lifted a hand to brush it away and he found himself staring into her widened tawny eyes that he realised who she was.

Even at that stage he might have saved himself if he had been content to render what assistance he could and leave it at that. But he was already half bewitched, and his day was free and so was hers . . . And at the end of it he kissed her, and his rational mind ceased to work.

He had been more emotionally moved than he could have believed possible to find that Lorne was still a virgin. Her sensuous beauty and her awareness of its effect on men had led him to suppose she might be wanton. He was enchanted and enraptured by her fresh youth, her firm young body which had appeared so deceptively slim, her uninhibited pleasure in his love-making . . . When he got home he lay awake, staring into the dark, thinking of her.

Alan had been well versed in conducting his affairs with discretion and secrecy and this time he took even more precautions than usual. Lorne gave him the key of her flat, and during the drive from Somerset West he would think of her curled up in bed waiting for him. He always arrived late at night and left early in the morning while the streets were still deserted.

Fully aware of all the risks involved, he had intended that their affair should end shortly before Maisie returned from her trip. But when the time came to break off their relationship, he found he did not have the strength to do so. He was unable to face the thought of losing her, even though he recognised that it was something he would have to face up to sooner or later.

So he left things as they were and said nothing, and continued to go to her whenever he could. Once a week. Twice at the most, if he could think of a feasible enough reason to give Maisie for going out. The few nights he now shared with Lorne served only to intensify his desire for her, and aggravated another far more difficult problem which was causing him some considerable anxiety.

. . . When Maisie returned from Europe he found that the very thought of having any physical contact with her filled him with abhorrence, and try as he would, he was unable to overcome this. She had fined down after having done a three weeks' specialised diet while staying in England, which she had undergone solely to please him. She was warmly affectionate and radiantly delighted to be back. But he was quite unable to respond, and no force of will could bring him to make love to her.

At no stage had Alan committed himself by telling Lorne that he was in love with her. It was a fact he had not even admitted to himself, but he now realised with considerable alarm how deeply involved he was.

He racked his brains to think of some convincing explanation he could give Maisie. He even toyed with the idea of telling her that he had caught a bug, or some such thing, but on thinking it over, decided against it. Knowing Maisie she would immediately call in a doctor and his complaint would then be disproved.

So in the end he said nothing at all, but tried to make up in other ways for not loving her. He turned on all his charm and formed the uncharacteristic habit of occasionally presenting her with a small extravagant gift. A bottle of her favourite perfume. A beaded evening bag. A silk scarf . . . She received these offerings with barely audible thanks and downcast eyes.

A less self-centred more perceptive man than Alan would have recognised the danger signs. He would have noticed how much quieter she was, and he would have noticed that she had become a compulsive eater and no longer cared about her appearance. He would have taken heed and known that if he ever intended ending his liaison with Lorne, it must be done at once.

When the break came it took him completely unawares, like a knife-thrust in the dark.

They were sitting in the study after dinner and he was telling her that he had come to agree with Andries van Eeden's opinion that if one were prepared to wait, pears in the long run were a better proposition than peaches. He was thinking of embarking on a three-year planting scheme which should ultimately treble the present pear crop, but this would mean scrapping the two oldest peach orchards on the farm which had been planted by her grandfather. Would she mind?

When she didn't speak he glanced at her and frowned slightly when he saw she was staring unseeingly ahead.

"Maisie—"

She looked at him. "Yes, Alan?"

"Did you hear what I said?"

"D'y mean about planting pears? . . . Yes, I heard."

"Aren't you *interested*?" he asked half angrily. "You've lived here all your life, and L'Horizon has belonged in your family for four generations and yet at times I think the place means more to me than it does to you."

She said: "Alan, I'm flying to Europe next Friday."

His brows lifted. "Next Friday? Isn't this very sudden?"

"No, I've been thinking about going for some time. I made all the arrangements several weeks ago."

His pulse quickened at the thought of the freedom this would entail.

He said: "Why haven't you mentioned this before? Aren't you leaving rather earlier than usual?"

". . . Yes."

The way it was said made him look at her and he realised with distaste how much she had let herself go these last few months. She was wearing the knitted coral suit she had bought in Paris last year when she had been at least a stone lighter. It was too tightly stretched across her breasts and unbecomingly rucked up over the bulges of hip and thigh. He wondered when last she had been to the hairdresser. Excess weight had made her face heavy and dull.

She stirred slightly as if she guessed his thoughts. "I've booked my flight from Port Elizabeth."

"Whatever for?"

"I want to spend a night at the shack on the way. It's nearly eighteen months since we've been there and I want to check if everything's all right. I'll take the Mercedes."

"I'll drive you up."

". . . No, Alan," she said slowly. "I'd rather go alone."

"I insist. I won't hear of your going alone." Turning on the charm. "In any case, what about the Mercedes—who would bring it back?"

"I can always arrange something."

"No, Maisie, I won't hear of it. I'd enjoy going with you and spending a night in the shack."

She gripped the arms of her chair. "Alan, I'll be gone two months which should give you ample time." She drew in a painful breath. “When I get back I don’t want to find you here.”

His body stiffened. She knew!

“What on earth are you talking about?” He spoke quite calmly though his face had tightened.

“I think you know what I’m talking about.”

“If I knew, I wouldn’t be asking you. Maisie, what’s the matter?”

“Don’t let’s be hypocritical, Alan. You’ve surely guessed by now that I must know about the affair you’re having with that—girl . . . I’ve known about it for some time.”

He could only stare at her. Shock always seemed to have this paralysing effect upon him.

“. . . I’ve seen her,” she said. “She’s very beautiful and very—young . . . I-I’m not surprised you couldn’t bring yourself to—” She gulped and stopped.

“Oh, for God’s sake! Maisie—”

“You only married me for my money, didn’t you? Everyone warned me at the time but I wouldn’t believe them. I believed *you* . . . You were a very convincing liar, Alan.”

"Who have you been talking to? Who has been trying to put you against me?"

". . . Or did you marry me for L'Horizon? Was that the reason?"

"I married you because I fell in love with you. You know that as well as I do."

". . . And do you still love me?"

"What's the matter with you? Of course I still love you." He pushed his blond hair back from his brow and she noticed how his set features enhanced the cold sculptured beauty of his face. "Look, Maisie, I think I can guess why you—I haven't wanted to alarm you because I knew how you'd worry if I told you this . . . I went to see a specialist while you were away. I'd been feeling off-colour for some time and it seems I've caught some bug which has had this effect on me. He said—"

"Don't you make love to her either?"

He felt entrapped as he thrust himself back in his chair. "You've got this all wrong."

"What have I got wrong, Alan?"

"I'll be honest with you. I won't deny that I had an affair. But it isn't of any importance—to *me*, I mean. That's what you don't seem to understand. It has nothing to do with the way I feel about you.''

''Why do you say you *had* an affair with her? Do you think I don't know you're still seeing her?''

How did she know? Had someone told her? Had she by any chance put a detective on to him? You could never tell how a woman would react.

She gave a humourless smile. ''Don't worry, Alan, I haven't had you followed.''

''Look, Maisie, she means nothing to me . . . This—thing started while you were away. I was lonely. Hell, I'm not the first man to look at another woman when his wife goes off and leaves him. But that was all it was and as I said—she means *nothing* to me.''

Her lip curled. ''D'you expect me to believe that?''

''I'll prove it to you by not seeing her again.''

She gave a harsh discordant laugh which startled him. ''Are you doing this because you don't want to lose me? Or is it L'Horizon you're frightened of losing?''

''Why won't you believe me?''

''You're in love with her, Alan, as far as

you're capable of loving anyone besides yourself . . . This is the first time you've had young flesh, isn't it?"

God, he thought, she was capable of being as bitchy as Linda at her worst.

"I've learned a great deal more about you now, and if I'd known the half of it I would never have married you. When I fell in love with you, Alan, I fell in love with a man who didn't exist. You've been a parasite all your life, living off rich middle-aged women like—like me. Well, try living off a young girl for a change. I know all about her. I know her name: Lorne Sellars—a pretty name for a pretty girl. I also know she's a model and I'm told does quite well: but she doesn't earn anything like the kind of money you'll need to lead the life you've become accustomed to."

"You've been listening to other people running me down. Surely these five years we've shared have proved *something*." He leaned forward, resting his hands on his knees, his face pale and intense. "I'm going on this trip with you, Maisie. We'll go to Europe together and I'll prove to you—"

"It's no use, Alan," she said wearily, suddenly looking desperately tired and old.

"As I said, I want you out of this house by the time I get back. I have all the evidence I need to divorce you, but I would rather not use it. I'll only use it if you force me to. Let's at least part with some semblance of dignity."

"Have you been discussing this with your friends?"

"I've discussed it with no one," and then added bitterly, "You've been very discreet. I don't think any of our friends have an inkling that you're in love with her."

"How many more times do I have to tell you that I'm not in love with her," he said angrily.

She reached for her bag which she had tucked behind her and got up. "Good-night, Alan," she said quietly, and went out.

He watched her go, dazed and bewildered by the speed at which his entire life had been disrupted.

God, what a fool he had been! What an incredible *fool* not to have ended his affair with Lorne months ago! No, not months ago, he should have ended it *before* Maisie came back. He flung himself back. He must have been stark staring raving mad to risk everything; *L'Horizon*, for an affair with a girl barely out of her teens.

His face darkened as he thought of Lorne with something approaching to hatred. *She* had done this to him! *She* was responsible for the mess he was in now. Every word he had said to Maisie was true, she meant *nothing* to him. God, he hoped he'd never see her again.

To lose L'Horizon! This was something he found he could not face.

He clasped his head in his hands and tried to think calmly and rationally. She was unreasonable and upset now, but he must get round Maisie. If anyone knew how to handle a woman, he should by now. His body slowly relaxed as his mind took over. He must have been insane to think he could get away with it; not to go near her all these months and think there would be no repercussions. There was obviously only one course to take, and strangely enough, he now found that the shock of her confrontation and the fear of losing L'Horizon had acted as the spur he had needed to wipe out whatever feelings of abhorrence there had been at the thought of approaching her.

. . . Later he went to her room only to

find the door locked. He tapped on it and repeatedly begged her to let him in, but she feigned sleep and in the end he went back to his own room to spend a restless and uneasy night.

A constant flow of friends filled the house for the next five days and gave him no opportunity of speaking to Maisie again and reopening the subject. Guests stayed until late at night and by the time he had seen them off, Maisie had nipped off to her room and locked the door.

This undeniably worried him but not unduly so. It reminded him somewhat of the technique Linda had employed at times to turn the screw on him when he had flared out at her for pushing him around once too often, and she wanted to remind him just who was supplying his bread and butter. He could handle this. Let things ride for the time being. But once they spent the night together in the shack, where there was no lock to the bedroom door, he was quite confident that he would make the break-through and win Maisie back.

The one thing that never crossed Alan's mind was the possibility that Maisie might no longer love him.

. . . She told him this when he tried to make love to her that night in the shack. But he was arrogantly confident of his hold over her and refused to believe her.

So Maisie set out to convince him. She told him that she knew him now for what he was. A cold-blooded fortune hunter who sold himself for money. A liar and a cheat. On top of that he was penny-pinching and mean, and she knew, though he may not think so, how much of the money from the farm was going into his own pocket. His vanity was ludicrous to a pathetic degree. She laughed in his face when she told him this. Did he think people didn't notice how he stared and smiled at himself whenever he passed a mirror? He was so vain he didn't even realise that everyone laughed at him. He was in love with himself, that was his trouble, and he was incapable of loving anyone else. And she would tell him something else; even though he had been well tutored by Linda and her friends, Jan van Stalen had still been the better lover. When she looked back now, it was inconceivable to believe that she had actually imagined she was in love with him. The only thing she felt for him now was utter contempt.

She knew there was one thing besides money that he loved almost as much as he loved himself, and that was L'Horizon. And L'Horizon was *hers*, and it gave her immense satisfaction to know just how much it was going to hurt him to lose it. One thing was certain, he would never marry that girl because she had no money. So he had better start looking around for another rich widow with a big farm. She laughed. Unluckily for him rich widows with big farms were far and few between . . . But there was one thing he must make quite certain of. He must see that he was gone, lock, stock and barrel by the time she got back!

And so Maisie finally succeeded in convincing Alan that his cause was hopeless, and in so doing signed her own death warrant.

10

KAREL MEYER swore violently and blasphemously when he saw the headlines of Sam Walker's report in the *Cape Argus*, and cursed again when he had finished reading it. He put out a hand and lifted the receiver to telephone Sam to tell him exactly what he thought of him, then changed his mind, banged it down and reached for his cigarettes instead. What was the use? It was done now and he would certainly get no satisfaction from Sam. The reverse, in fact. A row with him would resolve nothing and could only result in heightened blood pressure and loss of dignity.

He lit a cigarette and drew on it several times to give himself time to simmer down before he lifted the receiver and telephoned Lisa Lombard. When she answered, he asked politely if it would be convenient if he came round to see her for ten minutes. Equally politely, but infinitely more coldly, she agreed to see him.

He found that she had not read the *Cape Argus* and knew nothing whatsoever about the report, so he proceeded to tell her everything. He told her that the murderer had mistakenly killed Jannie Barnard, thinking it was her. That he must have read the report by now and would know she was still alive. That they were dealing with an utterly ruthless man who knew her name and address and where she worked. He didn't pull his punches but was blunt to the point of being brutal. This was done with the fullest intention of frightening her. Despite all he had told her, he still got the impression that she did not appreciate the seriousness of the situation, or that her life might be in danger.

He reiterated what he had said before—that it would be wiser if she moved from her flat—and added that he would be only too pleased to make all the necessary arrangements for her to stay elsewhere.

He glanced at her when she remained silent and noted the mutinous set of her chin and softened his somewhat peremptory manner to his usual smooth urbanity . . . This had merely been a suggestion on his part. If she felt she didn't want to move, then she should at least try to find a friend who would be willing to share her flat.

She looked at him with cool green eyes and pointed out quite reasonably that if, as he said, the murderer knew where she worked, it would be easy for him to follow her and find out that she had moved. Her present flat was burglar-proofed and no one could possibly make an entry unless she let them in, and as he himself had seen to it that her front door had a chain and a spy hole, no one could come in unless she identified them first. Furthermore, he had informed her that her flat was under constant surveillance at night and that she was being shadowed by day. She could hardly be safer if she moved elsewhere. He must see that another girl sharing her flat could offer her no extra protection, but would merely complicate her life unnecessarily and cause her a great deal of inconvenience and discomfort.

Though he fumed inwardly at her obstinacy he had to be honest enough to admit to himself that there was a good deal of truth and common-sense in what she had just said. He found himself unwillingly admiring her sturdy independence and the courageous calmness with which she faced a situation which would have reduced most women to a state bordering on panic.

She had noticed a great change in his physical appearance. He looked as if he had lost nearly a stone in weight and his clothes now hung quite loosely on his muscular frame. His sallow faced looked gaunt and strained with no sign of the smooth chubbiness she remembered.

He had barely taken leave of her when Mark telephoned.

He first enquired coolly and politely after her health, and then suggested as Karel Meyer had done, that she should either move or get someone in to share her flat.

She guessed at once that he must have read the report in the paper and told him that Lieutenant Meyer had just been in to discuss matters with her, and that it had been decided to leave things as they were.

After a short silence he said: "You mean *you've* decided to leave things as they are," and said goodnight somewhat abruptly and hung up.

This was the first time Mark had telephoned since he had driven her back from Knysna . . . The drive, which she had dreaded so much, had proved both better and worse than she had anticipated. Better, in so far that Mark had asked no leading or searching questions. But worse, in that he had chosen to adopt a polite impersonal manner towards her. No matter how much she argued with herself that he was fully justified in his attitude and that she could hardly have expected him to react differently, she was nonetheless left miserably depressed . . . And she had tortured herself further by comparing his cool indifference to the warmth and affection he had shown on the previous occasion they had driven back from Knysna . . .

The young police officer who drove Lisa to work each morning was a painfully tongue-tied young man who never spoke unless she addressed him first, and then he flushed to the roots of his hair before he stammered a reply. She found Warrant Officer Ben du Toit the very antithesis of Jannie Barnard, whom she had met once only, when he fetched her at the Royal to drive her to the police station. He had immediately started up a conversation and had chattered cheerfully all the way.

The following evening Ben du Toit dropped her at her flat just after six and she bathed, and changed into pyjamas and a dressing-gown before cooking herself a light meal. She always did this whenever she intended to work late.

She washed up, made herself a cup of coffee and then lay stretched out on the floor and smoked the one cigarette she allowed herself a day, while she thought about children's winter coats. She always found it easier to do the creative side of her work in solitude in her flat, rather than in her office where she was constantly being interrupted by the telephone or by people coming in. The winter clothes she had designed for the present season had been in the shops for weeks, and her summer range completed months ago . . . Now she was beginning to plan her range for the next winter, and found, as was usually the case at this early stage, that she was full of doubt and beset by the gnawing worry that she might run out of ideas.

She eventually rolled over and reached up to stub out her cigarette in the flat ceramic ashtray on the coffee table. Got up and took the coffee cup to the kitchen, rinsed it under the tap, dried it and put it away, and then went back to the living-room and settled down to work. Cleared the table first and set the lamp upon it to give herself better light. She soon became deeply engrossed, sometimes staring straight ahead deep in thought, and at others sketching quickly. Every now and then she crumpled up a sheet of paper and tossed it impatiently on to the floor. Occasionally she held up a sketch to scrutinise it through narrowed lids, her head slightly cocked, and if satisfied, put it on one side.

The sudden peal of the front door bell shattered the silence and brought her heart leaping into her mouth. The blond man she had seen on the beach immediately came to mind and she had a moment of panic. She moistened her lips and glanced at her watch and saw it was five to ten. Who would call at this hour? If it were the man, there was still no need for her to panic. He couldn't get in and she could identify him through the spy hole and telephone the police.

She pushed back her chair, took off her horn-rimmed spectacles as she rose, and placed them on her unfinished sketch. Crossed the room and leaned forward to put her good eye to the spy hole. Her heart gave another awful jolt. It was Mark.

Her fingers were uncertain as she fumbled awkwardly with the chain and then lifted a hand to turn the Yale lock and opened the door.

She smiled. "Hello, Mark."

"Hello." Abruptly said and without an answering smile.

She cast a quick glance at his face as he stalked into the room. It told her nothing. She shut the door and heard the lock click and when she turned, found him standing with his back to the fireplace, calmly surveying the room.

She said a little breathlessly: "I'm afraid the room's rather untidy, I always seem to create this chaos when I work. I-I've been busy for the last three hours." She bent to pick up three balls of crumpled paper and tossed them into the wastepaper basket.

"So I see," he said laconically and strolled over to the table to look down at her unfinished sketch. He picked up her spectacles, turned them between his fingers, put them down again. "Since when have you worn these?"

She couldn't gauge his mood. He was

different, taut. The strong bones of his face stood out hard.

"I've worn them since my accident—but only at night. The specialist in London advised me to wear them when I work: he told me my bad eye would tend to play up when subjected to any strain."

"I see." He continued his appraisal of the room.

. . . She had thrown her camel's-hair coat across one of the armchairs. Frivolous green slippers kicked off while she was working; one lay under the chair on which she had been sitting, the other upside down beneath the table beside a crumpled ball of paper, overlooked. An indented cushion on the carpet. Had she been lying on the floor? A cigarette end stubbed out in the ashtray. She didn't smoke. Or did she now? He could remember the flat she had shared with a friend and recognised that the taste and furnishing must have been hers. The small settee and its two accompanying armchairs were covered in coarsely woven material of the same shade of sulphur yellow. The black and yellow sulphur design etched on the white curtains was reminiscent of the same colour scheme.

The shaggy bronze chrysanthemums cascading from a copper vase pushed to the edge of the table where she had been working were arranged with the casual artistry he remembered so well. Books on art, interior decorating, fashion design. Novels. A couple of autobiographies he had given her. Several post-impressionist reproductions on the walls. A pleasing one of Utrillos's above the fireplace of lit apartments and the lights of a bistro reflected in the wet street at dusk . . . She held down a good job and would have inherited something from her father. She must be comfortably off.

He looked at her and found she was watching him uncertainly and deliberately looked her over. She was wearing a short-sleeved loose-fitting, primrose yellow dressing-gown which reached her feet and was buttoned from the slender column of her throat to the hem. Her feet were bare, narrow, high-arched. He remembered them well. Her fine silky hair had been tied back and she was wearing no make-up. Her face had a clean scrubbed look as if she had just had a bath . . . She was looking highly nervous and her dark-fringed green eyes were carefully avoiding his.

She felt increasingly uncomfortable and self-conscious under his long silent scrutiny and lifted a hand to smooth her hair and allowed her slim fingers to slide down her temple to shield the left side of her face from his gaze.

It needed only this small gesture to trigger off the rage which had been simmering within him for the last three hours.

"I want you to answer a few questions," he said abruptly, and saw her stiffen.

She pushed her hands into the pockets of her gown. "Not now, if you don't mind, Mark. I've a terrifying amount of work to do which I—have to finish tonight. Perhaps we could discuss this some other—"

"It won't do, Lisa. I intend getting the answers from you now, tonight, and I'm staying here until you give them to me."

He seated himself deliberately in one of the armchairs and looked at her pointedly until she crossed over to the settee and perched herself reluctantly on the very edge.

"First of all, I'd like to know something

about Vernon Blakely, the man who cut me out. That was his name, wasn't it?"

". . . Yes." She looked at him for a second and her heart lurched when she saw his face had thinned and become pale with rage.

"I'll refresh your memory. You had been gone exactly two months when you suddenly stopped writing, and it took three weeks before I got a postcard. A *postcard*, mind you, from Spain, in which you told me you were holidaying with this man you'd met. It took a further fortnight before I heard from you again and you then gave me his name and told me you'd fallen in love with him and were going to get married. Is that correct?"

She forced herself to look up and meet his penetrating deep-set eyes. "When I wrote to you, I told you how—sorry I was to—" She broke off and swallowed. "These things happen, Mark."

"I agree. They happen all the time, but somehow I never believed it could happen to us. I believed our—relationship was the one thing I could depend on. I would have staked my life on it."

She made herself keep on looking at him.

"Where did you meet this Vernon Blakely?"

"We met in London."

"Where?"

"At a drink party."

"How long did you know him before you decided on going off together on this trip to Spain?"

". . . Not so long."

"How long? A week—a month?"

"I don't *know*."

"Had you met him when you wrote me your last love-letter? The one I got three weeks before you sent the postcard?"

She said in sudden anger. "Mark, I won't be cross-examined!"

He felt for his cigarettes, held out the packet and offered her one. She shook her head, too tense to speak. He helped himself, lit it, inhaled deeply and blew out the smoke before he spoke. "What does Vernon Blakely do? What's his profession?"

She moved uncomfortably. "He's an interior decorator."

"So?" He sat back and stared at the tip of his cigarette. "You've always been interesting in interior decorating, haven't you? You must have found you had a great deal in common."

Was it sarcasm? Her knees were beginning to tremble and she realised she was sitting too stiffly and eased herself a little back.

"I take it you met before your accident?"

She cleared her throat. "Yes."

"You said you were going to marry him. Why didn't you?"

She looked down and didn't speak.

"Are you still engaged to him?"

She didn't look up. "No."

"Why not?"

"Mark, I won't be—"

"*Why not*?"

She wet her lips . . . "Things didn't work out."

"Things didn't work out," he mimicked. "Christ. Why don't you speak correct English!" He catapulted himself from his chair, paced the room once and stopped in front of her. "Did he walk out when he found your face had been smashed up?" he asked savagely. "Is that why you didn't get married?"

She flinched as if he had struck her. Later the memory of this would make him ashamed, but all he felt now was a queer perverted satisfaction at having wounded her.

"That's what you thought I would do, didn't you?"

When she made no reply he repeated angrily: "*Didn't* you?"

"You ask the questions and then answer them yourself. What's the *use* of going into this now—it's all finished and done with."

"I agree our engagement is finished and done with, I'm certainly making no mistake about that." He bent to grind out his half-smoked cigarette in the ashtray and went over to the chair and sat down again.

"To revert back to Vernon Blakely—"

She half shut her eyes. "Oh God, do you have to go on and *on* saying his name."

"Couldn't you have thought up a better one?" he flared. "*Vernon Blakely*. Christ!"

She stared at him silently.

After a second or two he leaned back and said in a conversational tone of voice: "I found a letter of considerable interest waiting for me when I got home this evening."

He was watching her and saw her face go still.

"Why do you tell me this?"

"Because the letter concerned you."

"Who was it from?"

"It was from your brother, Robert Lombard."

The colour drained from her face. "From *Robert*? B-but you don't even know him!"

"No, we've never met."

"But—why did he write to you?"

"He wrote in reply to a letter I wrote him. I asked a few questions I thought he would be in a position to answer."

"D'you mean to say you wrote and asked—you haven't the *right*!" she cried furiously, colour flooding back into her face. He noticed that the left side of her face had remained pale.

"Maybe I haven't the right, but at least I now have all the answers." He thrust himself to the edge of his chair. "Your lover, Vernon Blakely, never existed! He was nothing but a figment of your imagination. At the time when you were supposed to be having your affair with him in Spain, you were in actual fact lying in hospital in Wolverhampton, and it was from there that you sent me your postcard. Of course, when I got it I recognised the writing on the wall as I was meant to, and I was more or less prepared for the *coup de grace* when your letter came a fortnight later. The postcard of Madrid was authentic enough, but I was in no condition at the time to take note of the stamp. Were you successful in finding a Spanish one?"

She stared straight ahead and didn't speak.

"You fabricated Vernon Blakely to give yourself a reason for breaking off our engagement, because you reckoned it was going to be broken anyway, didn't you?"

She didn't look at him.

"You've never forgotten the conversation we had the night we got engaged, when you were so shocked at what you termed my ruthlessness." He felt in his pocket and took out a small parcel. He tore the paper off and leaned forward to put the deep blue toilet-box on the coffee table. "I offered this to you once before—I'm giving it to you now."

"I don't want it," she said in a stifled voice.

"Then give it away. Do what you like with it . . . You were certain if I were capable of getting rid of this because it was damaged, I would be just as likely to lose all interest in my girl if her face were damaged, weren't you?"

She continued to stare straight ahead as if he had not spoken, only the whitened knuckles of her clenched hands showed how tense she was.

"Or would the word disfigured be better? That's what you imagine yourself to be now, don't you? Because you've got a few scars down the one side of your face you feel you must hide it from me and everyone else."

"Why don't you go?"

"Well, we'll never know now, will we, how I might have reacted? Maybe it's just as well you didn't put me to the test."

Her pale composure and seeming indifference to what he was saying made him want to lash out at her and get some sort of response.

"Do you remember your father writing to you and saying that his decision to die alone could be interpreted as cowardice or a false kind of pride?"

She looked at him without answering.

"Which would you say it was?"

She whitened at the nostrils. "Leave my father out of this."

"Which was it with you?"

Green eyes blazing at him. Face pale and wild. "Leave me alone and stop cross-examining me. I'm not in the witness box. You're not in court now."

"You haven't answered my question."

"You don't need my answers. You and Robert between you have supplied all the answers . . . You had to go sneaking behind my back—"

"Yes, call it that if you must," he said angrily. "I went behind your back, and I'll tell you why I did. I wrote to your brother because you lacked the moral courage—the *guts*, to answer the question yourself . . . Just as you lacked the bloody guts to wait and see how I'd react."

She leapt to her feet white-faced, eyes lighter with rage. "You've said what you've come to say and if there's any more, I don't want to hear. Will you please go! *Get out*!"

"It's what I intend doing and I can't go quickly enough—"

She turned her back on him as he got up and he suddenly reached out and caught her arm and jerked her round to face him.

Her eyes widened and her face became pinched and frightened.

His fingers automatically tightened and bit into the cool firm flesh of her arm as a black wave of rage and lust engulfed him. In that second of horrifying self revelation he realised that he was as capable of rape and violence as the next man.

He abruptly released her and stepped back. "*Damn* you. Damn you for a lying cowardly bitch!"

Seconds later the front door slammed with a reverberating crash.

11

LORNE thought she heard the sound of footsteps coming along the passageway outside her flat and lifted her head from the pillow to listen. Seconds later she heard a key grate in the lock, and then the front door opened and shut.

She quickly sat up and switched on the bedside lamp. "Is that you, Alan?" she called huskily.

"Yes."

She heard the rustle of his coat as he took it off and hung it behind the door.

"Is it still raining?"

"Yes, it's been coming down steadily for the last half hour."

She tilted her head back and lifted her hands to free her hair and shook it loose. "What happened? Why didn't you come on Friday night?"

No answer.

She combed her fingers through her hair and fluffed it out to frame her face.

"You told me you'd come for sure. You *promised.*"

He came in and paused for a second in the doorway to look at her.

She was sitting up in bed, her slim young body as deeply tanned as his. Only her breasts white, gleaming luminously through the pale gold nightdress she was wearing. The light from the bedside lamp set her golden hair alight and threw a shadow across her face, making dark pools of her eyes.

"I thought something must have happened to you," she pouted, still combing her fingers through her hair. "Surely you could have phoned to let me know you weren't coming?"

He came over and sank down on the edge of her bed but didn't speak.

She regarded him sulkily from beneath her lashes, looking wanton and infinitely desirable in the subdued light. "Why didn't you come?" she asked again.

He stared silently at her as if he had not heard her speak, his handsome face so taut and strained it could have been chiselled from marble.

She felt her heart flutter once, uncomfortably. "Is anything wrong?" she asked.

He tensed his jaw and she saw a muscle ripple at his temple.

"Alan what's wrong?" Voice rising in alarm.

He reached for her and clutched her roughly to him, and held her crushed against him, his face in her hair. She could hear the thud of his heart and feel the slight trembling of his frame.

"*Alan.*" She was really frightened now.

He tightened his arms, gave a smothered sort of groan and buried his face in her neck. "Oh God, darling, I'm *finished.*"

She wriggled as frantically as a landed fish in his grasp until he loosened his arms, and then leaned back from the waist to look up into his face. "Tell me what's happened. Why are you frightening me like this?"

He put his hands on her shoulders, thrust her gently but firmly back until she subsided upon the pillows . . . leaned over her, searching her face.

She smiled uncertainly and put up a hand to brush his blond hair from his brow. "What is it? *Tell* me, darling," she whispered.

His throat muscles moved in an effort of speech . . . "Maisie's dead," he got out at last.

Her body went rigid. "*What?*" She stared up at him, pale, stupefied, mouth agape, eyes widened in disbelief. "Did you say your wife is *dead*?"

He slid his hands up her bare arms and clasped them above the elbows. "Lorne, do you love me?"

She was far too shocked by what he had said to respond as she would normally have done and said almost impatiently: "You know I do."

"Look at me and say it."

"Oh, Alan—"

"*Say* it."

She stared up at him. "I love you. Do I have to say it? Surely you know that by now . . . Alan, you said your—wife is dead. Has she been ill?"

"No."

"If she wasn't ill—what happened? Did she have an accident?"

He tightened his fingers round her arms. "*How* much do you love me?"

"Alan, I—"

"Enough to take what I'm going to tell you?"

"Stop frightening me like this . . . Wh-what do you want to tell me?" she stammered.

". . . I killed her."

Her body froze. "You're *lying*! You're trying to frighten me."

"Do you think I'd lie about a thing like this?"

"D'you realise what you're saying?"

"I killed her, I tell you," he said harshly.

"I don't believe you!"

He leaned further over her until their faces almost touched. "Don't you? Would you like me to tell you why I did it?"

She stared up at him, breathing as quickly as a bird trapped in the hand.

". . . It was because of you—"

"Oh God—"

She flung back the sheets and tried to scramble out of bed, but before she was half-way out he got his hands round her waist and pulled her back. She struck wildly at him as he drew her into his arms, twisted her body and turned her face away, but he followed and pressed his mouth to hers . . . He kissed her until he felt her body go limp in his arms.

After a time he loosened his arms but still kept them about her, and she stared up at him, tawny eyes, bright with unshed tears. He put his hands up to her face, held it and covered it with little kisses.

He said: "I love you, darling. I've never told you this before, have I?"

Her eyes filled with tears.

". . . *This* was why I killed her."

She covered her face in her hands and burst into tears.

"I couldn't take it any more—never seeing you. I told her about us, but she wouldn't give me a divorce. I tried everything . . . I love you, Lorne."

She gave an inarticulate cry and flung her arms about his neck and clung to him, sobbing as if her heart would break.

. . . She lay with her head on his shoulder in the dark, and after a time said in a small stifled voice: "How did you—what did you do to her?"

He drew her to him and held her close while he told her. He told her everything. The *relief* of sharing this with someone else . . . Inner tension had mounted to such a pitch during the last forty-eight hours that he had feared his nerve might break . . . He told her his plan had been foolproof and that not a soul would have suspected Maisie's death had been anything but a tragic drowning . . . He tightened his arms and kissed her. Even *she* would never have guessed it was anything but that, because if things had run according to plan he would naturally never have confessed to her. But now, with this girl having witnessed the drowning, the whole complexion of things had changed and forced him to tell her everything . . . She must realise, of course, that once the girl witnessed what he did, he had no alternative but to get rid of her.

She stiffened. "What d'you mean?"

"It meant I had to kill her too."

She moaned, struggled, tried to free herself, but he tightened his arms and pressed his face against hers.

"Darling, surely you can see I had to do it. The girl saw me drown Maisie—she saw me carry her up the beach. God knows how long we stood there staring at each other. She'd recognise me any time she saw me. Just as I would recognise her."

"Oh, Alan, I can't *bear* it! I can't—"

"Can't you see it was the girl or me? You surely realise I'd be finished if she testified against me."

When she didn't speak he added: "And she's a threat to *our* future. Can't you see that?"

She shivered . . . "What did you—do to her?"

He told her the rest. The long agonising wait while he hid in the car park, but how calm he had been at the end. The split second timing it had required. And that never-to-be forgotten second when his car had teetered at the very brink, nearly plummeting after her mini over the precipice. It still gave him sleepless nights and brought him out in a cold sweat to remember it . . . To have executed everything at such personal risk, to have barely survived and then to find it had all been for nothing! God, it hardly bore thinking of!

The seconds ticked by and then she asked in a cold little voice: ". . . Why do you say it was all for nothing?"

"The girl is still alive."

She stared at him in the dark. "But

how's that possible? You've just said you sent her car over the cliff. Did she escape?"

He loosened his arms and flung himself back on the pillows. "The driver of the car didn't escape. He was killed all right, but it wasn't *her*."

"What?" But I thought you said—"

"It wasn't *her*, I tell you! . . . A god-damned police officer was driving her car." he drew in her breath with a little hiss but didn't speak.

". . . It's the end—I'm finished."

"No."

"It's the end, Lorne."

"Oh darling, there must be *something* you can do—"

"There's only one thing that could save me. Only one."

"What?"

"I would still be safe if the girl could be written off. But tell me how I do it? I'm scared of even putting a foot in Cape Town in case she sees and recognises me. She would obviously have told the police everything and they'll have her tailed and whoever's following her would have been given a description of what I look like. If I made one move in her direction I would be arrested."

She said; "Alan, wouldn't it be better if you left the country?"

"No," he said harshly.

"But—"

"Can't you see that's exactly what they'd expect me to do? They'll have a pretty accurate picture of what I look like and they'll be on the look-out. Every exit from the country will be watched. I wouldn't have a snowball's hope in hell of getting away."

"Couldn't you disguise yourself in some way?" she said desperately. "Dye your hair or grow a beard—or something—" she ended lamely.

He moved impatiently. "For God's sake, try to be realistic, Lorne. How about my passport? Have you thought of that? And what if I met someone who knows me? However skilfully I disguised myself I'd still be recognisable. Then I'd really be in the soup. What feasible reason could I possibly give for the sudden change in my appearance?"

She drew a deep shuddering breath, oppressed to the point of suffocation. They lay without touching. She heard him breathing beside her.

". . . It's like a nightmare," she said after a time.

"Lorne, the girl works for Dryads Ltd., a clothing factory in Observatory." It was dropped like a pebble into a still pool.

"*Dryads*?" she said sharply.

His voice quickened. "Do you know the firm?"

"Yes, I know them well. I sometimes model their clothes."

"This was what I was hoping for. *Lorne*—" He raised himself and leaned over her.

For some reason she shrank from him.

"Darling, this is like a miracle!"

"What are you talking about?"

"The police obviously won't know that you are connected in any way with the man they're looking for."

She stiffened. "What do you mean?"

He slid his arms under her waist. "Can't you *see*?" He bent and kissed her. "Darling, this could be the answer to a prayer!"

"I still don't know what you mean."

"Use that beautiful head of yours.

Think! . . . It would be as easy as pie for you to scrape up an acquaintanceship with her—*wouldn't* it?"

He felt her body become rigid, and when she didn't speak, lay down, keeping his arms about her and drew her to him. "She dropped her bag when she ran away and I went through it and found out quite a few things about her. Her name's Miss Lisa Lombard and she lives at—"

"Oh, Alan, I *can't*—"

"*Listen*, darling. It's our future that's at stake. *My* life. Doesn't that mean anything to you?"

"Oh God, you know it does. But this thing you want me to do—"

"Don't you see, once we're rid of this girl I'll be *safe* and we can start planning our future?"

"What future can we possibly have?" she said hopelessly.

"*Marriage*. A family."

She moved restlessly in his arms. "Even if you got rid of the girl—what about your—what about—Maisie? What's going to happen when the police find she's missing? They must find that out sooner or later. What happens then?"

"*Nothing* will happen. I agree they must find out she's missing, but what will it prove? Maisie went on a trip overseas and it won't be the first time someone has done so and vanished without trace. There will be no reason to connect her disappearance with me."

"They may find she never left the country."

"Granted. That still doesn't prove anything. If the girl's dead they can prove nothing."

"Alan—"

"Yes, darling."

She lifted a hand to touch his face. "Please don't ask me to do this. I *can't*."

He jerked his face away from her fingers. "Christ, and you say you love me!" He thrust her from him and flung himself on to his back.

"You *know* I love you." She was half crying.

"So you tell me. But you obviously don't love me enough to lift a finger to fight for our future."

"That's not true! You *know* it isn't."

". . . Do I?"

"It's this thing you want me to do.

Darling, can't you see this is something—"

"Forget it!" he said harshly.

"I'll do anything in the world for you as long as I—"

"I said forget it!"

She bit her lip, trying to stem her tears.

"You know, of course, I'll swing?"

She began to cry silently, feeling the tears slide down her cheeks.

"It isn't as though I'm asking you to murder the girl."

She wiped her eyes with the back of her hand and dried her face on the sheet. "What do you want me to do?" she asked in a trembling voice.

He turned and put an arm about her. "Look, darling, if you feel you can't do this—"

"What d'you want me to do?" she repeated dully.

"Get to know the girl, that's all. You're more or less in the same trade, which should give you the necessary contacts—it shouldn't be too difficult to find some way of meeting her . . . And when you've done so, maybe you could dine together, or take her to see a show."

". . . And then?"

He laughed softly and slid the warm palm of his hand over her hips and up her back, bent his head to kiss her neck and shoulders. "Look, sweetheart, I'm not asking you to put arsenic in her tea, or anything like that. I'm not asking you to *do* a single thing to her. All I want you to do is to get to know her."

Despite her tension and the awful coldness enveloping her spirit, she was responding to his touch and knew he was aware of this.

He pushed his fingers through her hair and tilted her face back. "Are you prepared to do this, darling? After all, it's not such a terrible thing I'm asking you to do."

". . . Yes, I'll do it," she said in a hoarse low voice.

He kissed her gently on the mouth. "That's my girl. I knew once you'd really thought about it you'd turn up trumps . . . Now, to get back to the girl. As I said, her name's Lisa Lombard and I'd say she must be round about your age, or maybe a year or two older. Blonde and tallish. She lives below the line in Rondebosch at No. 6 Oakapple Crescent. Do you know the flats?"

She swallowed and nodded.

"She doesn't seem to have a phone. I looked up her name in the telephone directory but couldn't find it. It could be she's just moved in—you might check on this. I still think your best bet is to contact her through her job. I'm afraid I can't help you there, I haven't an inkling what she does."

She cleared her throat. "I could easily find out."

"That's my girl," he said again. "One thing's important—try not to take too long over this. See if you can't do something about it tomorrow morning."

She mumbled a smothered assent.

"Look at it from the angle that you're safe-guarding our future—and that she's a threat to it."

She had gone cold on him and was no longer responding to his touch.

"What's the matter?" he asked. "Is something else worrying you?"

". . . What are you going to—do to her? . . . How will you—"

He tightened his arms. "Don't think along those lines, Lorne. That's my department and the less you know about it the better. Your only concern must be to win the girl's confidence, and as I said, there should be some connection between your jobs to enable you to find a common interest . . . But time is the most important factor and we can't afford to waste it. In the situation we're in now, every minute could count, and the sooner you do something about this the better."

Nearly a minute passed before she spoke . . . "When will you—do it?"

"Don't you think about that either. When I've worked things out I'll tell you exactly what I'll want you to do."

She gave an inarticulate smothered cry and tried to twist away from him but he pulled her round and began to kiss her passionately.

". . . Alan, we're lost! We're caught in a trap and there's no way out . . . Oh darling, what have you done to us—"

12

MAJOR THERON, the District Criminal Investigation officer, telephoned Karel Meyer to tell him that a woman had been interviewed in Knysna who seemed to think she might have seen the man they were looking for. Her evidence had been taken down but didn't seem very conclusive. If he could spare the time maybe he would like to question her himself?

Karel Meyer agreed that this might be a good idea. There was a dual purpose in mind as he had intended to find time to pay a call on Miss Suzanna Nel, the girl whom Jannie Barnard had told him he wanted to marry.

He flew to George early the next morning and was met at the airport by the police car which took him to the police station in Knysna.

The interview with the woman was brief, unsatisfactory and unfruitful as he had somewhat gloomily suspected from the start it might turn out to be, and when it was over and he had courteously thanked her for granting a second interview, seen her to her car, he went in to have a few words with Major Theron.

The Major waved him to take a seat and he flopped down into the chair opposite the desk and felt for his cigarettes.

"You were right, of course. Her evidence was inconclusive and a mass of contradictions. She's no more seen the murderer than I have."

"I'm sorry your trip has been all for nothing."

"I was coming anyway. There's someone I have to see." He blew out a plume of smoke. "It's just on a week since Jannie was killed and the evidence we have to date is no more than we had at the start. We know what the murderer looks like and we know the colour of his car. We've interviewed dozens of people by now and not one of them has produced a shred of evidence worth having. I've never known such a case. Usually within the first forty-eight hours we're on the scent. We've notified every garage in the Western Cape to keep us informed if a damaged dark grey car is brought in for repairs, but once again we've drawn a blank. I'm beginning to doubt if he ever intends having his car fixed. I'm suspecting more and more, Major, that we're dealing not only with an utterly ruthless man, but also with an extremely clever one."

Major Theron plucked at his pendulous lower lip and nodded thoughtfully. "It looks as if you might be right. But sooner or later, lieutenant, a woman must be reported missing."

"True, Major, but when?" he asked smoothly, far more polite than he had been to Mark. "Miss Lombard is the one I'm worrying about. However closely we guard her, there are still twenty-four hours in the day and it just isn't possible to keep her under our eye every minute of that time. If this man is out to get her, and clever enough, he could always think of a means of doing it."

They discussed things for a further ten minutes and arranged to meet for lunch at one o'clock at the Royal Hotel. In the interval Karel Meyer decided he had better pay a quick visit to his mother. Sooner or later she would be certain to find out he had been in Knysna and he knew how mortally offended she would be if he had not dropped in to see her.

Even so, she was affronted because he could not lunch with her, notwithstanding his explanation that he was in Knysna purely on business.

She hardly ever saw him, she said, and when he did come he was only prepared to sacrifice a few minutes of his time. She looked him over, her downturned mouth tightening. Look at him! He was skin and bone. He looked half starved. It was quite plain for anyone to see he was undernourished. It was ridiculous that she should be living here in Knysna, while he lived in Cape Town with no one to look after him and see to it that he had his regular meals. Apart from anything else, it was a sheer waste of good money for them to be running two separate establishments. Did he know that the drought had more than doubled the price of fruit and vegetables in the district? It was scandalous what people were expected to pay. She had meant to write and tell him that the very day he left she had to sack the maid because she caught her thieving—it had taken two days before she could get another one, who was proving to be bone-lazy and cheeky into the bargain.

His time was limited and after glancing at his watch he cut short her complaints and took his leave. He was scheduled to fly back at four o'clock and if he were late for lunch it would leave him little time to visit Suzanna Nel.

He knew where Mrs. Nel lived, and as her house was within easy walking distance of the Royal Hotel, he decided on strolling there after lunch, and arranged with the Major that the police car should fetch him at the house at three o'clock.

Once he parted from the Major and set off on the short walk, he could feel himself becoming tense. For days he had been dreading this meeting with the girl, knowing how difficult it would be for him to remain calm and detached.

Few people knew of this weakness of his. Despite the nature of his work and having to frequently break the news of tragedy and death to those most closely concerned, he had never become hardened to the deep distress this always caused, and though he managed to hide his feelings successfully behind an urbane mask, it always tore him apart, and left him drained and depressed for days. Mrs. Barnard's grief when he had broken the news of Jannie's death to her was still painfully alive in his memory.

He knew when the purpose of his visit was divulged to the girl there was every possibility that she would break down. But it was something he felt himself compelled to do.

When he reached the house he saw the windows were shut and the lace curtains drawn. He had hoped as it was Saturday that he might find the girl in, but now wondered gloomily if anyone would be at home.

He pressed the bell and waited

He was just about to press it for the second time when the door was unbolted and Mrs. Nel opened it.

He knew her by sight and greeted her by name and introduced himself.

He was startled to see her face freeze, and for an unbelievable second he thought she was about to slam the door in his face.

"Mrs. Nel—" he said quickly.

She stared at him, the colour heightened in her cheeks, looking both angry and frightened at the same time. "Yes, Lieutenant Meyer, what do you want?"

She was a good-looking woman in her mid forties who could have made much more of herself. Her faded blond hair was unstylishly set, and she was neatly, rather dowdily, dressed in a countrified way, respectability written all over her. Anger and anxiety had slightly widened her beautiful dark blue long-lashed eyes.

He said: "I've come to see your daughter, Mrs. Nel. Is Suzanna in?"

She glanced quickly to the left to see if anyone in the neighbouring house might be watching and thought she saw the curtains stir in the front window. Would it be Stella Venter? Everyone knew how inquisitive she was. And everyone knew who Lieutenant Meyer was. If it *was* Stella, it would be spread all over the town that the police had called at her house.

Her eyes flickered back to him and she wet her lips. "Why d'you want to see Suzanna?"

"It's a personal matter, Mrs. Nel," he said smoothly. "Is she at home?"

A nervous tic twitched her cheek, "Come in," she said abruptly and stepped aside to let him into the passage and quickly shut the door. "Why do you want to see her?" she repeated harshly.

He smiled. "Mrs. Nel, there's nothing to be concerned about. Suzanna hasn't done anything. I've come to see her in connection with Jannie Barnard."

"Jannie Barnard!" She almost spat out his name.

The venom with which it was said took him aback and he remained quite silent looking at her through slightly narrowed lids.

"Did you say *Jannie Barnard*?"

"Yes, Mrs. Nel, he was one of our most promising boys. He told me—"

"Suzanna!" She twisted her neck round as she screamed her name down the passage.

Her shrill scream was earsplitting, deafening in the confines of the narrow passageway, and made the ensuing silence all the heavier.

"Suzanna!" she screamed again. "You can hear me. *Come here* when I call you!"

They were still standing at the head of the long dark passage. All the doors opening into it were shut and the only light came from the fanlight behind them.

She opened the door on the right and said: "Wait in here while I fetch her."

He went in and heard her hurrying down the passage.

"Don't tell me you didn't hear me!" she cried shrilly. "Why don't you come when I call you?" A door opened and shut.

The room was gloomy and stuffy and gave the impression that it was seldom used. All the windows were shut, and the net curtains drawn across them obscured most of the light. A mixed arrangement of artificial flowers on the upright piano half hid a coloured photograph of the Heads. Crocheted antimacassars protected the chintz-covered chairs and sofa. He went over to peer at a lurid oil above the fireplace of the setting sun reflected in the glass-like surface of the lagoon. Drew the curtains aside to look out at the small neat garden.

He turned from the window as the girl came in, closely followed by her mother.

Pretty, but strained and white. Long dark brown hair. Eyes beautiful, deep blue, long-lashed, like her mother's, but red-rimmed as if she had been crying a lot.

Dress neat and stylish. Fresh *clean*-looking. Not the type of girl he would have expected Jannie to fall for. The few girls whom he had seen Jannie escorting had been bolder, flashier, more sexy than this one.

He smiled, "Good-afternoon, Suzanna. Do you know who I am?"

Her eyes came up briefly to meet his. "Yes, Lieutenant Meyer."

He turned to her mother. "Mrs. Nel, would you mind if I had a few words with Suzanna?"

"What do you want to say to her?" Voice too shrill. "Why do you want to see her alone?" Her breathing quickened. "Do you think I don't know everything by now? Do you think there's anything you have to hide from me?"

He stared at her in puzzlement. "I don't know what you're talking about, Mrs. Nel."

"You pretend you don't know what I'm talking about! Didn't Jannie Barnard tell you? Isn't that why you're here?"

His pale blue eyes became coldly intent. "Would you like *me* to tell you?"

"Ma, *please*."

She turned on Suzanna as if she could

barely restrain herself from hitting her. "If you don't want me to tell him, *you* do it!" She caught the girl's arm. "Go on, you heard what I said, *tell* him!"

"Mrs. Nel, I think it would be better if you—"

"Didn't Jannie Barnard tell you that he made my daughter pregnant? Didn't he tell you that?"

He shut his eyes in anguish, as shock, guilt, remorse flooded through him.

Her mouth worked and tears oozed from the corners of her eyes. "And this is what my daughter does in return for all her parents have done for her. We gave her everything and brought her up to be respectable, decent and God fearing and this is how she repays us."

He was only half-listening to her, his mind still grappling with what she had just told him.

"From the second I clapped eyes on him, I knew Jannie Barnard was a bad lot. I know his type—when they take a girl out they're interested only in one thing. I tried to warn Suzanna but she wouldn't listen to me."

"I wouldn't listen because it wasn't true!

Jannie wasn't like that, he wasn't bad. If anyone should know, *I* should. Would he have asked me to marry him if he were as bad as you say?"

"And you let him take you in! That's an old trick, anyone but a fool knows that! They all try it on if they can't get what they're after. He would never have married you, I can tell you that straight. If your father had been alive today this would never have happened. The first time your Jannie Barnard tried to put a foot in this house he would have turned him out."

"Mrs. Nel—"

"That you, my own daughter, could let a man do this to you!"

"I've told you a hundred times, Jannie and I were engaged."

"You say you were engaged?" Her voice rose. "Does that mean you had to behave like a slut—like a street woman? Have you no shame? D'you think for one second that your father and I behaved like that when we became engaged?"

The girl stared at her pale faced.

"Do you think for one moment that your father would have dreamed of laying a finger on me before we were married?

Your father was a gentleman—that was the difference.'' She fumbled in her dress for her handkerchief. ''And you do this to me now, when I'm a widow and must bear the burden alone.''

''Mrs. Nel—'' Karel Meyer tried again.

She looked at him, deep blue eyes drenched in tears. ''Lieutenant Meyer, I want you to speak to Suzanna. I've told her she must get rid of the baby.''

A spot of colour came into the girl's pale cheeks. ''I've already told you, I—won't—do—it.''

''Are you utterly shameless! Haven't you realised the disgrace? Have you given no thought to how the neighbours will talk when they find out?''

''Unless you moderate your voice, Mrs. Nel, your neighbours are liable to find out right now.''

She wiped her eyes and blew her nose. ''Lieutenant Meyer,'' she said, lowering her voice, ''You surely can see it's imperative she should get rid of the baby. If Suzanna persists in going through with this, it could only ruin her life. What hope of marriage could she have with the stigma of an illegitimate child? And her reputation would be ruined."

Before he could speak she added: "And who will look after the child? Who's going to support it?"

"*I'll* support it. I've been saving—"

"How much have you saved, may I ask? Not more than a couple of hundred rand, I'll wager, and how far do you think that's going to take you? How long do you imagine it's going to last?"

"I'll work. I'll earn enough to support my baby and myself . . . Don't worry, I'll go away before any of your precious neighbours find out. I—I'll find some place where they will take me in, where I can have my baby, but *nothing* you say will make me get rid of it!"

Her defiance acted like a red rag to a bull. Her mother seized her by the arm and shook her roughly. "You'll listen to me!" she cried hysterically. "You're only nineteen and you'll do as *I* say. You're not having this baby and that's final! I've heard there are people who take babies away. Qualified people like doctors and midwives. I'll make it my business to find out where you must go." She wrung her hands in sudden distress, wondering how she could set about this. *Whom* to ask for advice without it being spread all over the town; because she knew however kind and helpfull people were they always talked. The *sordidness* of it, that she, a God fearing respectable woman should be called upon to associate with such low class people. She squared her shoulders. But she *must* do it. "I'll find out whom you must see, and I'll take you there myself."

"If you do that, Mrs. Nel, I'll have you arrested," Karel Meyer said quietly.

She stared at him, open-mouthed, aghast.

"If you insist on forcing your daughter to have an illegal abortion, you will leave me no alternative but to have you arrested." His pale blue eyes looked as cold as ice.

She reached blindly for a chair and collapsed into it, covered her face in her hands and burst into tears.

He said more gently: "Mrs. Nel, bar breaking the law, I'm prepared to do everything in my power to help you and Suzanna in this matter." He cleared his throat. "Jannie Barnard was one of my men, and I feel this to be my responsibility."

. . . It was entirely his responsibility. If it

hadn't been for him—if he hadn't ordered Jannie to drive the mini back, none of this would have happened. Jannie would be alive now and he would have married the girl. The boy had even told him of his intentions—and what was it he had said in reply? . . . "Why does a youngster like you want to get himself tied up? If you must have your fun, take it, but don't get yourself hooked" . . . It made him shrivel up inside to remember. Thanks to him, Jannie's child would now be born a bastard, and, as her mother said, the girl's reputation would be ruined. She was made of fine clay—anyone could see that. There was a cleanness and innocence despite everything. He would be prepared to lay his head on a block that she had been a virgin when Jannie met her.

He glanced sidelong at her, but could see no signs of thickening about the waist.

He asked her quietly: "When is your baby due?"

She flushed slightly. "In six and a half months," she said in a low voice.

"When I get back this evening I'll make enquiries about a suitable place. The Child Welfare have homes for unmarried mothers and there're other places as well. I'll make the fullest enquiries and let you have the particulars immediately. It would probably be just as well to make your arrangements early."

She murmured something inaudible, keeping her head bent.

Mrs. Nel looked up at him, dabbing at her reddened eyes. "Lieutenant Meyer, wouldn't it be possible to arrange to have the baby adopted?"

He rubbed his cheek with two fingers. "I imagine it could be arranged quite easily. I know there's always a long waiting list for—"

"No," the girl said quickly.

"Suzanna, it's the only answer," Mrs. Nel said urgently. "Can't you see that, my child? No one need ever know that you've had a baby and it will be assured of a good home—a better one than you could afford to give it."

The girl compressed her lips, stared at her silently.

"Are you going to brand the child as illegitimate and yourself as a woman of loose morals!" she said angrily. "Have you thought of—"

"I *won't* have it adopted."

"If your father were alive he'd take a whip to your back! That's what I should have done before now. I've spoilt you, that's the trouble. I've always given you everything you've wanted, and now—"

"Mrs. Nel," Karel Meyer interrupted. "This must be Suzanna's decision. It is for her to decide whether she wants to keep the baby or have it adopted. No one has the right to force her."

"I'm her mother. Does that mean nothing?"

"It still doesn't give you the right to force her . . . My suggestion is that Suzanna moves to Cape Town as soon as possible, where I'll be able to keep an eye on her. The sooner she leaves, the easier it will be to keep things quiet. I know of a woman with whom she can board—a Mrs. van Tonder. She's a widow, and she's kind and would be very understanding."

She wiped her nose but didn't speak.

"This is what we must do now, Mrs. Nel. We must do all we can to help Suzanna. She needs your help, and this is the time when you must stick by your daughter."

"I've always helped her and looked after her. No one knows that better than she does. And after all I've done for her she can still do this to me."

He knew it would be useless to appeal to her further. He could only hope that in time she would become more reconciled.

He turned to Suzanna. "You mentioned that you've managed to save something. I take it you have a job?"

"Yes, I work in an office."

"Shorthand and typing?"

"Yes."

"That is something else I'll fix. It shouldn't be difficult to find a job for you in the city. It will keep you occupied and enable you to pay board and maybe put aside a little more."

"The only reason why Suzanna was able to save anything was because I didn't make her pay a penny for her board, as any other widowed mother would have done. And what thanks have I got for it? What has she—"

"Hand in your notice tomorrow. If you don't want the neighbours to start talking, the sooner you leave Knysna the better." Privately he thought that the sooner she got away from her mother the better it would be for both of them.

"What does it matter when she leaves! Do you think someone from here won't meet her in Cape Town, when everyone on the streets will see she's pregnant."

He glanced at his watch, a faint frown creasing his brow. "Mrs. Nel, I'll have to leave in a few minutes and would like to have a word in private with Suzanna before I go."

She sat back looking as if nothing on earth would budge her.

"Would you please be good enough to leave us."

She stared at him angrily. It was on the tip of her tongue to refuse, but she could not quite bring herself to speak. His face had tightened and his steely eyes made her feel distinctly uncomfortable.

He went over to the door, opened it and stood waiting.

She remained seated for several seconds and then suddenly got up, lifted her chin and walked out of the room.

He looked at Suzanna as he shut the door. Something about the way she stood waiting for him to speak reminded him of

Lisa Lombard. The girl had the same obstinacy and dignity.

He fumbled in his pocket as he went over to her, found what he sought and held it out. "Do you recognise this?"

She stared down at Jannie's watch, cupped in the centre of his palm.

He saw tears bead her thick dark lashes, spill over. He found himself looking at the line of cheek, her lips.

Her throat moved convulsively before she could speak . . . "His watch . . . He told me that you gave it to him."

He nodded. "Yes, I gave it to Jannie on his twenty-first birthday . . . I think you have some idea how fond I was of him."

The watch had proved everything it had been vouched for. Waterproof, shock-proof and it had started ticking the very second he wound it. Only the leather strap had to be renewed.

He said: "I want you to know that Jannie told me the day before he died that you were going to get married. He hadn't confided this to his mother, but when I told her she agreed with me that Jannie would have liked you to have this."

She turned sharply and went over to the

window to stare out through the net curtains.

After a time she said in an uneven, thickened voice: "Jannie's the only boy I've ever—"

"I know," he interrupted quickly. "You don't have to tell me that."

"He told me that he wanted to call the baby after you if it was a boy—and—we were going to call it Carol if it was a girl."

He tried to say something but felt an obstruction block his throat, cleared it loudly and still couldn't speak.

"Jannie said he was going to ask you if you would consent to be our baby's godfather."

He cleared his throat again, and this time managed to speak. "I'll be very—honoured to be your baby's godfather." He coughed into his hand. "I'll always look after its welfare—you may rest assured of that." He had an awful fear that he might break down.

He put the watch on the table, not trusting himself to go over and give it to her. "The car's here—I must go."

She turned from the window. "Thank

you, Lieutenant Meyer . . . Thank you for—everything.''

He avoided her eyes, muttered something incoherent, opened the door and went out.

13

LISA looked up when there was a light tap on the door, but before she could speak it opened and Issy Goldberg came in.

Issy Goldberg was the only Jewish director on the board of Dryads Ltd. and also by far the youngest. He was not popular with the older directors who found him arrogant and insensitive, and there was no doubt that he could be gratingly brash at times. Despite their disapproval of him as an individual the members of the board were the first to admit that it had been solely due to his drive, enterprise and imagination that the firm had risen from the doldrums into which it had sunk in the sixties. He had forced them to recognise that they were too conservative, and that the firm was doomed unless they were prepared to move with the times.

Lisa liked Issy Goldberg. Before she had become engaged to Mark he had pestered her with his attentions but that was all over now. He was generous and warm-hearted and she had always suspected that it had been his suggestion that the firm should continue to pay her after the accident, and encourage her to keep on with her work.

She put down her pen and smiled. "Hello, Issy. Come in."

He gave his full-lipped upcurving smile. "I've brought someone who's anxious to meet you." He ushered a girl into the office and took her arm as she came through the doorway. "Lisa, meet Lorne Sellars—and Lorne, this is Lisa Lombard, whom you wanted to meet so much."

He kept his hirsute olive-skinned hand on the girl's bare arm. "Lorne was telling me she's a great fan of yours."

"Oh." Lisa managed to resist an impulse to raise her eyebrows. She found it difficult to imagine that this tall poised golden-haired girl could possibly be a fan of hers.

Issy turned his head to smile at Lorne and tightened his fingers round her arm. This was the closest he had managed to get to her, and as they were much of a height he found himself looking full into her tawny eyes. "Lorne's a model," he said, and with an effort tore his eyes from hers and looked at Lisa. "She saw some kids modelling your summer range last week and was so impressed that she telephoned me half an hour ago and asked if I could arrange a meeting."

Lisa was unable to prevent herself from flushing. "Needless to say I'm very flattered." She found praise always embarrassed her and at the same time gave her this warm glow.

He reluctantly released Lorne's arm. "I'll leave you two girls to it." He smiled at her and lowered his voice. "Let me know when you're leaving. My office is directly opposite, so just walk in."

She nodded without smiling and didn't look at him.

Her response was less warm than he had hoped it might be and he looked a little thoughtful as he went out . . . He would take the precaution of leaving his office door open, just in case she tried to give him the slip.

Issy Goldberg pursued women with the same ardent enthusiasm he tackled any problems connected with his work. He had been trying to date Lorne ever since he had seen her modelling in a fashion show at

Stuttafords. Up to now she had given him the brush off and a cold shoulder. He had hardly been able to credit it when she telephoned and asked him if he could arrange a meeting with Lisa Lombard. He had leapt at this opportunity of doing her a favour, feeling it not unreasonable to hope that this might be the prelude to a happier and closer relationship.

When he shut the door, Lisa said: "Won't you sit down?"

Lorne took the chair opposite the desk, sat down and crossed her long slim legs. "I do hope you don't think it's awful cheek on my part barging in on you like this."

Lisa smiled. "On the contrary, I'm highly flattered that you should have gone to so much trouble."

She was conscious of a feeling of faint disappointment. The girl's husky voice was of good timbre, but her diction over precise and too studied, which tended to make her speech affected . . . She still found it hard to believe that this beautiful, self-assured, elegantly dressed young woman should have sought her out for the sole purpose of telling her that she liked the children's clothes she had designed.

Lorne was studying her overtly and guessed more or less what she was thinking.

"It was just as Issy said. I'm a model—and I was in the fashion show they held at the President Hotel last week. I suppose you know about it—they were also modelling children's clothes."

"Yes, I knew about it. Issy mentioned it at the time and actually asked if I would like to go with him."

"Why didn't you?"

"I don't really like fashion shows very much and I get an inferiority complex when I see the other children's clothes—they always look so much better than mine."

"You're quite wrong, you know. In my job one comes to learn quite a bit about fashion design, and I thought yours stood out. Some people seem to have that extra flair for simplicity and style . . . It's funny how the two always seem to go together, isn't it?"

"I suppose it could apply to most things."

Lorne looked slightly confused . . . "Yes, I suppose so . . . Anyway, I can't tell you how impressed I was when someone mentioned that the children's clothes I liked so much had been fashioned by a girl of my own age.''

. . . Actually Lisa Lombard looked as if she might be a year or two older, but she'd probably be flattered to be bracketed in the same age group. She wondered what had happened to her—how she had got those two long purplish scars curving across her left cheek. It was easy to see she was self-conscious about her face by the way she pulled her hair across her cheek and hid the scars behind her hand. She was quite stunning in a rather withdrawn well bred way, and looked as if she might easily be stuck up . . . What on earth were they going to talk about once their present topic was exhausted? It was all very well for Alan airily to say that she would be sure to find they had lots in common. But *what*? She had found she didn't get on that well with her own sex. Nine times out of ten they were jealous and went out of their way to be catty. The ones who said the least, pulled faces and raised their brows, were the worst . . .

She said: "One of the other models happened to mention that you work for Issy . . . We often meet at shows and I've got to know him quite well, so I telephoned him this morning and said I'd like to meet you and—well, so here I am." She uncrossed her legs and put her feet together.

Lisa thought Lorne Sellars looked every inch a model. She was wearing a well-cut pale apricot midi and her long legs were encased in glittering bronze stockings. Her wet-look Italian shoes and handbag were several shades deeper than her frock. Her long deep-gold hair was very shiny and looked as if it had just been washed and combed. But for her tilted tawny eyes, she was wearing no make-up.

"You said you often meet Issy. Have you known him long?"

Lorne combed her fingers through her hair. "No, not so long. I've lived in Durban most of my life, but six months ago I decided I'd like a change, so I came to Cape Town and met Issy shortly after I got here. He seems to attend most of the fashion shows, so I suppose it was inevitable we should meet." She crossed her legs again. "Do you keep a record of the clothes you've designed? I mean—I wondered if you've kept a scrapbook or something like that?"

"Yes, I've kept a scrapbook of the better ones."

"You have? Oh, I'd love to see it sometime. *Could* I? Would you mind awfully?"

Lisa flushed slightly. "No, of course I wouldn't mind."

"The scrapbook isn't here by any chance?"

"No, there's no room for it here. I keep it in my flat."

". . . Oh." Looking charmingly and slightly sulkily disappointed.

Lisa fidgeted, picked up her pen, put it down again. "If you're really interested I could bring it in sometime."

"Of course I'm interested. I thought I'd convinced you of that by now. But I don't want to inconvenience you in any way." She was holding her handbag on her lap and her fingers tightened unconsciously round it as she braced herself to take the plunge. "I wondered if you wouldn't let me drive you back to your flat after work this evening and maybe I could see the scrapbook then—"

She saw Lisa's face close and she seemed to withdraw slightly.

She immediately realised that she had

rushed her fences and flushed painfully; this made her appear surprisingly young and unsure of herself. "Only if you've nothing else on, of course—" she added quickly.

Lisa had been on the verge of pleading a previous engagement but was now completely won over by the girl's flush and uncontrived confusion.

She smiled and said: "As a matter of fact, I'm not doing anything."

". . . May I fetch you then?" Lorne asked hesitantly.

"Won't it be miles out of your way?"

"Not at all. I'll be in town all day and could pick you up on my way home." Her confidence was slowly returning. "You live in Rondebosch, don't you? I—seem to remember someone mentioning it. Issy, possibly."

"Yes, I live below the line at Rondebosch, in Oak Apple Crescent. Do you know the flats?"

"Not really, but I have a rough idea where they are. I'm not so far from you: my flat's in Kenilworth. I hope you'll come and see it sometime."

"I'd like to," Lisa murmured politely.

Lorne pushed her hair back from her shoulders. "Would you have dinner with me later?" She flickered a look at her to see how she was taking this. "I could book a table at Geneva's which would be close, and we wouldn't have to trail into town or all the way out to Sea Point."

Lisa could not but be warmed by the girl's obvious desire to be friendly and said impulsively: "No, don't book at Geneva's. If you're prepared to take a chance on my cooking, let's rather have a bite in my flat."

The surge of relief which flooded through Lorne felt somewhat akin to triumph. This was more—far more, than she had dared hope for. She thought of Alan's surprise—how pleased he would be with her when she telephoned him in the morning. For the moment the purpose behind it all had been forgotten.

She said: "Are you quite sure this won't be too much trouble?"

"None at all, provided you don't mind a very simple meal. There's fillet and some new potatoes and we could have salad."

"I'll make it," Lorne said quickly. "And I'll buy what we need. *Please* let me."

"If you want to. But—"

"*Please*, Lisa . . . And cheese—I'd like to bring some cheese, if I may."

"Don't feel you have to contribute anything towards the meal."

"I don't feel that way at all, I'd *like* to bring something. Have you any preference in cheese?"

"None, provided it doesn't stink." Remembering unwittingly Mark's penchant for ripe cheese.

Though Lorne had achieved her purpose she found she was experiencing a feeling of being entrapped—of wanting to escape. Lisa's friendly response to her overtures had stirred up a conflict of emotion within her.

She glanced at her watch and gave a contrived little gasp. "Good grief, I had no idea it's so late! I'm afraid I'll have to rush. I've an appointment in twenty minutes and daren't be late." She rose in one fluid graceful movement. "What time would you like me to pick you up?"

"If you can get here just after five I'll be waiting for you at the entrance."

"I'll come at five past. Please don't get up," she said quickly as Lisa pushed back her chair. "I know my way out." She gave her warm sensuous smile. "See you later." Opened the door and went out.

A second or so later Lisa heard Issy shout "*Lorne*, wait!"

She smiled as she reached for her pen and wondered how much headway he would make with the girl.

She twirled the pen absently between her fingers, and stared straight ahead, the faintest line between her brows . . . Despite Lorne's flattery and friendliness, she hadn't felt she was entirely sincere and it puzzled her why she should feel this way. Had she gathered this impression because of the somewhat refined, affected manner in which she spoke? Or was it something else? . . . She half shrugged and dismissed it.

Once Lorne entered her flat and shut the door, she felt curiously deflated and jaded. Though it was only shortly after eleven o'clock, for once she took off her clothes and flopped into bed without bothering to do anything about her face. She found her legs and arms were aching and realised how tense she must have been all evening. And there was this awful feeling of degradation and shame. She had *spied* on Lisa; there was no other word for it. Peeking and prying round her flat and asking all those personal questions . . . If only Alan could have been here now to restore her self-confidence and build up her morale. Surely there would have been no risk if he had come tonight.

". . . Try and find out every single thing you can about her," he had said when she followed him to the front door to see him off. "Get her to swop confidences with you the way I'm told you girls always do. Make her talk about herself. The more you can find out about her the better. Who her parents are, her background, if she's got any brothers and sisters. From what I saw of her, she's presentable, so there's sure to be a boyfriend in the offing. Get her to talk about him. Ask her his name, which part of the Peninsula he lives in. What does he do for a living . . ."

She had said with a certain desperation: "Oh, Alan, how can you expect me to fire all these questions at her."

"That's just what I don't want you to do. If you did she could become edgy and dry up. But if you're subtle enough and handle things the right way she'll talk about herself and tell you everything you want to know . . . You've got a way with you, Lorne. I watched you that night at the van Eedens and was amused to see how in no time at all you had everyone eating out of your hand. If you're prepared to put your mind to it you could make *anyone* talk." He smiled, took her chin between finger and thumb. "Take a look at me. You've got me eating out of your hand like the rest of them."

. . . But it wasn't true. The truth of the matter was that it was *she* who ate out of *his* hand. And they both knew it. From the start of their relationship he had been the dominant partner. He was the more experienced, older—nearly twelve years her senior, but it wasn't only that. She had heard it said that in most sexual relationships there was usually one partner more deeply involved than the other. She knew—she could feel that in her relationship with Alan, *she* was the one. She had never thought she could be capable of feeling this way about anyone. It was like being possessed. She was *insanely* in love with him. Nothing he said or did made the slightest difference to the way she felt about him. He could be a rogue, a cheat, a liar, a thief, a *murderer*, and it would make no difference . . . And he could charm her, even when she knew it was deliberate, as it had been then . . . He could even make her forget *why* she was doing this . . .

Nothing had been as easy as Alan had made out. Firstly, she found that she and Lisa Lombard had very little in common. One of the chief drawbacks had been that they came from different backgrounds; and beyond their work shared no common interest. All those books, for instance, on art and God knows what. Had she read them all? And if she had, when did she find *time*? As far as she was concerned, that sort of reading was for the birds. And those rather badly painted pictures on the walls—had she done them? They didn't go for the same kind of music. She seemed keen on that highbrow classical stuff which had no message for her . . . But she *liked* Lisa, and found she wasn't stuck up as she had first supposed she might be. Lisa was classy, and she wasn't, that was the big difference. And she had proved to be one of those girls who didn't talk about her private life. She had that "touch me not" air which discouraged one from asking the personal questions one wouldn't hesitate to ask any other girl. In fact, most of the girls she knew gave all the intimate details of their private life without being asked. She had tried taking Lisa into her confidence and had told her that she was in love with a married man, and that they were having an affair. Lisa had listened in that quiet well-mannered way she had, but hadn't reciprocated by confiding anything to her . . . At one stage she had plucked up the courage to ask if she had ever been in love. Lisa had said nothing at first, and then gave a slight smile and said: "Let's say I haven't managed to get this far and remain unscathed." What on earth had she *meant*? Could it be connected with the roses? Because there had been no doubt that Lisa had changed colour when they entered her flat and she saw the yellow and white roses. They had been arranged in a white pedestal vase which stood on a low table in front of the settee and she had said: "*Roses*" rather breathlessly. ". . . They must have come while the char was still here" and tossed her handbag on to the settee and bent over to smell them. The envelope from the florist had been taped to the pedestal and she seemed to have difficulty taking it off and sliding the card out of the envelope, as if her hands weren't quite steady. She had stared at the card for a second and then dropped it on the table and said: "Let's have a drink. I'll fetch the ice" and went into the kitchen . . . Lorne shifted uncomfortably as she remembered how despicable she had felt—as if she were doing something deceitful and dishonest when she went over to the roses ostensibly to sniff at them and looked down at the card. Fortunately it had fallen the right way up, as she very much doubted if she would have had the nerve to twitch it over in case Lisa came back and caught her doing it . . . Only one word had been written on the card. "Mark". Not "With love from" or "With thanks". Just his name. Mark. It seemed rather odd and abrupt. When Lisa came back she had made a point of remarking on how lovely the roses were and how well they matched the colour scheme in her room. She had hoped to draw Lisa out, but she had merely smiled and said coolly:

"Yes, they do go well with the room, don't they?" and then changed the subject.

Despite Lisa not opening up about herself, she had still managed to find out most of the things Alan had wanted to know. Lisa had told her that both her parents were dead and that her father had been professor of something or other at Rhodes University. She had mentioned what subject he lectured in, but it had conveyed nothing to her and she hadn't wanted to display her ignorance by asking Lisa to enlighten her. She had also mentioned that she had a brother who was a doctor and that he had settled in England.

She could now tell Alan that there *was* a telephone in the flat and she had written down the number quite openly. She would also be able to tell him that she had noticed a young man sitting in a car outside Dryads when she fetched Lisa and that he had followed them to her flat. Lisa had gone over to say a few words to him before they went in which made it look as if he were right and she *was* being followed and watched. She had also spotted a peep-hole in the front door and had noticed that it was chained.

She shivered, curled up her legs and clasped her arms . . . Was Alan right about the other things too?

He had said, as he shrugged himself into his coat: "Look, darling, until things are—settled, it would be better not to see each other."

She had been unable to stop herself crying out: "Oh, Alan, *why*?" Not to be able to see him *now*, when she needed all the reassurance he could give her.

He put an arm about her and drew her to lean against him. "I know how you feel about this, darling, and I can assure you I feel the same way. But we've got to play this safe. We can't afford to underestimate the police. There's just a chance they may check on you when they see you're going round with the girl, and things being what they are, you can surely see that it would be madness for me to risk coming here . . . In fact, I daren't even 'phone you."

She had twisted her head round to stare up at him. "Are you saying that I'm not going to see you—and that I'm not even going to *hear* from you?"

He tightened his arm and drew her closer. "We'll talk to each other every day.

You must ring me—not from here, of course, the telephone may be tapped."

He couldn't be serious! He was making it all sound like melodramatic fiction. Like those improbable thrillers one read.

"You think I'm crazy, don't you? We must anticipate every eventuality, Lorne. We can't afford to take the smallest chance. That's how most people slip up and get caught; by omitting to take precautions which should have been obvious at the time."

"Where do you expect me to 'phone from, if I mustn't do it from here?" she had asked sulkily.

"Isn't there a telephone booth anywhere near?"

She admitted that there was one round the corner.

"Then what could be easier? Ring me from there and I'll reverse the call and we can talk for as long as we like. I should think that the best time to ring me would be between eight and nine in the morning." Smiled down at her. "What do you say?"

When she made no reply, he put his other arm about her and gave her a long kiss which left her breathless and weak in the knees.

Then he tilted her chin and made her look at him. "*This* is what we're fighting for, darling. What does a short separation matter when we've got the rest of our lives to spend together? I've every confidence in you and I know how well you'll cope. That's what I admire about you. Your independence and your strength and efficiency." He kissed her again. "It's not only *this*. You're wonderful in all the ways that matter."

14

IT was shortly after half-past eight when Lorne made her way down the pavement to the telephone booth.

She was relieved to find it unoccupied, and quickly dialled Trunks and then the number Alan had given her.

The receiver was lifted the second the telephone rang. "Hello." His voice was unmistakeable.

She said: "It's me, darling. Have you been waiting long?"

"I've been sitting on tenterhooks for the last half hour. Give me your number, hang up and I'll call you back."

As soon as the connection had been remade he said: "Have you managed to make any contact with her?"

". . . Yes," she said a trifle sulkily, piqued that this should be his only concern.

"You *have*?" His voice immediately quickening. "Did you speak to her?"

"Not only have I spoken to her, but we dined together in her flat."

"What?" He sounded incredulous. "Did I get you right? Did you say you dined together in her flat?"

"Yes," she said coolly.

He guessed at once why she had gone cold on him and cursed himself for his stupidity. Surely he knew by now how a woman had to be handled.

He said: "I can hardly believe it." His voice warmed. "You're fabulous, darling. I knew I wasn't overestimating what you could do, but must admit that I didn't think even you could manage to get things moving as quickly as this."

"It wasn't so difficult really." Slightly mollified.

"I think it's fantastic! Tell me how you set about it."

"Once I'd found out what job she did, I knew I had the necessary contact to meet her."

"Don't keep me in suspense, darling. Hurry up and tell me exactly what you did."

She told him, and everything else that had followed. He interrupted her twice to question her closely on a point, and once to ask her to repeat Lisa's number while he wrote it down, but for the most part listened in silence.

When he was satisfied that she had told him everything he said: "So I was right, the police are watching her. Did she mention this?"

"No, not a word."

"Didn't she say anything about what happened on the beach?"

"No, nothing."

"It seems strange."

"You wouldn't think it strange if you knew her. She's like that."

"D'you mean she's secretive?"

"No, I wouldn't say it was that. She just doesn't like talking about herself. I think she'd have to know someone very well indeed before she'd ever confide in them."

"She'll confide in you before long, you'll see. She won't be able to help herself. Have you arranged to meet again?"

"Yes, we're going to the flicks this evening."

"What a girl! You really are wonderful, you know."

". . . Alan, I—"

"There's only one little thing that bothers me," he interrupted.

"What?"

"That you weren't successful in finding out if there's a boyfriend. Remember, I told you it would be just as well for us to know. You didn't think of asking her?"

"I asked her indirectly, and fished a bit, but she wouldn't bite."

"Why didn't you ask outright?"

"Oh, Alan, I *couldn't*! I keep telling you, one can't ask her those sort of questions."

"Haven't you allowed yourself to become a wee bit over-sensitive about this? My experience has always been that most women are only too eager to talk about their boyfriends."

"Well, this one *doesn't*. She's not like that—she's different."

"Try and find out tonight. If you feel you can't ask her directly, maybe you could do it in a roundabout way. Let's face it, an unknown boyfriend in the offing could prove not only an embarrassment, but also highly dangerous."

After a longish pause she said somewhat reluctantly: "There were those roses—"

"Roses?" Immediately sensing it could be important. "What roses? What are you talking about?"

"Someone called Mark sent her roses yesterday. I—happened to see his name on the card." Feeling as if she were betraying a confidence.

"See if you can find out who he is," he said urgently. "He could be the very man we want to know about. It shouldn't be difficult to get to talk about him."

She shifted her stance. "You don't know how awful I felt *spying* and asking all those questions. And when I read his name on the card I felt despicable—as if I were doing something dishonest . . . I *like* her," she added desperately.

"That's all to the good," he said soothingly. "If you like her, darling, then you can be pretty sure she likes you too. It always works both ways. How could she help herself anyway. *Everyone* likes you."

"Oh God, you don't understand—" she said hoarsely.

"*Lorne*, listen to me. While I was waiting for you to 'phone I sat here thinking about you, about *us*. Planning all the things we're going to do once this is all over. And this is what you must do, darling. Think of our future, make that your goal and keep it in mind all the time. Don't allow yourself to be sidetracked or upset by the small things, and above all, don't become emotionally involved with this girl."

"It's easy for you to talk. You don't know her and you don't have to do these awful things . . . Alan, couldn't you come tonight? Surely there'd be no risk?"

"Darling, I want this as much as you do, but there *would* be a risk, and we both know this now. You can't have forgotten that you told me only a few minutes ago that the police are watching her."

She couldn't speak and felt her eyes fill with tears. She drew a deep uneven breath and leaned back against the side of the booth.

"And as I said, if they're watching her, the chances are they may check on you . . . Try to be patient, darling. Things won't be this way for long."

She wiped her eyes with the back of her hand. "It's being alone—not seeing you—"

"We've got so much to look forward to, Lorne. Whatever we do, we mustn't take the smallest risk of jeopardising our future. Just think of making friends with the girl and don't let anything else intrude . . . And think of one other thing. Remember I love you. Think of this when you're feeling the least bit down."

Lorne had arranged with Lisa to pick her up at her flat at a quarter to eight. But she was ten minutes early when she rang the bell.

Lisa opened the door, wearing a long pale yellow dressing-gown which she hadn't bothered to fasten but held wrapped about her. "I'm just changing into something warmer. You're early, aren't you?"

"I'm afraid so, but don't bother about me, I'll amuse myself while you're getting dressed."

"You'll find the latest *Vogue* and *Life* on the table. I won't be more than a couple of minutes." She twitched off her gown as she went into the bedroom.

Lorne saw that the roses had been moved to the mantelshelf above the fireplace where they showed to better advantage and she went over to smell them. She picked up the little dark blue china box, held it to the light to look at it. Put it back and strolled across to the table and picked up *Vogue*, leafed through it. She was about to sit down when the telephone rang.

"Do you mind answering that?" Lisa called from the bedroom. "Tell whoever it is to hold on, I'll be along in a minute."

The telephone stood on a small long-legged mahogany table near the door and Lorne lifted off the receiver as it rang for the third time. "Hullo," she said huskily into the mouthpiece.

"Is Lisa there?" a man's resonant voice asked.

"She's nearly dressed and said I must tell you she'll be along in a minute . . . Who shall I tell her is calling?"

There was a longish pause. She was beginning to doubt if he intended replying when he said somewhat abruptly: "This is Mark Standish speaking."

Her heart gave a distinct thump. *Mark*, the man Alan wanted to know about.

She said over-precisely: "I don't know how long Lisa will be. Would you like me to give her a message?"

"Thanks. I'd prefer to wait and speak to her myself."

She reddened, feeling snubbed and a little angry, and then Lisa came in, wearing a high-necked red frock of some soft woollen material, carrying a camel's-hair coat slung over her arm.

Lorne said: "Oh, here Lisa is now," and held out the receiver and dropped her voice. "A man wants to speak to you—a Mr. Mark Standish."

"Oh." She took the receiver and dropped her coat over the back of the chair. "Hello, Mark," she said evenly.

"Who's the affected inquisitive female?"

She caught her lip beneath her teeth. "A friend," she said carefully and glanced sidelong at Lorne who was still standing beside her, absently feeling the texture of her coat. His voice had sounded frighteningly loud. Could she have heard?

She said: "Thank you for the roses, Mark. They're lovely. I've already written to thank you, but you probably haven't received my note yet. They match my room perfectly."

"I've been feeling pretty ashamed of myself since I saw you last."

" . . . You told me so when you sent the roses," she said in a low voice.

"I want to apologise for the language I used."

"As I said, you've already apologised and don't have to do so again."

"But don't get me wrong. I'm apologising for the language, but I'm not taking back anything I said."

She looked down and ran her finger along the edge of the table.

"As far as I'm concerned the topic is now closed," he said.

She cleared her throat but didn't speak.

"But I hope we can both be civilised about this and at least remain friends."

When she still didn't speak, he added: "I'm the first to admit that my behaviour the other night was anything but civilised and I couldn't blame you if you don't want to see me again."

Her eyes followed Lorne as she went over to the settee and sat down . . . "We were both at fault. I certainly bear you no ill will."

"I didn't think you would." He abruptly switched the subject. "Do you remember Judge Hanley?" he asked.

Her brows knitted in an effort of memory. "Judge Hanley? I'm not sure if I do."

"You dined with him and my mother two days before you left. We played bridge after dinner and I remember you took rather a shine to each other."

Her face cleared. "Oh, do you mean that dynamic old man with the blue eyes and leonine mane of snow-white hair?"

"An apt description." By the way he said it she could tell he was smiling. "Though he wouldn't be flattered to hear you referring to him as being old. I believe his hair went white in his early thirties. He has barely reached his half century."

"Oh." She had stiffened, guessing what all this was leading up to.

"He's dining with us tomorrow night and my mother has just informed me that our fourth for bridge has telephoned to say she's down with 'flu. This is very short notice, I know, but I wondered if by any chance you're free and if so, whether you'd be—civilised and come."

. . . It would be easy to give the excuse of a previous engagement and make it sound authentic. Especially as his invitation was so belated . . . To spend an evening in Mark's company constituted in itself a big enough strain, but the thought of having to face Mrs. Standish positively frightened her.

He said quietly: "If you feel you couldn't stomach the evening, I'd quite understand."

She knew his pride and what it must have cost him to deliberately lay himself open to a rebuff. She couldn't wound him again. It would be petty and ungracious on her part not to meet his gesture halfway.

So she said: "Thank you, I'd like to come."

"Good, I'm glad you can make it. I'll fetch you just after a quarter past seven. Hanley informed me this morning that his car will be out of commission for the whole of this week, so I'll be picking him up first."

Fluttering relief to know that at least they wouldn't be alone in the car.

"What shall I wear?" she asked.

"Oh, something informal I should imagine, but I'd better make sure. Hang on a moment." She heard him call: "What dress tomorrow night?" Then he muttered something under his breath . . . Back to her. "Sorry, it's formal. I'd forgotten Hanley makes rather a thing of it. I suspect he thinks the garb suits his flamboyant looks."

He repeated what time he would fetch her, said goodnight and hung up.

She lifted her coat off the back of the chair and glanced at Lorne as she shrugged it over her shoulders. "Sorry you had to wait. Shall we go?"

Lorne put *Vogue* down and reached for her handbag. She was wearing a dark blue midi suit, the sleeves and collar edged with red and white piping. She smoothed her skirt over her hips as she crossed the room.

"He's got a super voice," she said huskily.

"Has he?" Lifted a hand to turn the Yale lock.

"Is he English?"

"No, South African, through and through. His mother's family are Afrikaans speaking."

"Mark Standish is rather an English sounding name." Her eyes flickered instinctively to the roses as she said his name, and guessing Lisa would have noticed this, added quickly, by way of explanation: "I couldn't help overhearing you thanking him for the roses."

Lisa pushed the door open and stood aside to allow her to go ahead. "Don't let's take the lift, it's only one flight down."

. . . So she wasn't going to talk about him. This was the thing she had tried to explain to Alan.

They went abreast down the stairs and when they were halfway she said: "You think I'm inquisitive, don't you—like he does?"

Lisa flushed in discomfort. So she *had* heard.

"Do you also agree with him that I'm affected?"

Lisa said awkwardly: "I'm sorry. You must have overheard what he said."

"I could hardly fail, could I, as I happened to be standing right next to you." She laughed. "You don't have to look so embarrassed about it Lisa. It couldn't worry me less."

"He would be horrified if he knew you'd overheard."

"I must say, he was very short on the 'phone. Is he always so abrupt and—rude?"

"You mustn't take any notice of Mark. He can have an abrupt manner at times, but he doesn't mean to be rude."

"What does he do?" Sensing that Lisa's

embarrassment had broken down some of her reserve.

"He's an advocate."

"Oh. Do you mean he's one of those people who argue in court?"

"Yes."

"Have you known him for some time?"

". . . For quite a while."

They had reached Lorne's Volkswagen by now and separated to get in.

Lorne didn't speak again until she turned the car into the main street.

"I couldn't help overhearing you thanking him for the roses. When you're sitting in the same room it's almost impossible to divorce yourself from what's being said on the 'phone. Does he often send you flowers?"

"No."

"You quarrelled with him, didn't you? Isn't that why he sent the roses?"

". . . I suppose one could say it was that."

Careful, Lorne said to herself, don't push it. You've made a break-through at last. Leave it now.

She pushed her hair back from her shoulders and said: "Your friend Mark Standish is probably right. When I come to think of it, I suppose I have got an affected way of speaking."

Lisa moved restlessly. "Oh, *Lorne*, I wish you'd forget what he said."

Lorne turned her head to give her a quick smile. "Don't let it worry you. It hasn't upset me, I promise you . . . You see, Lisa, I'm no class and no one knows this better than I do. It's the big difference between me, and you and your advocate. You have both obviously learned to speak the way your parents did, just as I learned to speak like Mum. My mum's a Cockney and even though she came out to South Africa to settle in Durban over eighteen years ago, when I was still a baby, she's never lost her Cockney accent . . . I never knew my father. I don't even know what he looked like. Mum says she's a widow, but I've always suspected I'm illegit."

Lisa drew up her legs and pulled the camel's hair coat closer about her.

Lorne grinned. "You didn't like my saying that, did you? I'll tell you something, I've never said this to a soul before. I suppose it's because I've never trusted anyone sufficiently."

"Why do you suppose you're illegitimate?"

"Mum's getting on and she knocks the bottle. But when she was young she must have been a very pretty girl. I've good reason to think that a boy of better class got her into trouble. Firstly there were no photographs of my father, who was supposed to have died just before I was born, and secondly, though Mum had to be careful, we were never *poor*. In fact, we seemed reasonably well provided for, by a monthly cheque from England. I asked her once where the money was coming from and she got a bit flustered and said something vague about an inheritance."

Lisa was watching her and saw her lips curve in a smile.

"Let's face it, a woman of Mum's class would be unlikely to inherit anything from her ancestors, bar a weakness for gin—and she's inherited that all right." She slowed down and stopped at the traffic lights.

She slammed in the gear as the lights changed to green and the car shot up the hill towards De Waal Drive.

"Mum has a fantastic flair for dressmaking, and she started doing this in a small way. It didn't take long for people to realise how good she was, and in no time she was making clothes for the snob lot and making them pay through the nose for it. This made a big difference to our finances and we moved into quite a decent flat in a good area. Mum was ambitious for me and sent me to a good school. I hated it. Most of the girls were better class than me, and let me know it. Mum made all my clothes and though I was the best dressed girl in the class and the prettiest, none of them would have anything to do with me. Whenever I was within hearing distance of a group in the playground one or other would imitate the way I spoke and they'd all laugh." She flicked her hair back. "I hated them so much it ate right into me and used to keep me awake at night. But I got my own back in the end: I could pinch any one of their boyfriends if I wanted to, and that's just what I did. I hated them too. Pimply-faced conceited little bastards. Though they ran after me I knew they thought I was common, and that I'd be an easy lay. I'd lead them on until they were crazy for me and then I'd tell them to go to hell. And when I told them this, I used all the choicest words I'd learned from Mum when she was drunk."

They flashed past Groote Schuur Hospital ablaze with lights, on the right, and soared up the hill.

Lorne was sitting very erect, eyes fixed on the road, long mane of golden hair flowing down her back.

"I was sixteen when I won a beauty contest on the Natal Coast. I had lied about my age and of course my picture was in all the papers and the school made a big fuss. I persuaded Mum to let me leave and take up modelling. She wasn't keen at first, being so ambitious for me, but gave in after I threatened to run away. My first pay cheque went towards a course in speech training. I knew by then exactly what I wanted, and where I was going. I intended to become one of the snob lot who despised me so much, and I knew if I wanted to do this, I'd have to marry one of them. And the other important thing was that he must have oodles of beautiful lolly." She slanted a glance at Lisa. "Does that shock you?"

"No, why should it?"

"You're one of the the snob lot, but you're different . . . It didn't take me long to learn to speak well. Maybe I enunciate too carefully and sound affected like your friend Mark Standish says, but at least I speak like a lady. Do you agree?"

"You speak extremely well. I never—"

"Forget what he said, Lisa. As I told you, it couldn't worry me less . . . I also hung on to my virginity. Don't make the mistake of thinking that this was due to any high-minded misguided principles. I did it solely because I knew by now how men always boast about their conquests and ruin a girl's reputation. It's part of their immaturity. I wasn't going to risk getting a reputation and spoiling my chances. I also knew that if I wanted to make the grade I'd have to leave Durban, where people could find out about my background. And with Mum in the background I wouldn't stand a chance. Mum's as common as dirt and knocks the bottle, and when she's tight she lifts the roof. If any of the neighbours are foolhardy enough to come in to complain, she yells and swears at them like a trooper. She's never yet been evicted from a flat because she's got a heart of gold. She's big and generous and warm-hearted and would give the coat off her back to help a friend:

so when she goes on the rampage the neighbours tend to turn a deaf ear . . . Mum's the only real friend I've ever had. I love her and I'm goddamned ashamed of her. Can you believe that anyone can be as mixed up as that?"

"Yes. I think I would probably have felt the same way."

"When I told Mum I was going to live in Cape Town she cried at first. She's like me, or rather I'm like her. We both cry easily even though we're tough. But when she got over it, I remember her saying: 'You've got good blood in you, Lornie. Better than what I've got, and you're prettier than I was. You take more after your Dad. Don't you make the same mistake what your old Mum did. If you play your cards well, you could marry a prince.' So I think she guessed what I was after."

They were now swooping down towards the bright lights of the city. The curved bay gleamed like pewter beneath the twinkling stars and the thin sliver of the new moon.

"When I first came to Cape Town I was chased by the usual bunch of urging wolves. You know the type. Your friend Issy Goldberg was amongst that lot."

"I thought he was a friend of yours."

"Issy has the contacts and can be useful at times. We're friendly, but I've never gone out with him. I gave him, and the whole bunch the brush-off, and for a time I was as lonely as hell. When you come to a new place, unless you know someone it isn't easy to meet the right people. I was almost getting desperate when I went to a drink party given at the Mount Nelson by one of the big firms and met this boy. I knew at once that he came out of the top drawer. I could tell by the way he spoke and by his clothes. He was a little shy, nice—I *liked* him. His father was managing director of one of the biggest firms in Cape Town and he was the only son. There was no shortage of the lolly I wanted. I could see right away I was big time with him, you can always tell, and we started going out. Things were more or less buttoned up when I met this married man I told you about." She gave Lisa a quick glance to see if she remembered. "I went to a dance in the country one night while the other boy was away on business and I noticed this man at once. He's fantastically handsome in a blond Nordic way. In fact, I think he's the handsomest man I've ever seen. We didn't even speak to each other, but there was something alive, electric between us. We both sensed it and have spoken of it since . . . It was literally an accident that we met the next day. It was raining and my car got into a skid and I ended up in the ditch and he happened to be driving behind me. To cut a long story short he followed me to Cape Town and we spent the rest of the day together. By the evening I knew I was crazy about him. I've never felt this way about anyone before. If a man tried to get fresh, no matter how much I liked him, I could always check him at a certain stage and tell him there was nothing doing . . . But when he started making love to me I didn't even try to stop him . . . I didn't want to—" She cleared her throat. "I told you how I'd hung on to my virginity. I'm glad now I did . . . It seemed to mean a lot to him—"

"Lorne, is there any future for you in this relationship?" Lisa asked impulsively. "Will he divorce his wife and marry you?"

Lorne jammed her foot down on the accelerator and the volkswagen leapt forward.

When she didn't speak Lisa stole a glance

at her and saw that she was staring straight ahead, gnawing at her lip.

Lisa drew her coat closer about her, huddled into it. Oh, Lord, she thought miserably. I've put my foot in it.

15

KAREL MEYER stared at Ben du Toit through slightly narrowed lids. "You say Miss Lombard mentioned she's only known the girl two days?"

"Yes, sir." The young warrant officer was standing stiffly erect on the other side of the desk. "I knew they'd spent the last two evenings together, so when I drove Miss Lombard to work this morning I asked her if they're old friends." His rather heavy fair-skinned face reddened suddenly in recollection of how hotly he had flushed when he had finally plucked up the courage to ask her this. "She told me she has only known Miss Sellars two days." He was painfully aware of Karel Meyer's cold blue eyes watching him. "You t-told me to keep my eyes and ears open, sir," he stammered.

"So I did," Karel Meyer conceded, leaning forward to put his clasped hands on the desk. "You did right in reporting this to me," he said grudgingly.

He had noted the flush and was experiencing his usual difficulty in repressing the impatience and irritation which invariably assailed him whenever the boy was in his presence. He knew he was unfair in allowing almost everything about Ben du Toit to set his nerves on edge. His gangling calf-like clumsiness, largely due to his huge feet. The stiff ungainly way he walked. The ready blushes and the occasional stammer when he was nervous. Even the boy's keenness on his job; his earnestness, gauche and sincere, acted as an abrasive.

No one could possibly have been more opposite to Jannie Barnard, into whose shoes he had stepped. Karel Meyer knew he erred in comparing the two, and that it was always to Ben du Toit's disadvantage. He was also guiltily aware that the boy probably knew this. Just as he was aware that Ben du Toit had all the qualities which should make him a first class police officer. Integrity, responsibility, application and courage. All he lacked was the necessary self-confidence, and he had done nothing to help instil this. He had neither encouraged the boy nor had he done anything to bolster up the confidence in which he was so sorely lacking.

He reached for a pencil. "Do you know the girl's full name?" he enquired abruptly.

"Yes, sir. Miss L-Lorne Sellars."

He wrote it down, looked up again. "Profession?"

"She's a model, sir."

"Model," he wrote. "Do you know where she lives?"

"Yes, sir, I made enquiries. She lives at Jacaranda Court, Smith Street, Kenilworth, in Flat 12."

"Flat 12." He smiled interrogatively. "Good-looking?" Watching him, anticipating the flush.

It came in a hot wave, which made him sweat slightly. "Yes, sir, she's a very pretty girl."

"Hmm." He dropped the pencil and sat back, lifting a hand to stroke his cheek. After a second or two he said: "I want you to check on her menfriends. See about this right away. You've been given a description of the man we're looking for, not so?"

"Yes, sir."

"You've seen the identikit drawing of him?"

"Yes, sir."

"Well, check the men she goes round with and see if by any chance she knows someone adding up to his description."

"Yes, sir."

"I'll put someone on to watch her flat at night in case she has any nocturnal visitors." He continued to stroke his cheek, watching the boy. "He'll be told to report to you. I want you to handle this."

'Yes, sir." Face aflame, a barely perceptible straightening of his shoulders.

"If anying should crop up, you're to report back to me. Understood?"

"Yes, sir."

"You realise, of course, that the chances are a hundred to one you'll be wasting your time?"

Ben du Toit looked at him silently, not wanting to venture a reply.

"But this is beside the point . . . Always remember that in our department of the Force it's our duty to explore every possible channel, no matter how unlikely it may seem. Is that clear?"

Ben's prominent Adam's apple jumped as he swallowed. "Yes, sir." He was feeling increasingly uncomfortable under the pale blue discerning eyes.

"You've been given the details of the case, so you should know what to look out for."

"Yes, sir."

"Well, what are you waiting for? Get moving!" he said with sudden impatience.

Ben turned, stumbled over his own feet, half lost his balance and blundered against the desk. He glanced quickly at Karel Meyer and apologised, red-faced.

Karel Meyer sat back and watched as he walked stiff-legged and self-conscious over to the door. He fumbled awkwardly with the handle, twisted it the wrong way and tried to force it open. Realised his mistake, more fumbling and he finally succeeded in opening the door and went out.

Karel Meyer gave an exasperated sigh as he helped himself to a cigarette from the packet he always kept at hand on his desk. When it was alight he settled himself in his chair, put his head back and absently puffed out a smoke-ring to the ceiling and continued to stare upwards, deep in thought. Nothing would evolve from this, of that he was certain. But as he had said to

Ben du Toit, it was a case of exploring every channel. Ten days had now passed since he had interviewed Lisa Lombard at the police station in Knysna and he could truthfully say that they had not advanced a single step since then. Whatever clues they had followed had led to a false trail, ending in bitter frustration. They were up against a blank wall, there was no other word for it.

He straightened at a sharp knock on the door and called: "Come in."

The duty constable opened the door. "Are you busy, sir?"

"I'm always busy. What is it?"

"A young lady would like to see you, sir."

His brows rose. "A young lady? It isn't often I have that pleasure." He showed his white teeth in a sardonic smile. "Is she pretty?"

The constable grinned. "Yes, sir."

"Well, show her in. What are you waiting for?"

The constable turned to speak to someone and a second later ushered Suzanna Nel into his office.

Though she had been much in his thoughts, she was the last person he expected to see and he found himself totally unprepared. He rose too quickly from behind his desk and nearly sent his chair toppling over backwards. He knew he was flushing and the unpleasant thought flashed through his mind that he must be looking just about as ridiculous as Ben du Toit.

"*Suzanna*, what on earth are you doing here?" He came round and pulled a chair from the wall and placed it for her opposite the desk. "Sit down."

He glanced at the constable and caught the grin on his face. His eyes immediately steeled and he jerked his chin towards the door.

She looked unsure of herself and a little frightened. Even younger and more defenceless than when he had seen her last. She tied back her hair which made her look like a schoolgirl. Her neat blue woollen suit brought out the intense blueness of her eyes. Her face was rather pale and there was a darkish bruise below her right eye. She still had the drawn haunted look of someone deeply unhappy.

He smiled and indicated the chair. "Sit down," he repeated and went behind his desk and sat down himself.

He waited until she looked at him. "What can I do for you? Can I help you in any way?"

She was sitting clasping her handbag tightly on her lap. She said: "Lieutenant Meyer, I got your letter two days ago. You must be wondering why I haven't written to thank you."

"Two days is a short time. I didn't expect to hear from you so soon."

"You will never know how grateful I've been for all you've done—the trouble you've gone to."

He had left his cigarette smouldering in the ashtray and took it between his strong fingers and stubbed it out. "It has been no trouble, I assure you."

"Lieutenant Meyer, you mentioned in your letter that your friend, Mrs. van Tonder, very kindly said that I could stay with her—" She faltered to a stop and he watched her hands clench over her handbag.

"Yes, Suzanna?" he enquired gently when she didn't go on.

She lifted her eyes. "You did say, didn't you, that she said I could come any time?—"

He nodded. "Yes. Is this why you're here?"

". . . I've brought all my things. I know I should have given you some sort of warning. Written or 'phoned—"

"Have you been having trouble with your mother?" he asked.

She looked down . . . "I think she hates me now," she said in a low voice.

"I was afraid of this." His eyes dwelt on the dark bruise on her cheek. "Did she hit you?" His bland sallow face gave nothing away.

She didn't meet his eyes. "She makes me say things to her that I never dreamed I could—that I'm ashamed to remember . . . We're bad for each other, Lieutenant Meyer. It is much better that I should leave now."

"I agree it's for the best. But you must understand, Suzanna, how any mother would feel—"

"Oh, but I do. Please believe me when I say I don't blame my mother . . . It is only that I can't—take any more—"

He picked up the pencil, twisted it between his fingers. "I'll give Mrs. van Tonder a ring and tell her that you're here.

She'll quite understand. What have you done with your luggage?"

"I came by train and left it at the station."

"Did you tell your mother you were leaving?"

Eyes down, hands twisting the handle of her bag. "I left a note."

"Let me have the ticket and I'll send someone along to collect your luggage." He watched while she searched for it in her bag. "As soon as we've got your luggage I'll take you to Mrs. van Tonder's and once you're installed, you must ring your mother to let her know that you've arrived safely."

She stared at him with the slightly widened eyes of a frightened child. He thought, God how young she is.

He smiled. "Or would you prefer me to do it?"

"Oh, *please* ring her, Lieutenant Meyer," she said in a trembling voice, looking as if she were about to cry. "I know it would upset my mother less if you were to speak to her."

"OK, I'll ring her." Stretched his hand across the desk. "And now let me have that ticket."

An hour later he drove her to Bessie van Tonder's cottage in Tamboerskloof.

Bessie van Tonder had been a widow for three years. Her husband was shot at point blank range by a thief who had entered their tobacconist shop just before closing time and it was Karel Meyer who tracked down the murderer and ultimately arrested him.

Karel Meyer, as a regular customer, had come to know Willem van Tonder and after his death went out of his way to befriend and help his widow. He saw to it that she got good price for her husband's small thriving business and assisted her to find a cottage in Tamboerskloof, cheap enough and with enough accommodation to take in three P.G.s.

He knew she felt deeply indebted to him, and that he could safely entrust Suzanna Nel to her care.

He had told her the whole story and as soon as she saw Suzanna she put an arm half about her and greeted her as if she had known her all her life.

"I've had your room ready for days; ever since Karel told me you were coming." She noted how strained and unhappy the girl looked.

". . . I hope I haven't inconvenienced you by coming so unexpectedly."

"Not at all, my child, I'm delighted you've come." She saw Karel Meyer glance at his watch. "I suppose you're in a hurry as usual?"

"As you know, Bessie, I've a demanding job and we're handling a particularly tricky case at the moment."

"You look tired, Karel, and you look as if you've lost weight. Why not come and have supper with Suzanna and me tonight and put your feet up and relax for a change?"

He hesitated and saw the girl look at him imploringly. It brought home to him how lonely and alien she must be feeling.

He said: "I'd like to say yes. But you know how things can go. I may have to let you down at the last minute."

"We'll take a chance on that," she said comfortably. She had caught Suzanna's imploring look and had seen how his eyes had rested on the girl's face. "If you can get away, try and be here by half-past six."

"I'll be earlier if nothing unforeseen

crops up." He glanced at the girl who was standing silently between them. "I'll see about that job for you when I get back. There's something more or less lined up and you could start at once."

She nodded and bit her lip.

He hesitated in slight embarrassment. "You seem to have left home in rather a hurry. Are you all right for cash?"

She coloured. "Yes, thank you, Lieutenant Meyer. I cashed a cheque before I left."

"Well, then, I must be off . . . I'll ring your mother and let her know you're safe and sound."

Her eyes filled with tears and she quickly averted her face.

Bessie van Tonder took her arm. "Come, Suzanna, let me take you to your room, and then we'll have a nice cup of tea . . . It is Suzanna, isn't it? Or are you called Sannie, by any chance?"

". . . Most of my friends call me Sannie," she said in a muffled voice.

Karel Meyer was frowning slightly as he got into his car, . . . Sannie. He didn't like the name. Never had. He remembered now that Jannie Barnard had called her that . . .

16

MRS. STANDISH was wearing black velvet and her pearls. She had been sitting for the last ten minutes in the wing chair with Toby stretched out like a fox stole on her lap. As the door opened he leapt off and she rose when Mark ushered Lisa and Judge Hanley into the room.

She went halfway across the room to meet them and greeted Lisa first, holding out a cool capable hand and enquired politely how she was.

Mark saw her smile had stopped at her eyes, and glanced at Lisa and saw at once that she had noticed this.

If there had been warmth lacking in Mrs Standish's greeting, there was certainly no lack of it in the ecstatic welcome Toby gave Lisa once he had tentatively sniffed at the hem of her frock and realised who she was. He scrabbled at the skirt of her long white dress, whining and sneezing in excitement.

"He'll tear your frock," Mrs. Standish said.

Lisa caught him up and half turned her back as she hugged him and pressed her face into his silky musky fur. He wiggled and licked her cheek, disarranging the wing of hair she had so carefully placed across it.

"He hasn't forgotten you," Mark said.

She fondled Toby and didn't turn round.

"How about a drink. What can I get you?"

She put Toby on the floor, turned, with a hand up to her face. "Could I have a dry sherry?"

"You must be cold," Mrs Standish said. "Come and sit by the fire. No—not there. Sit in the wing chair."

Lisa went over to the wing chair and sat down, and in a second Toby took a flying leap into her lap and thrust a cold moist questing nose into her hand.

Mark put the glass of sherry on the coffee table beside her and she glanced at him briefly and murmured her thanks.

"How about you, sir?" Mark asked Hanley.

"A whisky and water, no ice, and make

it long." He rubbed his hands briskly and stretched them out to the fire. "It's been as cold as charity all day. It looks as if we might be in for an early winter. Have you had much rain?" he enquired of Mrs. Standish.

"We had a few showers before lunch, but it's hardly stopped since."

"Well, God knows we need it badly enough . . . I don't suppose you've started pruning your hydrangeas yet?"

"No, it's much too early. I never touch them before the end of June." She went to sit in the armchair opposite Lisa.

Lisa remembered they had discussed gardening before.

He turned his back to the fire and clasped his hands behind him. "Well, Jess, you'll probably be surprised and shocked to hear that I cut mine back last weekend. You've never seen such dead wood from lack of water. You've got your own water here, which makes all the difference. I sometimes wonder if you appreciate just how lucky you are. What with the water restrictions enforced this year and the drought, my garden has barely survived the summer."

He nodded as he took the glass Mark proffered him.

Mrs. Standish saw Lisa smile down at Toby and run the back of her fingers along his pointed muzzle. He was lying on his back staring up at her, dark brown eyes deep with meaning.

She said coolly: "I don't think Toby should be lying on your lap, he could ruin your frock."

Lisa looked up quickly and gave a slight strained smile. "I'm sure he won't . . . I'm so—touched that he has remembered me."

Unsmiling, she fingered her pearls. "A dog's memory and affection can often be more lasting than ours."

Lisa felt herself flush and dropped her eyes and went on stroking Toby.

"He hasn't had a bath for weeks and I wouldn't like him to dirty your white frock." She snapped her fingers and in a flash Toby leapt off Lisa's lap and landed full toss into hers and her arm automatically enfolded him as he snuggled up to her.

Mark slanted her an oblique glance as he went over to stand beside Lisa's chair.

"If I may say so, your frock is an extremely becoming one," Hanley said, smiling down at Lisa. "I always like to see a woman in white."

Hanley's appearance was somewhat theatrical. This was largely due to the striking contrast between his mobile clever unlined face and his white sideburns and flowing mane of snow-white hair. He was slim, small, foppishly dressed. He was attractive to women, and there had been rumours of his affairs.

"I agree with you, Charles, Lisa's dress is quite lovely." She smiled at Lisa with her lips only. "Did you buy it in London?"

"Yes," Lisa said and reached for her glass.

She sipped delicately at the pale gold sherry, very conscious of Mark standing silently beside her chair. She wondered if he remembered that he had told her once that he and his father always knew if his mother had taken a dislike to someone. "My father always referred to it as 'the lethal politeness your mother employs whenever she's taken a dislike to some poor wretch'." He had laughed when he told her this and she had laughed with him . . . It would have been unthinkable then to have believed that she would one day be a recipient of this deadly politeness.

She felt wretchedly miserable and horribly oppressed by the thought of the interminable evening stretching ahead. She was angry with herself for not having had the strength of character to refuse Mark's invitation, irrespective of whether it might have hurt him. And she was also bitterly resentful that he had placed her in this invidious and untenable position.

Half an hour later the maid came in to announce dinner and when they went in it was to find the dining-room much more brightly lit than usual. The central light had been switched on and the usual candles were missing from the dining-table. The two elaborately branched candelabra had been moved to the mahogany sideboard and placed on either side of the pedestalled wine-cooler, which Lisa saw still held the same arrangement of dried leaves she remembered from last year.

She also remembered Mrs. Standish telling her that any form of smoke tended to stoke up Judge Hanley's asthmatic condition. This would account for the absence of candles, and also explained why Mark hadn't smoked before dinner. She thought it would be unlikely to have improved his temper.

The two central leaves of the long dining-table had been taken out and it was now circular and seated four. The arrangement of translucent single pink camelias in the centre of the table could have been a cluster of water lilies, and were the same delicate shade of pink as the lace-edged Italian table mats and napkins at each place.

The housemaid was wearing a pink striped uniform in keeping with all the rest, and murmured good-evening as she put a steaming bowl of savoury-smelling soup before her.

Hanley as usual was holding the floor, and Mark was sitting back, a hand resting on the table, listening to him. Lisa glanced at him sidelong and thought again how much his narrow introspective face reminded her of a Van Dyck portrait. All he lacked was the pointed beard and the lace at throat and wrists.

He turned his head and caught her looking at him, and she immediately put up her left hand to shield her face.

He felt a flicker of irritation, bordering

on anger, as he pushed back his chair and went over to the sideboard to fetch the sherry.

He filled her glass and let his eyes rest deliberately and dispassionately on the white nape of her neck. She had put up her hair and carefully swept a silky pale gold wing to lie becomingly across her left cheek. He noticed that she hadn't succeeded in quite hiding the two long scars, and it was apparent that she knew this. He had also noticed that if she were addressed she instinctively lifted a hand to shield the left side of her face before speaking. Each time she did this, he felt the same unreasonable deepening anger towards her. Even her withdrawn look, her face as expressionless as a mask was beginning to infuriate him. Nor had his mother's damnable politeness done anything to improve his humour . . . He should have realised that the position was futureless and hopeless, and that the evening could be nothing but disastrous.

But just how disastrous it would prove to be, he was yet to find.

Old Lizzie, who had cooked for Mrs. Standish since her marriage, was the one to deliver the first crippling blow to the evening.

She poked her head round the door leading to the kitchen when they were halfway through dinner and cleared her throat sufficiently loudly to catch their attention.

She gave Mrs. Standish a toothless ingratiating smile when she looked up. "Excuse me, Merrem—"

Mrs. Standish's straight brows twitched, but her handsome well-bred face hid her annoyance. "Yes, Lizzie, what is it?"

"Excuse me, Merrem, I jes like to say good-evening to Miss Lisa. Merrem say she come tonight, and as Merrem know it long time I not see her."

"Very well, come in, and for goodness sake shut the door. There's a tearing draught," she spoke a shade impatiently, knowing quite well the real motive behind Lizzie's request.

Lizzie came in and shut the door, stood a little bent, washing her hands obsequiously and smiled at Judge Hanley. "Good-evening, Your Worship."

He smiled affably. "Good-evening, Lizzie. How are you?"

No one knew Lizzie's age, least of all she.

But her wiry bush of hair on which her cap was somewhat precariously perched, was every bit as white as Hanley's, and she had always assumed that they must be much of an age.

She said: "I can't complain, Your Worship. But you and I is getting no younger."

His faun-like face lit up with amusement. "Get along with you. Each time I see you you look younger and prettier."

She bridled and gave a high cackle of laughter. "His Worship always make jokes." She sidled over to Lisa's chair, washed her hands again and gave her toothless smile "Good-evening, Miss Lisa."

Lisa turned to smile at her, a hand up to her face. "Good-evening, Lizzie."

"And how Miss Lisa keeping?"

"I'm very well. And you're looking well too, Lizzie. You're still exactly the same."

"As I says to His Worship, I can't complain, Miss Lisa, but we's getting ole." She winced, clapped a hand to her back and grimaced in pain. "Ag, eina!"

"What's the matter?"

"It my poor beck, Miss Lisa. Ai, now in dis cold weather my beck give me lot of troubles. When you get ole like me, Miss Lisa, you needs someting extra to keep out the cold." She cocked a rheumy eye at Mark who was watching her with a slight smile.

He twisted the long stem of the crystal wineglass between his fingers. "You can have my old fishing jersey—that should help keep out the cold."

"Ag, Massa Mark, you mustn't make jokes with poor ole Lizzie." She winced again, hand still clapped to her back. "It my rumateik—it bed tonight. It damp air what done it . . . Ag, Massa Markie, give poor ole Lizzie a doppie."

He glanced at his mother to see if she were agreeable and when she nodded unsmiling, he pushed back his chair and got up to fetch the brandy bottle from the drink tray in the sitting-room.

He paused on his way out to peer behind the wine-cooler on the sideboard, found what he sought and held the tumbler aloft. "How did this get here?"

"I puts it there, Massa Mark," Lizzie said, unabashed. "I puts it there jes in case my beck give troubles again."

Mark and Hanley exchanged a grin as he went out.

Lizzie clasped her gnarled hands over her stomach and gave her attention back to Lisa. "We not see Miss Lisa for long time. I tinks it over a year now."

"Yes, it must be just about that."

"Did Miss Lisa have a nice time?"

"Yes, thank you."

She cocked her head on one side and looked her over. "Miss Lisa got tin."

"Do you think so?"

"Yes. Last time I see Miss Lisa you's much fatter."

Mark came back with the brandy bottle and went over to the sideboard and picked up the tumbler.

Lizzie, her back forgotten, bent well down to peer into Lisa's face. "When Merrem tell me Miss Lisa coming tonight, she say Miss Lisa got hurt bed while you's away."

Mark stiffened, the bottle poised above the tumbler. What the hell did his mother have to tell her that for?

He heard Lisa say in a low voice: "Yes, I—I had an accident."

He poured out a generous measure and

screwed the cap on the bottle. "Here's your dop, Lizzie," he said abruptly.

Lizzie was still peering, and when Lisa clasped her hands in her lap, she saw the two long purple scars curving across her cheek.

Her wrinkled old face puckered up like a child's about to cry. "Ag, foeitog, Miss Lisa!" Her mouth turned down and emotional tears welled into her eyes. "When Merrem tell me, I not know it so bed. Foeitog, foeitog, foeitog, Miss Lisa."

Mark said harshly: "Do you want your damned dop, or don't you? Here—" He came over and held out the tumbler. "Take this and get out!"

She straightened and stared at him with startled eyes, mouth agape.

"What the hell are you doing in here anyway?" he said angrily. "Why aren't you in the kitchen where you belong?"

"Mark—" his mother said.

He thrust the tumbler into Lizzie's hand. "You heard what I said. Take this and get out! He looked capable of seizing her by the scruff of her neck and throwing her out.

She backed from him, eyes widened in exaggerated consternation, then turned and scuttled over to the door and opened it. She stood framed in the doorway, knowing that with the possible exception of Lisa, they would all be watching her. She clasped the tumbler to her spare bosom and looked at each one in turn until her eyes came finally to rest on Mrs. Standish.

"Tomorrow I hands in my notice," she said in a quavering voice and lifted her apron to her face and burst into tears.

She left a heavy silence and for the remainder of the meal the atmosphere was distinctly strained. But once they were back in the sitting-room, Hanley, while savouring his cognac, set out to dispel the cloud that had settled over the party since Lizzie's dramatic departure.

Despite a tendency to hold the floor he was a delightful conversationalist and a raconteur with a quick wit and an unusual twist of phrase. This, combined with his mobile expressive face, gave his anecdotes an individual freshness and humour.

He concentrated mostly on Lisa. Mark remembered that he had taken a great liking to her when they met before. He was well known to have an eye for the women and for his ability to charm them.

It didn't take him long to have Lisa under his spell. Mark was grateful to him in one way, and irritated in another.

Nonetheless it would be Hanley who unwittingly dealt the second crushing blow to the evening.

At the end of a racy anecdote that had them all laughing, he consulted his watch and suggested it was time they settled down to bridge. He was an excellent bridge-player with a passion for the game. At times his bidding could be erratic and over-optimistic, but he more than compensated for this by the play of his hands and by his brilliant defence.

He cut Mark for the first rub, which proved to be an up and down affair lasting nearly an hour. They would have won the rub if Hanley hadn't tried for an optimistic slam and Mark hadn't misplayed a game bid.

Hanley and Mrs. Standish cut together for the second rub and when Mark sat down opposite Lisa he realised that this was the first opportunity he'd had all night of really studying her.

And this was what he proceeded to do the first time he was dummy. His closed face gave nothing away as he eased himself back and sat and watched her. The light from the standard lamp which had been placed between her chair and his mother's shone down on her pale gold hair and bare shoulders. It seemed that for once she had forgotten about her face and was giving her full attention to the play of the hand. She was in a tricky contract of four spades which had been doubled by Hanley with brisk confidence, and with what Mark deemed unnecessary emphasis. Lisa's face had become still and intent and he noticed how this emphasised its delicate bone structure. Her slim brows were faintly drawn together and her mouth firmed at the corners. He watched her long-fingered hand play a card, gather up the trick. He believed himself to be dispassionate as his eyes strayed over her fine-skinned shoulders and the curve of her neck. She was wearing the intricately coiled gold brooch he remembered, pinned to her frock above the swell of her breast.

Hanley suddenly thrust himself back in his chair and tossed the last two cards on the table with ill-concealed petulance.

He cleared his throat. "Hurrumph!"

Tension of any sort tended to constrict his breathing. "You've got me, Lisa. The last trick must be yours. I could see what you were up to, but there was nothing I could do to prevent it. Well played." He pushed himself a little further back and thrust two fingers into his collar to ease it. "Well played indeed," he repeated more heartily, having got over his initial disappointment. "Did you see that, Mark? Did you see how she played the hand?"

Mark looked slightly blank.

"Did you see what she did? I had to make the Ace of clubs, the Queen of trumps, and sat over her with the Ace, Queen of hearts. It looked as if it must be a sitting double. But what does she do? She draws only two rounds of trumps, strips the hands until we're down to three cards and throws me in with her last trump—and has me on toast. All I can do is to cash the Ace of hearts, and her King becomes good."

Mark's attention had been elsewhere and he had taken scant note of the play.

He smiled at her and said: "Well played."

"Well played, he says," Hanley repeated sarcastically, feeling the praise to have been lukewarm. "Let me tell you something, Mark, Lisa could teach you a thing or two at this game. If you had adopted similar tactics in that four spade contract you made such a muck of just now, you wouldn't have gone one down and we would have won the rub." Conveniently forgetting his own lapse.

"Yes, sir." His eyes were still on Lisa's face and when her eyes came up he rubbed his nose and winked at her poker-faced and saw her catch her lip beneath her teeth to suppress a smile . . . It was the only warming moment there had been all night.

It was by no means a warming moment for Mrs. Standish who had intercepted Mark's wink and Lisa's suppressed smile. She felt bitterly resentful towards the girl for what she had done to him, and her chief fear now was that he might become involved with her again.

She smiled coolly at Lisa, fingering her pearls. "I agree with Charles, you played the hand beautifully. Didn't you mention once that your father taught you to play bridge?"

"Yes." The withdrawn look had come

back. "He taught Robert and me to play when we were children."

"Wasn't he one of the leading bridge-players in Grahamstown?" Mark asked.

She glanced at him briefly with cool clear eyes, putting up a hand to finger the silky wing across her cheek. "Yes."

"It doesn't matter who taught her. If Lisa didn't have card-sense, no one could have taught her to play the game of bridge she does." Hanley ran a well-kept hand over his flowing white hair. "This is something one is born with, and if it's missing, no amount of teaching can instil it. Take your father, for instance, Mark—and I'm sure you'll bear me out on this, Jess." Slanting her a glance across the table. "There was a man with a brilliant intellect and someone who had made a study of the game. Yet he remained an indifferent player all his life."

Lisa had cut the cards and he picked up the pack and dealt.

"Card-sense. That's the thing to be born with." He gave Lisa a smiling glance. "And that's what you've got, Lisa. And you were also fortunate enough to be taught by a good player. Your father must have found you a rewarding pupil . . . Now take our friend Mark here. He's got card-sense and twice the flair for the game his father had. His trouble is that he doesn't play enough tight bridge. The only way to improve at this game and acquire expertise is to play in a tough school for high stakes and be made to pay heavily for your mistakes. That was the way I learnt." He fingered his jaw and smiled slightly. "I'm not sure how much humility Mark's got. I suspect not much. But if he isn't over-loaded with too much masculine arrogance to be willing to learn from his wife, you should be able to improve his game considerably."

She sat staring down at her lap.

He blundered on oblivious. "The last time we met, you two had just become engaged. When are you thinking of getting married?"

Eyes still down, hand half hiding her face . . . "We're no longer engaged."

"Hurrumph!"

"Mark," Mrs Standish said calmly. "Get Charles a drink. I'm sure he'd like one."

"A whisky and water, sir?"

"Yes, thanks, Mark. Long. No ice . . . Hurrumph!"

The evening dragged on for another hour.

Mark thought it would never end. His nervous system had been craving a cigarette all night and twice when he was dummy he got up and went into the study and smoked half a cigarette. When he came back he stonily ignored the sharp glance Hanley cast him and all the humming and hawing which followed because he had kept them waiting. He ceased making any contribution whatsoever to the conversation.

He blamed himself for not having forseen that the evening would be bound to be disastrous. He was annoyed with his mother, and that bumbling old fool, Hanley. But unjustifiably, most of his anger was directed at Lisa. Her pale withdrawn look and her hand constantly up to her face had now got on his nerves to such a degree that he could scarcely bring himself to look at her.

When the evening finally dragged to a close he stood at the front door listening with detached cynicism to the exchange of insincere inanities passing between Lisa and his mother.

When they went out it was to find that the rain had stopped though it was imminent any minute. The moon and stars were masked by heavy cloud and it was pitch dark. The night air felt damp and a bitingly cold wind made them hunch their shoulders as they made their way to the car.

Hanley opened the door and suggested that Lisa should sit at the back with him. Mark waited until they were both in before he switched on. He drove in silence and listened with the same detached cynicism to the monologue coming from Hanley at the back, which was directed solely at Lisa. He told her one or two amusing anecdotes, and then after a considered pause, said how much he hoped she would dine with him one evening. Mark couldn't catch what she said in reply to this, but assumed that she had murmured an assent. Hanley said he would arrange a tough game of bridge. He would try to get hold of Dr. Munro, and Leftwich, the advocate, who rather fancied themselves as a couple. He chuckled. He couldn't wait to see their faces when they saw that he was being partnered by a beautiful young woman. They would doubtless make the mistake of assuming they were in for easy pickings. It was going to be enormous fun disillusioning them.

Mark wondered sourly if that was all Dr. Munro and Leftwich would have in mind when they saw her.

As soon as he slowed down and drew up at her block of flats Hanley leapt out and opened the door for her with a flourish. The beam of light from the entrance fell upon him, hat in hand, his snow-white crest of hair blown by the wind, his young faun-like face alive . . . It had been a great pleasure meeting her again. He was looking forward to having many more games of bridge. He would contact Munro and Leftwich and give her a ring within the next few days. She thanked him, and they shook hands and said goodnight.

Mark and Lisa went in. He lit a cigarette as they mounted the one flight of stairs. Her latchkey was in the pocket of her coat and when they stopped at the door of her flat she had the key in the lock and the door open before he could make a move to do it for her.

. . . And now there would be the same

inanities that had passed between her and his mother . . . Thank you, Mark, for a lovely evening . . . Don't mention it, Lisa. It's been enormous fun. We must do this more often. Next time I'll arrange a tough game of bridge and you can give me a few tips on how to improve my game . . .

She pocketed the key and turned to say goodnight. The light in the small bare foyer was harshly bright and she was standing in the full glare of it. As she opened her mouth to speak she instinctively lifted her left hand to shield her face. That did it.

His smouldering anger erupted. "For Christ's sake, stop doing that!"

She stared at him. Her lips trembled, but it was with anger.

"You never forget your face for a second, do you?"

Rage had quickened her breathing. She still didn't speak.

"OK, so you've got a few scars on your face. When the hell are you going to face up to that fact and learn to live with it?"

"You m-mean I haven't got the bloody guts to live with it. That's what you mean, don't you?"

"It's as good a way as any of putting it."

She had gone dead white. The scars stood out like purple weals across her cheek. "Wouldn't a cowardly bitch be a better way of putting it? That's what you said last time." She took a deep breath to steady herself. "Leave me alone in future, Mark. We can forget about being civilised. I don't want to see you again."

She went in and shut the door in his face.

17

BY nine o'clock Alan was beginning to sweat thinly and his face had become pale and fine-drawn, as if he were ill. He sat tensely gripping the arms of his chair for another ten minutes, then suddenly leapt to his feet and began pacing the room.

So Lorne had decided to do the same thing today that she had done to him yesterday morning. Keeping him sweating on a string for an hour without telephoning him.

As he strode past the armchair he dealt the back of it a violent blow with his clenched fist. The *bitch*, that she could do this to him!

When she hadn't telephoned him yesterday morning, tension had mounted steadily during the day until finally against all wisdom and common-sense he had telephoned at eleven that night, only to end by slamming down the receiver in frustration when she didn't answer. When he tried again at one o'clock, and once more after two, the result had been the same. He had stood by the telephone cursing her for three whole minutes, out of breath with his own rage. *Knowing* she was in the flat. Visualising her lying in bed listening to the telephone ringing and making no move to get up and answer it.

He continued striding restlessly up and down trying to contain his rage. He couldn't remember when last he had been so angry. If he had *ever* been so angry. It burnt him up like something consuming him. The appalling mess he was in now was all due to her. If he had obeyed his first instincts and steered well clear of her, none of this would have happened.

He flung himself into the armchair and let his head fall back and stared up at the ceiling . . . It was obvious that by not telephoning him, Lorne hoped to blackmail him into going to see her. And she could do this knowing the risk involved! *This* was what infuriated him so much. That she was prepared to endanger his life when she said she loved him. It was also obvious by now that she would do nothing about saving him unless he pressurised her into doing so.

He straightened, sat back and thought things out and finally came to the conclusion that he had no choice but to go and see her . . . But everything must be cut and dried when he went. Planned, so that whatever had to be done could be executed with the minimum delay. One thing was certain; the girl must be written off within the next few days, before Lorne lost her nerve. He would have to build her up and on no account let her suspect his rage. He must be careful not to let her feel that she was being coerced into doing what was necessary. He must get her into the frame of mind where she would feel she was doing what he asked only because she loved him, and because of their future.

He had been thinking things over for the last few days and had thought of a way in which he could dispose of the girl. But before he could finalise his plans he must literally explore the lay of the land . . . Not only must he be able to tell Lorne what he wanted her to do, but he must also be able to describe the exact spot where the girl must be taken to. . . . Within half an hour he had changed his clothes and left the house . . .

If Lorne had been asked why she hadn't

telephoned Alan for two days she would have been hard pressed to find an answer. But blackmailing him into coming to see her had never entered her mind—even though she had desperately needed the reassurance of his love.

Several factors had contributed towards her reluctance to speak to him . . . There was this awful feeling of being entrapped in a nightmare, and with it the growing horrifying realisation of her reason for cultivating Lisa's friendship. Getting to know her, and liking and respecting her more than any girl she knew had increased this feeling tenfold, and had now made her situation intolerable . . . When she hadn't telephoned Alan, nor made any further effort to contact Lisa, she was reacting like a frightened child. Slamming the door and locking it. Hoping that if she did nothing and didn't think about it, that somehow everything would be resolved by the morning.

But of course *nothing* was different in the morning. If anything, it was worse because she now felt guilt for not having telephoned Alan, and also a little frightened for not answering the telephone during the night when she had known it could only be him. . . . She had a long appointment with a photographer to model a range of dresses for the forthcoming spring and summer seasons and because she was nervous and highly strung, her session with him proved to be a particularly exhausting and trying one.

The photographer, recognised as one of the best in the Republic, was newly arrived from Johannesburg and of Latin origin. Slightly effeminate, thin, dark, long-haired and civil enough at the start.

It didn't take long before it became apparent that he was a perfectionist with little consideration for his model. Time was of no importance. He had her posed for ten minutes, a quarter of an hour, concentrating only on achieving the maximum effect from the light. Then he made her raise her chin, move a leg an inch or two back.

Normally she would have recognised his worth, and would have been co-operative. But in her present mood she found him pernickety and maddeningly slow. And she made no effort to hide this. He didn't react at first, but then abruptly became provocatively insolent and arrogant, treating her almost with contempt. She lost her temper, flared out and told him what she thought of him. He screamed back in Italian. She couldn't understand what he said, but there was no mistaking what he meant. She yelled at him, her language uninhibited, Cockney accent evident, and he shrilly flung the worst words back in broken English . . . She froze and didn't speak again. Looked right through him and obeyed his orders with cold disdain.

He was utterly delighted with her. The more she glared at him from blazing tawny eyes when he flicked her with his tongue, and the more icily contemptuous her manner became, the better pleased he was. In this lay the secret of his success, and explained the ice and fire which emanated from his models.

When the session was over and she finally swept out without looking at him, she found Issy Goldberg waiting in the corridor by the lift where he had been for close on an hour. Lorne had by now become an obsession with him, and by devious means he kept track of her movements and contrived to meet her whenever he could, pursuing her with dogged persistence despite being repeatedly rebuffed.

She didn't look particularly pleased to see him, but he was undeterred, and walked with her to her car, gallantly opened the door and asked tentatively if she would dine with him that evening, not expecting for one second that she would comply. She looked at him a long moment, as if she were summing things up, and then somewhat ungraciously accepted.

The unpleasant session she had just endured with the photographer had been the last straw, and she now felt that anything would be preferable to spending another evening alone in her flat, with every possibility of the telephone ringing as it had done last night, jangling her nerves and leaving her rigid, frightened and trembling by the time it stopped.

It was well after one when Issy Goldberg brought her home and said goodnight at the door of her flat. He made no move to kiss her, nor did he make any suggestion that he might come in; and she rewarded him for this with a warm sensuous smile and thanked him quite graciously for a pleasant evening.

She had enjoyed herself more than she would have believed possible. Issy hadn't pushed his luck. Beyond holding her closely when they danced and making his admiration evident by the way he eyed her all night, he had seemed more intent on impressing her with his sophistication and wealth. He had taken her to dine at the Grill Room in the Mount Nelson. The "Nellie" as he called it; and it was obvious by the welcome and service from the staff that he frequently dined there and it also looked as if he must be a lavish tipper. He was almost obsessively interested in food which probably accounted for his carrying too much weight. Once the course was put before him she noticed that he only opened his mouth to fork something into it. But for the rest he had proved surprisingly good company and unstinting in lavishing only the best on her. If there was brashness and vulgarity, so too there was warmth, generosity and humour. She had to admit that no one had ever wined and dined her better . . . She suspected that she and Issy were much of a kind, and that his origins were no better than hers.

When she said goodnight and went in, her eyes automatically flickered to the telephone and she wondered if Alan had tried to ring her again. She immediately felt chilled, though still warm and relaxed from the food and wine.

Trying to hold on to her relaxed mood, she filled the bath and lay stretched out in the hot steaming water . . . If only she and Alan could lead a normal life. Spend an evening together like she had done with Issy tonight. Dine in a gracious restaurant, eat exotic food, drink only the best French wines, with champagne at the end. She was so proud of him. She wanted to be *seen* with him—to proclaim her ownership of him to the world. They'd had *no fun* together. No companionship. Only their furtive meetings at night, and now not even that. She knew so little about him. He spoke scarcely ever about himself and when asked, usually turned the point the other way. He never mentioned his childhood nor what he had done before he married Maisie and became a farmer. He often spoke of L'Horizon, and she could tell by the way his voice deepened how much he loved the place. It would be strange living on a farm, after the tempo and bustle of city life. How long would it take before she could lead a normal life with Alan and be seen with him? . . . Oh God, there could be no future for them until Lisa—She scrambled out of the bath, picked up her towel and began drying herself.

She didn't hear the key in the front door but as she reached for her gown the door opened and Alan came in.

"*Alan*. Oh, darling, you've come."

He caught her to him and kissed her. Then he lifted her in his arms and carried her through to the bedroom.

. . . He made no reference to having telephoned her during the night, nor did he ask why she hadn't telephoned him for two successive mornings.

He said: "Were you out with her tonight?" and felt the muscles in her back tighten.

". . . No," she said a little defiantly. "I haven't seen her for two days."

He felt a hot murderous spark of rage which he had difficulty in suppressing and waited until he could speak calmly before he asked: "But you've been out, haven't you?"

"Yes. I've been wined and dined like a queen," she said with the same defiance.

"Oh."

"You can hardly object. Do you expect me to sit here night after night?"

"No, naturally I don't. But I'm still only human, Lorne, and I can't say that I like the thought of your spending the evening with someone else . . . I take it you were with a man?" He was experiencing sudden alarm that he might be losing his hold on her.

She twined her arms about his neck and kissed him. "Yes, it was with a man, and I wouldn't care if I never saw him again. Don't you know you're the only man I want to be with. But I never *see* you."

"You know it won't be this way for long."

"While I lay in the bath I was thinking about us. How we've never done any of the things other couples take for granted. Like going for walks, or seeing a show, or dining together. I haven't even danced with you . . . We've had no *fun*."

"Don't you think this is fun." He kissed her, slowly tightening his arms.

At first she responded passionately but then freed herself half petulantly. "Oh God, you know what I mean. You know I wasn't talking about *this*."

"But *this* is what's important. Without it, none of the rest would matter."

". . . We've never danced, and I adore dancing."

"There'll be plenty of time for that. We'll have the rest of our lives to learn to keep in step."

She pushed her fingers caressingly through his hair. "I adore dining in madly expensive restaurants and eating exotic food—like snails. Do you like snails?"

"I loathe them," he said shortly. "But if you like dining out we'll do that too." Trying to instil some enthusiasm into his voice.

. . . He'd had more than his fill of dining in exclusive restaurants during the time he had squired Linda. She had always insisted on dining out at least twice a week, which had bored him, and it had also sickened him to think of all that money being spent on food and drink . . . Linda had made a habit of occasionally insisting he should pay and he had noticed that on these occasions she seemed to go deliberately out of her way to order the most exotic dishes and the highest priced imported wines. He did what he could to save his purse by ordering something simple for himself, which had never failed to elicit a nasty smile and the caustic comment that he had the palate of a peasant. "Or is it only that you're as mean as one, darling?" . . .

He said: "Lorne, don't you realise that I also find our present mode of life frustrating? Do you suppose you're the only one who's suffering? I want it to end as much as you do, and what's more, I want it to end *now.*" He drew her to lie against him. "Only one person in the world can stop us having what we want, and there's no future for us until I get rid of her. You realise this, don't you?"

She nodded but didn't speak.

"Then I've got to do something about her right away. Are you still prepared to go through with this and help me?"

She nodded again.

"Are you sure, Lorne? I don't want to force you—"

"Yes."

"I want to get this thing over and done with and I've worked out everything now." She was lying very still and he tightened his arm about her. "Remember what I said, you don't have to *do* anything to her. All you must do is get her to the right place at the right time."

". . . Where is this place?"

"The top of Table Mountain. I want you to take her up by cableway. Suggest having lunch there."

". . . When d'you want me to do this?"

"On Thursday morning. This is important: being a weekday there'll be fewer people about. If there's any difficulty about her being able to get off, do you think you could manage to wangle something?"

She knew she would only have to ask Issy. "Yes, I could fix it," she said in a rather small voice. "But she mightn't want to come—"

"Then it will be up to you to talk her into it. If she seems at all hesitant, tell her you want her advice or hint you're in some sort of trouble. It shouldn't be difficult to persuade her to come."

She stirred restlessly.

"I went up the mountain yesterday. I didn't want to risk taking the cableway so I walked up Skeleton Gorge. I felt I must get the complete lay of the land before I spoke to you, so that I could give you exact instructions of where you must take her. I've now found the perfect spot. It's about a mile from the tearoom and once I've described it to you, you won't be able to miss it. But to be on the safe side I'll draw a diagram before I leave. Timing is an important factor. I want you to take the ten-thirty car up the cableway, which means you should reach the spot shortly after eleven."

". . . What must I do when we get there? . . . Will we see you?"

"No. Take her to a ledge I'll describe to you and sit there with her for a few minutes. Then make some excuse. Ask her to wait for you and tell her you'll be back, and beat it."

"D'you mean I must go back to the cableway? Go home?"

"No, you obviously can't do that. You'll have to report that she's missing."

"But what do I say has happened to

her?" Her voice rose. "I can't just say she's vanished—"

"Nothing could be easier," he said soothingly. "When you leave the girl, wander around on your own for a bit. Give yourself, say, half an hour and then go to the tearoom and ask if she's there. Tell them you got separated."

"But—will they believe me?"

"Of course they will. Can't you see it's foolproof, darling? This won't be the first time someone falls down the mountain and gets killed. It happens year after year."

". . . Alan, will she—see you? I couldn't bear to think of her being terrified out of her mind. I mean—"

"Look, darling, I promise she won't see or hear me. I'll come up from behind and she won't even know what hit her."

"But what if—"

"Lorne don't *think* about it. Let me do the worrying. Once it's all over we can forget the whole thing and start planning our life together."

She suddenly put her arms round him and clung to him. "Alan, do you love me?"

He smiled. "Haven't I proved that to you yet?"

"Oh God, I don't know. I sometimes wonder if—"

He kissed her and stopped her from saying anything more.

18

KAREL MEYER didn't look up but continued writing until he had finished his letter and signed it, then he dropped his pencil, leaned back in his chair and looked Ben du Toit over. The boy had been standing stiffly at attention on the other side of the desk for close on five minutes.

Ben du Toit straightened his back a little more under his scrutiny and Karel Meyer felt the familiar flickerings of irritation. "Well?" he said shortly, in his most peremptory manner. "What is it?"

The boy flushed darkly and stretched his neck as if he found his collar constricting. "I've come to report that Miss Sellars had a visitor last night, sir."

"So? . . . A man, I take it?"

"Yes, sir."

He raised his brows half ironically. "I seem to remember your mentioning she's a pretty girl. It wouldn't be considered surprising these days to find a pretty girl entertaining a male guest at night." He fingered a cigarette expertly from the packet on the desk. "How long did he stay with her?"

"Miss Sellars went out with Mr. Goldberg earlier in the evening sir." He cleared his throat. "Mr. Goldberg is one of the directors of Dryads Ltd., the firm for which Miss Lombard works—"

"I'm aware of that," Karel Meyer said testily and struck a match and drew at his cigarette. He glanced at Ben as he shook out the match. It seemed the boy had been struck dumb by the interruption. "Go on. Get on with it!" he said impatiently.

Ben swallowed before he spoke. "The man—the—er—visitor I mentioned, came to her flat half an hour after Mr. Goldberg brought her back, and he remained with her for about four hours." Another painful flush at what was inferred.

Karel Meyer shifted his weight impatiently but refrained from speaking.

"It was drizzling when he arrived and he was wearing a hat and coat: this made it difficult for our man to get much impression of what he looked like. But he was able to station himself close to the entrance, where the light would shine directly on the man's face when he left."

Karel Meyer had been studying him and noticed there was something different about the boy. Could it be that he had a shade more confidence? He hadn't stammered once and looked slightly flushed.

"Yes, go on."

"Luckily the man was carrying his hat in his hand when he left and our man could get a good look at him."

"Well?" Karel Meyer said quietly. "What did he look like?"

"He was tall, sir. Fair. Our man, Visser, said he was a very striking, good-looking man."

Karel Meyer's sallow face remained impassive, only his pale blue eyes seemed to become more coldly intent. "Was he wearing his coat?"

"Yes, sir."

"Could Visser get any impression of his physique?"

"Yes, sir. Visser said he had very broad shoulders and looked like an athlete. He mentioned that he looked very fit and suntanned."

Karel Meyer stroked his cheek with two

fingers. "How about his car? Did Visser check on it?"

"Yes, sir. He said the car was a white two-door 1970 Triumph and that it had a Somerset West registration number."

"Humph."

"I asked him to give me the number and after I dropped Miss Lombard at work I went to Caledon Square to find out to whom the car belongs."

Karel Meyer nodded his approval but didn't express it verbally.

"The car, sir, belongs to Mrs A. S. Lincoln, who owns the farm L'Horizon in Somerset West."

"Did you check on Mr. Lincoln's car while you were about it? It would seem likely he'd have one."

"Yes, sir. Mr. A. S. Lincoln owns a Mercedes 280 S.E."

"What colour?" he asked sharply.

Ben du Toit almost permitted himself a smile. It showed at the corner of his mouth. "Dark grey, sir."

"Dark grey, eh?" The cigarette bent between his fingers until it snapped. He stared at it for a second and then stubbed it out in the ashtray. "Anything else?"

"Yes, sir." His confidence was increasing by leaps and bounds with each question he answered. "When I finished at Caledon Square I telephoned Mrs. Lincoln. I wanted to find out if she—"

"What?"

The boy stopped, stared at him in silence.

"Let's get this straight. Did you say that you telephoned Mrs. Lincoln?"

"Y-yes, sir," he stammered, unnerved by the ominous manner in which the question had been asked.

"Who gave you permission to do so?"

Ben flushed and then the colour drained quickly from his face.

"I'm asking you. Who gave you permission to ring her?"

"N-no one, sir. But I thought—"

"I'm not interested in what you thought! You were told to report back to me, not to do anything off your own bat. You've no authority whatsoever! You're a junior police officer, nothing but a pipsqueak! God in heaven, do you realise what damage you might have done?"

Ben du Toit wet his lips and stared at him pale faced.

"What possible reason can you give me for having telephoned her?"

"I—wanted to find out if she was there, sir." His lips twitched as he gulped and swallowed. "I had been given a description of the man, and I knew a woman was missing, and I—I thought if I telephoned to—"

"You didn't have the bloody *right*! You could be demoted for this. Do you know that?"

The boy couldn't speak. The cold blue eyes seemed to be boring right through him.

Karel Meyer stared at him for a long minute . . . "Well," he said eventually. "Was she there or wasn't she?"

Ben du Toit cleared his throat. "She wasn't there, sir."

"Who spoke to you?"

"The cook, sir."

"What did she say?"

"She said Mrs. Lincoln has gone away."

"Did she say where she's gone?"

"Yes, sir. She said Mrs. Lincoln had gone overseas . . . She mentioned she went by air."

"Did you ask her when she left?"

A little colour had ebbed back into his

face. "Yes, sir. She said Mrs. Lincoln left eleven days ago, on the 8th April."

"The 8th April," Karel Meyer repeated slowly. "Does that date convey anything to you?"

"Yes, sir. It was the day before Miss Lombard saw the woman drowned."

"Exactly . . . Did she tell you anything more?"

"No, sir. I didn't want to risk asking too many questions . . . I—I'm sorry I telephoned Mrs. Lincoln, sir. I didn't realise I was exceeding my duty—"

"You can forget what I said. You've shown initiative and discretion, both the qualities we look for in the officers of our Force. Good work!" He saw the hot wave of colour suffuse the boy's face, but for once it didn't exasperate him. "You've guessed, of course, this could be our man?" he asked conversationally.

The boy met his look. "Yes, sir."

"But we could just as likely be barking up the wrong tree again. It's the timing and the location of the murder that worries me."

Ben watched him silently.

"We'll have our facts and we should

know a great deal more by the end of the day." He had been sitting forward somewhat tensely and now eased himself back in his chair. "I want you to check on what line Mrs. Lincoln was booked. Check the passenger lists and make sure if she collected her ticket and boarded the plane. Is that clear?"

"Yes, sir."

"Well, we've no time to waste, so get moving."

"Yes, sir." This time he managed to avoid bumping against the desk.

"Ben—"

The boy stopped at the door and turned red-faced to look at him. It was the first time Karel Meyer had called him by his Christian name. "Yes, sir?"

Karel Meyer grinned showing his even white teeth. "Do you know something? I'm holding thumbs you'll draw a blank."

Ben ventured a hesitant smile but didn't speak.

"I'll be putting someone on to the same job in Port Elizabeth, and I'm hoping he'll be the one who has the luck."

The boy's heavy-featured face tightened.

"Do you think she might have booked her flight from there, sir?"

"Let's say it's what I'm hoping for. If that's what she did then everything falls into place and the location and timing would no longer worry me . . . Report back as soon as you have the facts."

"Yes, sir."

Karel Meyer pressed his thumb on the bell as Ben went out.

. . . As he predicted, they knew a great deal more by the end of the day. In record time he had a well-trained highly efficient team of detectives on the job. He called them into his office in pairs or one at a time, and succinctly gave them his instructions. Once his own staff was organised and things on the move, he began casting his net farther afield.

One of the first things he did was to telephone Major Theron at the Knysna police station. The genial Major was delighted to hear that there seemed a possibility of a breakthrough. Karel Meyer asked him to check if a Mr. and Mrs. A. S. Lincoln had booked accommodation in one of the hotels in the surrounding district on the night of April 7th. At the same time he might check if the Lincolns owned property along the coast where they could have spent the night. He added as an afterthought that Mrs. Lincoln had previously been a Mrs. van Stalen, and that it might be a good idea to check on that name as well.

He put a call through to the police station in Port Elizabeth and arranged for one of their men to go through the passenger lists of all planes leaving the airport on April 8th, and to verify if Mrs. Lincoln had booked a passage, and if she had gone aboard.

He had been told that Alan Lincoln had previously lived in Johannesburg and asked police headquarters there to let him have whatever information they could about him.

He remained incarcerated in his office, the telephone close at hand, chain-smoking while he waited for news to come in.

And as he sifted, evaluated and made notes of the slowly accumulating evidence, he became more and more convinced that Alan Lincoln was their man. By the end of the day he knew him for what he was; a young man who had never held down a job but lived off older married women. As such he would be coldly calculating, and his marriage to the older, wealthy widow, Mrs. van Stalen, the owner of the farm L'Horizon, was in keeping with what he now knew of his character.

Surprisingly enough, he was finding some difficulty in procuring a photograph of Alan Lincoln, but the police officer in Johannesburg who had given him the information he wanted, had assured him that there was every possibility of letting him have one by the next day. Once they had shown this to Lisa Lombard, they should know where they stood. Certainly the description Visser had given him of Mr. Lincoln tallied with the one Lisa Lombard had given of the murderer.

By midday he knew that Mrs. Lincoln had been booked to fly by South African Airways from Port Elizabeth to Johannesburg on April 8th, but her name had been missing from the list of passengers who boarded the plane. He had tracked down the travel agency with which she dealt and they had sent him the complete itinerary of her trip overseas and were now checking on whether she had stayed in any of the hotels in which she had been booked.

No one knew better than Karel Meyer how long it could take before it would definitely be established that Mrs. Lincoln was missing . . . And, as he had said to Mark and Major Theron, it would take far longer than he could afford to wait before making a move. He was frankly alarmed by Lorne Sellars' sudden friendship with Lisa Lombard. It seemed likely she was Alan Lincoln's mistress, and if he *was* the man they were looking for, it could only mean that it had been a deliberate manoeuvre on his part that the two girls should meet. This made Lisa Lombard's situation extremely vulnerable, and doubly dangerous. Her safety was his responsibility. There was this feeling of urgency that he should act at once . . . He might have to make a move, even at the risk of jumping the gun.

A further piece of information which came through in the late evening, finally convinced him that they were on the right track.

He was sipping at a scalding cup of coffee in lieu of dinner, and smoking the inevitable cigarette, when a call came through from Major Theron. The moment he spoke, Karel Meyer sensed a difference in his voice and drew deeply on his cigarette as he felt himself tense. The Major said they had been successful in finding that Mrs. Lincoln owned a cottage on the lonely strip of coast between Knysna and Plettenberg Bay. If the name van Stalen hadn't been mentioned it was unlikely that they would have discovered this, as the cottage was still owned under her first married name. He and two of his men had driven down to look the place over. It was the typical seaside holiday cottage one would expect, and they'd found no difficulty in forcing an entry. The signs were all there that it had been recently occupied, and they had managed to take several sets of finger-prints which would be delivered to him first thing in the morning. They had combed every inch of the property and the immediate surroundings but had found nothing.

Karel Meyer had every reason to be satisfied with all the evidence that had piled up during the last twelve hours. In only one respect had the investigations borne no fruit. There was still no trace of Alan Lincoln's dark grey Mercedes. It could just as well have disappeared into thin air. The one vital piece still missing.

He lit one cigarette from another and ground out the stub in the ashtray. If *he* wanted to hide a car which might be used as incriminating evidence against him, where would he hide it? It was unlikely that more than the fender had been damaged and the car would still have been road-worthy. If it *was* Alan Lincoln who had stopped at Riversdale to fill up, it would mean he had holed up somewhere during the day and driven back through the night. This made it almost certain that the car must be hidden somewhere on the farm L'Horizon. The more he thought about this, the more convinced he became. If it were hidden in an unused out-house, it could moulder there for years and no one the wiser.

He knew that he would be rushing things unnecessarily if he arranged to make an early call on Alan Lincoln the next morning. It would be against his nature and against all his training to make so definite a move at this early stage of their investigations. In less than twenty-four hours they should have a photograph of Alan Lincoln, and if Lisa Lombard identified him as the man she saw at Roosklip, they would have him where they wanted him. Yet every instinct was urging him not to wait, but to move at once.

By midnight he had come to a decision.

Before he left in the squad car early the next morning he put a call through to Ben du Toit and told him to keep a watch on Miss Lombard until he heard from him again. If anything untoward were to take place, he must be contacted immediately.

19

IT was just after nine when Karel Meyer and Detective Sergeant Smith climbed the wide shallow flight of steps at L'Horizon and rang the front door bell.

The front of the house got the full benefit of the morning sun which beat down on them as they stood waiting on the stoep.

Detective Sergeant Smith expanded his chest. "Nice day, for a change."

Karel Meyer grunted and pushed the bell again.

A second or so later a younger African houseboy came through a door into the hall. As soon as he saw the two men standing at the door he instinctively guessed that they were plain-clothes policemen and the smile froze on his face.

"I'd like to see Mr. Lincoln," Karel Meyer said.

The houseboy's eyes rolled, showing the whites, and the detectives saw sweat break out and bead his forehead. The shock of the confrontation had rendered him speechless.

Karel Meyer guessed at once that he probably wasn't registered and that he must now be under the mistaken assumption that they were here to arrest him. He gave a bland smile which was meant to be reassuring, but if anything it frightened the boy more.

"Tell your master we'd like to speak to him."

The boy ducked his head. "Yes, Massa." Turned quickly and went back through the same door.

Detective Sergeant Smith grinned. "Do you want to take on a bet he isn't registered?"

Karel Meyer looked at him unsmiling. "Do you think I want to chuck my money away?" he growled.

The bottom half of the front door was shut and bolted. It was waist high and he rested his hands lightly along the top and surveyed the long, rather dark hall which ran the full depth of the house. The massive antique furniture along the walls would have swamped a modern house with lower ceilings. He noticed that the shelves of the magnificent stinkwood armoire near the front door were crammed with blue and white Nanking china. He always wondered why people set so much store by it; to him it looked as thick and cheap as kitchenware. A huge blue and white bowl from the same stable stood on an ebony-black, brass-bound kist between two doors. He saw that the hands of the marquetry grandfather clock were pointing to ten past nine, and automatically consulted his watch to see if it tallied. He could catch a glimpse of a high-walled garden through the long sash windows at the far end of the hall. He got an impression of brilliant sunshine, sweeping green lawns and great tall trees.

He turned his head as a big respectable-looking coloured woman came through the same door the houseboy had used.

She was quite unruffled and smiled at him calmly. "Good-morning, Massa. Can I help you?"

She was light-skinned, very tall and of vast proportions. She was not so much fat as massively solid-looking, and would have dwarfed most men. She was wearing an immaculate dove-grey overall and a stiffly starched apron and cap. Her spectacles gave her an added air of respectability.

He said: "Yes. I would like to speak to Mr. Lincoln."

"He not here, Massa."

Karel Meyer's face tightened. "Do you mean he's gone away?" he asked sharply.

She looked at him in faint surprise. "No, Massa. He jes gorn out for the day."

"Did he say when he'd be back?"

"Yes, Massa. Mr. Lincoln say he be beck sometime before dinner tonight."

He lifted a hand to stroke his cheek. "Did he mention where he was going?"

She was watching him wary-eyed and suspicious. "Mr. Lincoln come into the kitchen last night to tell me he going to climb mountain again today, like he done two days ago. He say I must make coffee and sandwiches like I done last time."

"Is he climbing one of the peaks on the farm?"

"I don't tink so, Massa."

"Did he mention which mountain he was climbing?"

"No, Massa."

He felt in his pocket for his cigarettes. "When did he leave?"

"Mr. Lincoln tell me he want breakfast

early, and he leave jes after seven o'clock."

"Did he take his car?"

". . . He take Merrem's car, Massa."

He didn't say anything and she watched while he struck a match and drew at his cigarette. When it was alight he asked: "Have you worked for Mrs. Lincoln for a long time?"

"Yes, Massa."

"How long?"

Her body lengthened as she drew herself up. "I jes turn fifteen when I comes here to L'Horizon to work for Merrem and Massa Retief. Dey my Merrem's parents, and she only a few weeks ole then, when I looks after her. Dere no other chillun, and Merrem and Massa Retief was ole when my Merrem was born . . . Too ole, Massa, to unnerstand and be bothered with a small chile."

He nodded understandingly.

"Later on I becomes cook, and after dey die in car accident, and my Merrem merry Mr. van Stalen, I stays on as cook and runs the house."

He smiled in a friendly way. "So you've known Mrs. Lincoln all her life?"

"Yes, Massa."

"You must be very fond of her."

"I never merry, Massa. I has no femily of my own . . . I love my Merrem like she my own chile," she added emotionally.

He nodded again. "And I'm sure your Madam must be very fond of you."

"Many times my Merrem says I's the best fren what she got." She had been searching his face while she spoke, and suddenly asked: "Massa, is there any troubles?"

He glanced down to knock the ash off the end of his cigarette as he debated on how much he should commit himself.

When he didn't speak at once she became visibly agitated. "Massa, I not hear from my Merrem like I usually does. When she go away, always four, five days after she gorn, I get postcard from her. Twice a week, Massa, I get picture postcard from where she stay, and she tell me how she is. Now nearly two weeks is gorn and I not hear nothing from her yet . . . My Merrem not happy when she gorn away, Massa. She not been heppy for long time, but she not tell me why."

"What is your name?" he asked quietly.

"Rosie, Massa." She suddenly clasped

her hands. "Massa, why is you here? Is my Merrem orl right?"

He evaded her question. "Rosie, do you know Mr. Lincoln's car?"

The very ordinariness of the question served to calm her down. "Yes, Massa."

"Where is it?"

Her eyes sharpened whilst she thought round what his reason could be for asking her this . . . "I not see Mr. Lincoln's car since he take Merrem to Port Elizabeth nearly two weeks ago."

"Did they go there on a holiday?"

"No, Massa. Merrem tell me dey go to spend a night in the house what she got by the sea. She want to see if everything in the house orl right, and then she say Mr. Lincoln going to take her to the airport in Port Elizabeth the next morning."

"And you say you haven't seen Mr. Lincoln's car since then?"

"No, Massa."

"Not even when he came back?"

"No, Massa. Mr. Lincoln come back late at night. I light sleeper, and wakes up when I hear the car come, and I look at my alarm clock and I sees if after one o'clock."

"Did he come straight into the house?"

Her features set as she thought round this as well . . . "No, Massa," she said slowly. "After a time I hears the car go away again, and it long time before it come back."

He nodded as if her answer had not been entirely unexpected. "Thank you, Rosie, you have been very helpful." He glanced at Detective Sergeant Smith who had been standing silently beside him all this time and said: "We'd better have a look around."

"Massa, is my Merrem orl right?" she asked in a trembling voice.

". . . I don't know."

She stared at him, trying to read what was in his mind . . . "I know where Mr. Lincoln's car is," she said abruptly.

"Is it somewhere on the farm?"

"Yes, Massa. Jan Titus, one of the volk, tells me he look through the creck in the door of the ole shed near the cellar what is never used no more, and he see Mr. Lincoln's car's there."

"Is there a key to the shed?"

"Yes, Massa. Dere big bunch of keys what Mr. Lincoln always keep in the top drawer of the tall-boy in his room. It will be with them keys. Would Massa like me to fetch it?"

"I'll come with you. I'd like to see Mr. Lincoln's room." He jerked his head at Detective Sergeant Smith to accompany them.

They crossed the hall, which had a rather pleasant musky smell, and turned down a passage by the grandfather clock. It was flagged with red tiles, and lit along only one side by tall sash windows overlooking a small grassed courtyard. Colourful old prints of birds hung at regular intervals down the length of the passage.

Rosie opened the third door on the right and moved her vast bulk aside to allow them to precede her into the room.

At first sight it could have been a typical masculine bedroom, which had been furnished in better-than-average taste. Despite the early hour, the bed had been made, and the room swept and dusted. The olive green edge-to-edge carpeting and the deep tangerine bedspread picked up some of the psychedelic colouring of the glazed cotton curtains which hung from a brass railing, ten to the floor. The gleaming old-fashioned brass bedstead, and the great double mahogany wardrobe occupying almost the entire length of one wall, and the rosewood tall-boy all had a rich patina as if newly polished. A pile of magazines were neatly stacked on the bedside table.

There were the photographs one would expect to see in a man's bedroom. They hung mostly on the walls and four had been placed on top of the tall-boy. While Rosie was searching for the keys Karel Meyer wandered round the room, hands clasped behind his back, and studied them one by one. With a growing feeling of distaste he realised that they were all of one subject. Alan Lincoln, the occupant of the room. Several of him playing tennis; serving, hitting a backhand, being presented with a cup. Alan Lincoln water-skiing. Alan Lincoln smiling brilliantly. Laughing, head thrown back. Half frowning. Another of him, face thinned, intense, incredibly handsome, staring straight at the camera.

Karel Meyer turned as Rosie spoke and took the bunch of keys she handed him. He nodded his thanks and looked deeply thoughtful as he thrust them into his pocket.

She watched as he reached up and took one of the photographs off the tall-boy.

He held it up and turned it to the light to view it better . . . It was a good likeness taken on the beach. He was wearing brief white bathing trunks, which gave one the full impression of his magnificent bronzed physique. Drops of water glistened on his muscled torso, and his blond hair, slightly ruffled, appeared more silver than gold.

Karel Meyer studied it for several seconds before sliding it deliberately into his pocket.

Rosie had been watching him, and their eyes met. Hers showed doubt and anxiety.

"Ja, Rosie," he said heavily, as if he were sad, and immeasurably tired.

She knew then that something must have happened to her mistress and turned her back on him, and covered her face in her hands.

When she began to cry he put a hand on her shoulder and pressed it compassionately. He sought words but could find none that would give her reassurance or comfort. He caught Detective Sergeant Smith's eye, nodded silently and they both went out.

When they reached the foot of the steps

he went over to the squad car to have a word with the driver.

"Anything come through?" he asked.

"No, sir."

He looked around and spotted the gabled cellar and a group of outhouses a hundred yards from the homestead, half hidden behind the oaks.

"We think we may be on to something. If a call comes through you'll find us in one of those sheds." He pointed to them. "Give me the torch, we may need a light."

The driver opened the cubby-hole, pushed a cloth aside, found the torch and handed it to him.

"We may be some time, all depending on what we find."

"Yes, sir."

The two police officers didn't converse as they walked over to the outbuildings. Karel Meyer whistled softly and tunelessly between his teeth, jingling the keys in his pocket. A golden labrador joined them and he stopped to pat it. He turned and saw that a small group of bare-footed coloured children, ranging from between four and eight years, had materialised from nowhere and were following in their wake, at what they deemed to be a safe distance. When they saw that he was standing staring at them they stopped dead and huddled a little closer to each other as if in mutual protection, looking at him with frightened widened eyes.

"*Weg is jy!*" he barked suddenly.

Detective Sergeant Smith laughed as they scattered like chaff before the wind.

They found two rambling dilapidated outhouses with double-doored barns at both ends, all padlocked. The original thatched roofs had long since been replaced with corrugated iron, rusted and badly in need of a coat of paint.

It immediately became apparent that a car could only be housed in one of the four double-doored barns. This made their search easier and they didn't have to waste time speculating on where they should start. Detective Sergeant Smith peered through a crack in the door of the second barn they approached and he was just able to make out the shape of a car parked far back in the dim interior.

The only time wasted was the interval during which Karel Meyer endeavoured to find the right key to fit the padlock, and once he had done this it required their combined strength to push open the one half of the old warped door, which creaked and groaned in protest before they finally succeeded in pushing it wide to let in the light.

Great sagging cobwebs, heavy with dust, were festooned across the dingy windows high up on the walls and permitted little light to filter through. Karel Meyer flicked on the torch as they went in and beamed the ray of light on to the empty shelves lining the walls, the long deal tables, the broken boxes stacked untidily beneath them and scattered with balls and streamers of wood-wool over the floor. Everything was smothered in thick layers of dust.

"Hasn't been used for years," he commented.

When they reached the car he veered the light on to it. "A Mercedes all right." He played the light over the car. "No number plate." A film of dust made the big car appear colourless. He brushed the palm of his hand over the rear fender to get rid of some of it and bent to peer down. "Dark grey," he said tersely.

They went round to the front of the car and he shone the light full on to the left fender and stared at it for a minute before he spoke.

"Hold this," he said abruptly and handed the torch to Detective Sergeant Smith. "Shine the light full on to that mudguard while I have a closer look."

The detective took the torch and shone the light on to the fender. Karel Meyer felt for his handkercheif and painstakingly wiped the dust off the crumpled metal and then leaned forward to examine it with still instensity. The touches of pale green paint against the dark grey looked almost phosphorescent in the bright pool of light. He pointed them out wordlessly, glanced up, and the other nodded meaningly.

"We've got him!" Karel Meyer said exultantly. "We've got the bastard at last!"

He turned as a figure loomed in the doorway and shut out some of the light.

"Who's that?" he called sharply.

"It's me, sir," the driver answered.

"What is it? Has a call come through?"

"Yes, sir. Warrant Officer du Toit has just called. He says it's urgent."

He straightened, feeling a sudden coldness grip him. "He says it's urgent, hey? Did he say what the trouble is?"

"Yes, sir. He said I must tell you that Mr. Goldberg gave Miss Lombard a lift to Cape Town and dropped her in Adderley Street where she met Miss Sellars. He says that during the interval in which he parked his car, they disappeared, and he's lost all contact with them. He seemed to think it was important you should know this, sir."

"Smith, I'm leaving you here. Contact the Somerset West police station and tell them to send two men along to guard the car. Make any enquiries here you think fit, but use your discretion."

"Yes, sir."

He sprinted across the barn. "Get moving!" he shouted at the driver. "What the hell are you waiting for? Get that goddamned car started!"

20

BY the time Alan left, he was satisfied that Lorne knew exactly what she must do. He had made her repeat everything after him so that there would be no possibility of a hitch due to any misunderstanding.

He had seized upon one important factor. When Lorne casually mentioned Issy Goldberg's infatuation for her, he instantly saw how this could be manipulated to their advantage.

"This could be providence, darling!"

She stared at him blankly.

He caught her arms and shook her gently to emphasise his point. "Can't you see? It's been worrying me for some time how we could possibly shake off the man tailing the girl. If you fetched her yourself, or arranged to meet her somewhere, he'd have no trouble following you, and I've been trying to think how we could handle this."

"Why should it be providential that Issy Goldberg's crazy about me? I don't follow how this could help solve your problem."

"You'll see once I've explained what I'll want you to do. Firstly, you must ring the girl at the last minute and ask her to meet you on Thursday morning. This means that she won't have a chance of discussing her plans with anyone else. But before you ring her, I want you to 'phone this Issy Goldstein—or whatever his name is. Ring him, say, at 9.30, and ask if he'd be prepared to let her off. Tell him there's something urgent you want to discuss with her. He's sure to agree, and once it's settled, ask him if he'll do you a favour and drop her in Adderley Street at 10 o'clock outside Stuttaford's. If he's as crazy about you as I think he is, he'll jump at doing it. See that you have your car parked in St. George's Street. You'll have to do something about this pretty early if you want to be certain of finding a parking place. Be waiting in Adderley Street when this character drops the girl and rush her straight through the store to your car. Try to have it parked as close to the St. George's Street entrance as possible. The man tailing her will have the problem of parking his car before he can follow you; and it's never easy to park in

Adderley Street—unless he wants to risk being fined. Even then, it would take time. If you're nippy enough you should have made it by the time he enters the store: and even if you haven't, he'll be unlikely to guess that you've gone straight through."

. . . His plan had worked perfectly. Issy, as predicted, had been only too pleased to do as she asked. But Lisa had proved less tractable. She was firm in saying that it would not be possible for her to leave the office for a lunch date at that hour of the morning. On being told that everything had been arranged with Issy, and that he had agreed to drop her in Adderley Street where they could meet, she suddenly froze.

Lorne had sufficient intuition to guess why.

She said: "Lisa, don't be angry with me. I know I should have consulted you first. I should have 'phoned and asked you before I spoke to Issy." She paused and added impulsively: "Won't you please forgive me and come?"

"It isn't a question of forgiveness, Lorne. It just happens that I'm exceptionally busy at the moment, and I simply can't spare the time—"

Lorne's fingers tightened round the receiver. "I know I'm sticking my neck out by asking you to do me a favour. I'm only doing it because there's something I simply *must* discuss with you."

"Couldn't we discuss it some other time? Tonight, if you like. Come back and have a bite with me and we could talk things over then." The coolness was still there, but not so marked.

"This can't wait . . . I wouldn't have 'phoned you otherwise." When Lisa remained silent she added desperately: "*Lisa*, I need your help."

There was a longish pause, then Lisa said . . . "All right, I'll come—"

Lorne hung up and stared ahead with a sort of angry defiance, while she battled with her conscience . . . It was no use pretending that the tactics she had used to persuade Lisa had been anything but despicable. She made herself believe she didn't care. What did it matter, as long as Lisa came. She almost talked herself into believing that she felt *nothing*—nothing at all.

. . . When Issy Goldberg's flamboyant ruby red Alfa Romeo drew up silkily at the kerb, Lorne was waiting on the pavement and smiled brilliantly at Lisa as she clambered out, and bent to smile and wave at Issy behind the wheel.

He smiled back warmly and watched her as she went through the entrance of the store with Lisa. He eyed the long length of her legs, and the sinuous movement of her hips in the narrow sheath of her clear yellow frock.

Ben du Toit had stopped immediately behind him and tapped the horn twice to tell him to move on. The Alpha Romeo was occupying the only available spot where he could park in an emergency. He wondered bleakly if he would be called upon to pay the incurred fine.

Issy turned round to glare at him and then realised he was looking straight at the young police officer who had been driving Lisa to and from work every day since her car had been damaged. He quickly changed to a conciliatory smile.

It fussed him and he stalled the engine. Over a minute passed before the Alpha Romeo glided away and Ben du Toit was able to edge in, park his car and leap out.

By this time Lorne and Lisa were well across the store. Lorne had set the pace, stretching out her long legs, striding ahead and weaving her way through the throng of shoppers. She looked over her shoulder and saw that they were now hidden from the Adderley Street entrance and stopped to allow Lisa to catch up.

"Sorry to rush you like this."

"What's the hurry?"

"I'm worried that my car may be ticketed. A traffic cop was making his way up St. George's Street when I went to meet you." It slowed them down to walk two abreast and she shot ahead again.

She nearly barged into a man as she went through the St. George's Street entrance like a projectile. He quickly stepped aside to avoid her, but this very act made it impossible to stop himself from colliding head-on with Lisa, who was immediately on her heels.

Lisa gave an involuntary gasp as the impact knocked the breath from her, and for seconds they were tangled together like lovers, his arm about her as he steadied himself, and her face pressed against his chest.

They quickly separated and she flushed hotly when she saw who it was. "Sorry,

Mark," she said breathlessly. "I didn't look where I was going."

In the split second of mutual recognition his face had been unguarded. He said: "The fault was mine as much as yours. I hope I didn't hurt you."

"All you did was to knock some of the breath out of me."

"Are you sure?"

"Yes, quite sure."

"Where are you off to in such a hurry?"

"Lorne is worried, her car may be ticketed . . . Oh, Lorne, this is Mark Standish. And Mark, I don't think you've met Lorne Sellars."

They both acknowledged the introduction, but Lorne had become so tense by now that she could barely bring herself to smile at him, and her eyes quickly slid away from his, to anxiously explore the store. She felt sweat break out on her forehead, and her hand shook as she lifted it to push back her hair. Oh God, this could upset all their plans. Why did Lisa have to meet someone *now*, of all times!

She made a pretence of looking at her watch. "Lisa, we *must* hurry."

"Where are you off to?" Mark asked Lisa for the second time.

"We haven't discussed it yet. Where *are* we going, Lorne?"

Lorne moistened her lips, hesitated for a fraction of a second, as if debating whether she should reply or not, and then said over-precisely: "I thought it might be fun to go up the cableway and have lunch on top of the mountain. I've always been meaning to do it."

Her answer was unexpected, and Lisa's eyebrows lifted in surprise; then she smiled and said: "I agree. It should be fun."

"I envy you," Mark said.

"Why aren't you in court?" Lisa asked. "I thought you were halfway through a murder case."

He half smiled. "Homicide. There's quite a difference. My client, the accused, has gone down with 'flue. He has a temperature of over 102° and can't appear in court today, so I have a day of unwanted leisure on my hands."

Lorne's heart gave a jolt as the thought entered her mind that he or Lisa might suggest that he accompany them.

"Lisa, we *must* go!" she said shrilly.

Mark glanced at her, gave her a considered look and then turned back to Lisa. "I won't keep you any longer. Enjoy yourselves." He nodded at them both, half lifted a hand in farewell and left.

He looked thoughtful as he made his way through the store. As soon as Lorne spoke he had recognised her voice as belonging to the girl who answered the telephone in Lisa's flat, which made it look as if they were seeing a lot of each other. This surprised him. He wouldn't have imagined somehow that she was Lisa's type. She was pretty enough, but looked as if she might be spoilt and sulky. Something about the girl disturbed him. It wasn't the fact that she had obviously been nervous and strung up. There was something else about her that made him feel vaguely uneasy. If she had been a witness under cross-examination he would have said that she was both guilty and frightened. He had seen the signs often enough in the witness box. Firstly, the impression given of being entrapped, and secondly, the sweating, unsteady hands, eyes furtive, sliding away to something out of range.

He took himself in hand. He was becoming fanciful. Guilt and fear? It was preposterous . . . Nonetheless the thought continued to niggle away at the back of his mind.

Lorne and Lisa didn't speak for the first five minutes. Lisa was thinking of Mark, and Lorne was concentrating on manoeuvring the Volkswagen through the heavy traffic.

Once she had turned from Wale Street into Long Street she said abruptly: "So that's Mark Standish."

Lisa continued to look ahead and didn't speak . . . Lorne had been cool, almost unfriendly when she had introduced her to Mark. It looked as if she had been offended by the remarks she had overheard him make, despite what she had said to the contrary.

"Don't make the mistake of thinking that I give a bloody damn what he said about my speech. As I said to you before, it couldn't worry me less . . . He's quite something, isn't he? Distinguished and interesting-looking. There isn't the slightest doubt that he belongs to the snob lot." She thought he would be round about Alan's age.

She glanced at Lisa when she remained silent. "You're not going to talk about him, are you? You even hated my mentioning his name."

"Why should I object?" Lisa said a little stiffly.

"Probably because you think I'm being thick-skinned and inquisitive. You dislike talking about anything concerning your private life, don't you?"

"I've no objection to talking about Mark, if that's what you want to do."

". . . I'm not sure if I do want to talk about him. In fact, now that I come to think of it, I'd—rather not know if there's anything between you."

"There's nothing between us."

She gave a brittle, humourless laugh. "D'you think I'm blind?"

"I don't know what you mean by that remark."

"I saw how you reacted when those flowers came from him, and I could sense there was something between you when you spoke to him over the 'phone. It was confirmed when I saw you two together just now.''

Lisa gave a forced smile. "You've allowed your imagination to colour your judgment.''

"Why did you blush then? Why did you go absolutely scarlet when you saw him?''

". . . Because I was taken by surprise, and very embarrassed.''

"Why should it embarrass you—just bumping into someone you know?''

Lisa cleared her throat. "It was embarrassing because I was once engaged to Mark.''

Lorne's brows shot up. "So *that's* it! . . . What went wrong? Why was your engagement broken off?''

Lisa didn't speak.

"All right, forget I asked. Don't tell me if you don't want to. It's none of my business anyway.''

They drove in silence until they reached the traffic lights and Lorne stopped the car with a jerk. "*You* broke it off, didn't you?''

Lisa stiffened. "Lorne, I'd rather not discuss this.''

"*Why* did you do it? I know you're still in

love with him . . . And he—why did you *do* it, Lisa?"

Lisa averted her face to look out of the window, instinctively lifting a hand to shield her cheek.

The lights changed to green and Lorne slammed in the gear and the car shot away. "You *fool*! I might have guessed—" She gnawed at her lip, driving too fast. She flashed past a delivery van and had to swerve sharply to avoid an oncoming car . . . "How did it happen?" she asked. "Did you have an accident?"

"I was knocked down by a car."

"Where did it happen? Here, in Cape Town?"

"No, in London, over a year ago."

"And when you found what had happened to your face you wrote to him and broke off your engagement? You didn't have much faith in him, did you?"

Lisa flushed. "You're hardly in the position to judge. You don't know the circumstances."

"But that was how it would have looked to him. Does he know that this was your reason for ending your engagement?"

"I'm not prepared to discuss this with you."

"*Does* he know?" she asked with such intensity that Lisa glanced at her and saw that her eyes had filled with tears. "*Tell* me, Lisa."

". . . He knows now."

"Would you have stopped loving him if the same thing had happened to him? I don't even need to ask. Yet you thought it would make a difference to him . . . You know he's still in love with you, don't you?"

"You don't know what you're talking about," Lisa said coldly.

"I know all right," she choked and swallowed. "I bloody well know. I saw his face just now when he suddenly realised who you were." She was pushing the Volkswagen with reckless abandon and put up a hand to dash the tears from her eyes. "Oh God, what does it matter whether he loves you or whether he doesn't. Why should I care? What the hell does *anything* matter! Oh *God*."

Lisa gave her a startled glance. "Lorne, what's wrong?"

"Nothing's wrong," she cried shrilly.

"Why do you imagine anything's wrong?"

"It's only because you seem so upset . . . When you rang me, you mentioned that you needed my help. If there's anything I can do—"

"Shut up!" Lorne shouted hysterically. She cornered too fast, and the tyres squealed as the car heeled over.

"You'll write us off if you're not careful."

Lorne eased her foot off the pedal and let the car slow down. "Oh God, I'm sorry—" She took a hand off the wheel to wipe her eyes. "Why do you have to be so bloody nice? Why can't you be a bitch like the other ones I know."

There was no reply Lisa could give to this, and neither of them spoke again until Lorne parked the Volkswagen in the parking lot below the ugly blocklike building of the cableway station.

She got out and glanced at her watch and muttered: "We'd better hurry if we don't want to miss the next car going up."

As they went up the steps she saw Lisa open her bag and search for her purse.

"I'm paying," she said harshly.

"Nonsense," Lisa said easily. "We'll go Scotch."

"I said, I'm paying!" She lengthened her stride and went on ahead.

Lisa followed more slowly in her wake. She was beginning to regret that she hadn't been more firm in her refusal.

During the trip to the mountain-top regret changed to resentment. There were only four other passengers closeted with them in the tiny windowed compartment in which they made their journey. A middle-aged English couple, obviously married, and another younger couple who seemed to be related to them, and also responsible for organising their excursion. They all crowded at the windows and the elderly woman in particular exclaimed at the panorama unfolding like a colourful map beneath them as they slowly rose. The faint haze had lifted from the city but still misted the densely populated northern suburbs which stretched across the Cape Flats almost as far as the range of the Hottentot Holland mountains. Beyond lay range after range of the Capefold mountains, and even, pale, washed-out blue against the skyline. An assortment of craft dotted Table Bay.

Two heavy tankers lay anchored far out, and three funnelled liners were in dock. The calm sea was a strange opaque greenish grey, flat as paint.

There was a nip in the air, but sunny and not a wisp of cloud visible in the sky.

Lorne had relapsed into a heavy preoccupied silence since her outburst in the car.

Lisa tried to speak to her once or twice and drew her attention to something, but Lorne barely bothered to look, and turned away without making any comment. She seemed oblivious of her surroundings and made it clear that she didn't wish to talk but wanted to be left alone.

Only when they reached the top and disembarked did she speak for the first time. "Let's go for a walk, I need some exercise."

It was on the tip of Lisa's tongue to refuse. Though she recognised that Lorne must be under some stress, she had become angered by the cavalier way in which she was being treated. She hesitated for a second, then shrugged inwardly and held her tongue.

It was her suggestion that they leave their

handbags with the woman in the tearoom before setting out. The bracing air made Lisa shiver at first, but once they started walking briskly she soon warmed up and began to experience an exhilarating sense of well being. Lorne set a sharp pace and seemed to know where she was heading. The territory was rocky and comparatively flat, the predominant colours slate grey rock, brown reeds and stunted russet-leaved heather. Lorne kept on the footpath along the edge of the mountain overlooking the city. At times they clambered down, and once in the lee of upthrusting rock found the vegetation luxuriant; proteas towering above them, and the flowering heather feet high. They walked in total silence, Lisa having made up her mind that she wouldn't speak unless Lorne spoke first.

After ten minutes she began to feel too hot and stopped to take off the jacket of her suit.

When Lorne saw her stop, she waited and stood watching her, strangely still and tense.

They set off again and she suddenly spoke. "Tell me more about your accident. What *were* the circumstances to make you break off your engagement? You can't tell me you weren't still in love with him." She glanced at Lisa when she didn't speak. "Oh God, Lisa. I'm sorry I've been such a bitch—"

"What's the matter, Lorne? What's happened to upset you so much?"

"Forget about me. Let's talk about you first. I know it's none of my damned business, and it's cheek on my part to ask, but I'd like to know why you did it?" She touched Lisa's arm. "*Please* tell me. Lisa. I'm not just being inquisitive. I—*like* you."

". . . It's a long, rather dull story."

"I'd like to hear it all the same, if you wouldn't mind telling me . . . Have you ever told anyone?"

"No."

"You wouldn't, of course. It's something I admire in you, but I still think you tend to bottle things up too much. Discussing things with someone else sometimes helps." She smiled. "The old saying—troubles shared are troubles halved. But if you'd rather not, of course—"

Lisa cleared her throat. "I don't mind talking about it, if you're really interested."

Their pace automatically slowed down

while she spoke, and Lorne listened to her with an almost painful intensity, her face as wrapt and expressive as a child's. Twice she bit her lip and tears welled in her eyes, and she quickly dashed them away. She didn't speak until Lisa finally relapsed into silence.

Then she said: "From what you've just told me, I gather that the plastic surgeon must have done a fantastic job on your face."

"Yes, he did. My brother Robert knows him personally and said he's recognised as being one of the leading plastic surgeons in the world . . . It was Robert who got him to operate on me."

"Those scars you've got, Lisa, are nothing! They must fade in time, and with make-up no one will notice them. Why didn't you *wait* before you broke off your engagement? Why didn't you at least wait to see what the surgeon could do for you? Didn't he tell you it wouldn't be as bad as you thought?"

"Yes, but I didn't believe him. You see, I knew exactly how extensive the damage was . . . I've already told you this—"

"Have you told Mark?"

"No."

"*Why not?* . . . Lisa, when you quarrelled with him the other night, was it because he'd found out that you hadn't fallen in love with someone else, but had broken off your engagement because of your face?"

". . . Yes," Lisa said, loath to talk about it.

"Didn't you tell him the whole story, like you've just told it to me?"

"No, it wasn't possible. He was too angry—and I also lost my temper . . . Lorne, let's forget about this. Things have been finished between Mark and me for over a year."

"Oh, you fool! You *idiot*!" She had been walking more and more slowly and now stopped and stood biting her lip, tears streaming unchecked down her cheeks.

Her excessive emotionalism embarrassed Lisa and she said a little awkwardly: "Lorne, you mustn't take my troubles so much to heart."

"You're still in love with him, aren't you? . . . OK, so you don't want to answer, but you don't have to tell me, I *know* you are. You say things are finished between you and Mark. If they were, would he bother to send you flowers?"

"It was Mark's way of apologising for losing his temper. Nothing more."

"Why did he get that look on his face when he realised it was you he had bumped into?"

Lisa smiled, albeit in a strained way. "As I said before, you've allowed your imagination—"

"It *wasn't* my imagination. I've got eyes, haven't I? Lisa, *listen* to me. I've been thinking about what you've just told me, and I know what you should do—" She broke off abruptly, swallowed and didn't go on.

She stared with wide haunted eyes at the outcrop of granite rock at the mountain's edge, less than fifty yards ahead, which Alan had been at such pains to describe to her . . . "You can't miss it, if you keep along the path at the edge of the mountain all the way. It should take you roughly twenty minutes from the cableway station to get there. You'll see a promontory of rock jutting up against the skyline almost completely square, skirted by two cylinders of rock which are a little taller, like chimneys on either side of it. Immediately below this you'll see that the slope is thickly overgrown with indigenous stuff, protected from the southeast wind by a bulwark of rock on the right. You'll find a footpath going through a virtual forest of protea, standing eight feet high. This will bring you to a spot where a couple of old trees have pushed their way through the rock, and once you've gone past them you'll have to do a bit of a climb, nothing much, just a matter of clambering up the rocks, and this will bring you to a wide sloping grassed ledge on the very edge of the mountain, completely hidden from view. The outlook from there is quite something: breathtaking in fact, which will give you the excuse to sit there. Relax with her for a few minutes. Don't rush it—take your time. Then get up, tell her you'll be back in a few minutes and go. As I said, that will be all you'll have to do. Nothing else! I'd suggest you give yourself an hour before you go back to the tearoom to report that she's missing . . ."

When Lorne suddenly stopped speaking, Lisa looked at her and saw that the blood had receded from her face, leaving her looking sallow and ill.

"Lorne, are you feeling all right?" she asked.

"Lisa, *run*!"

Lisa stared at her as if she had taken leave of her senses.

"Didn't you hear what I said, you stupid bitch—*run*!" Lorne screamed hysterically.

"I think we should go back—I'm sure you're not well."

"Do you want to be killed?" she asked shrilly.

Lisa stiffened and searched her face. What did she know of Lorne beyond what she had seen fit to tell her? She looked wild-eyed and unhinged and her behaviour all morning had been disquieting, even alarming. Could it be that she wasn't quite sane?

She said calmly: "Frankly, Lorne, I've walked far enough. D'you mind if we go back now?"

"I asked you a question. Do you want to be killed?"

Lisa went pale . . . "Who would want to kill me?" she asked hoarsely.

"You don't believe me, do you?" She was having difficulty with her breathing and had to take a deep breath before she could go on. "You think I'm mad. That's what you think, don't you?"

Lisa wet her lips but didn't speak.

"Can't you think of anyone who would want to murder you?" When Lisa didn't answer, she said harshly: "What about the man you saw at Roosklip? The one you saw drowning a woman? Don't you thing he would want to?"

Lisa had gone dead white. "How do you know I saw someone drown a woman? I've never told you this."

"No, you never told me. *He* told me. *Now* do you believe me? Why are you still standing there? Lisa, for God's sake, *run*!" She screamed, distraught.

Lisa turned without a word and ran for her life. In her blind panic she assumed that the man must be coming up from behind, and bolted in the wrong direction.

21

WHEN Lorne saw that Lisa was running straight on, away from the cableway station instead of towards it, she screamed: "Lisa, *stop*. You're running the wrong way! Go *back*, you bloody fool! Go back to the tearoom!"

Lisa heard Lorne scream but the shrill words were unintelligible and only served to galvanise her into lengthening her stride. She found that the jacket slung over her right arm interfered with her running so she cast it from her, stumbling and nearly falling as it threw her off balance.

Lorne screamed again, swearing at her, calling her every filthy name she knew when she took no heed, and then stood watching in frustration until she ran down a slope and disappeared from view.

She gave herself ten minutes before going on . . . Alan would be wondering by now why there was still no sign of them. She was a little afraid at the thought of meeting him, knowing he would be angry when she told him. But she was certain that once she had explained how impossible it had become for her to do what he asked, he would understand. Now he would be forced to change his plans—and it would be all for the best.

She was within twenty yards of the towering square block of granite when she saw the footpath going sharply down, which Alan had told her she must watch out for. She found the rough path steep going at first and clambered down it very carefully, but then it cut across the slope and levelled out, and once she was underneath the upthrusting rock, found herself in a deep thicket of tall nerifolia; the same pale pink black-bearded protea Lisa had pointed out, which seemed to flourish below the crest of the mountain whenever offered enough shelter from the prevailing winds. The narrow path was completely shaded, wet with dew, and the rocks slippery and treacherous underfoot.

Once through the thicket she found herself unexpectedly in a small grassed clearing up against the sheer face of a cliff. It was deeply shaded by the overhanging branches of a wide-spanned, many-boled wild laurel which had thrust its way through a split granite boulder. Delicate, fernlike fronds of Newlands creeper had twined themselves about the cork tree-trunks and snaked up into the lower branches. Tall bracken and lush arum leaves carpeted the ground beneath the tree and pushed up between the moss-encrusted rocks. The air was still, cold and smelt of mouldering leaves.

She was halfway across the clearing when he suddenly spoke.

"Where is she?"

The grass had muffled the sound of his footsteps and she gasped and gave a scream half stifled when she turned and found him looming over her. "Oh, my God, Alan, you nearly frightened the life out of me!"

"Where is she?" he repeated. "Why isn't she with you?" His face looked set and so pale as to appear greenish, almost luminous in the filtrated light.

Her heart quickened its beat. "Alan, I *couldn't* do it. I did everything else you said I must, and it all—worked out, and no one followed us to the cableway station. I *tried*, darling, but just before we reached here, at the very last minute, I found I couldn't do this to her."

"Where is she?" he asked for the third time.

"She's—gone. I told her to run away. Darling, won't you try to understand," she said desperately. "I *like* Lisa. I like her more than any girl I've ever met . . . She's unhappy, Alan. She even confided in me at the end. She told me—"

"You say you told her to run away," he cut in. "Just what did you say to her? What reason did you give to convince her she must do so?"

Lorne had been a fighter all her life, unafraid and well able to fend for herself. She had never as yet found herself in any predicament or situation with which she was unable to cope; nor had she at any stage experienced extreme physical fear. But she recognised that what she was experiencing at this moment must be something closely allied to it. Her hands had gone clammy and the heavy suffocating beat of her heart had quickened her breathing. His cold inflexible face, and the quiet almost menacing manner in which he had asked the question had done this to her.

"What did you say to her?" he repeated more loudly when she didn't speak.

". . . I told her that her life was in danger."

"Did you enlighten her and tell her why?"

". . . Yes," she said eventually. "I told her that if she didn't do as I said, if—she didn't run away, she'd be murdered—"

"And did you tell her who would murder her?"

She swallowed and stared at him in silence.

"*Did* you or didn't you?" he asked savagely.

"I—Oh, darling, can't you see—"

"Answer my question. Did you or did you not tell her who was going to do it?"

She drew a deep breath . . . "When I told her she would be—murdered if she didn't run away, she didn't believe me. I could see she was wondering if I was—mentally unstable. The only way I could convince her was to tell her it would be—the man she saw on the beach that morning," and added quickly: "Oh, darling, don't look like that! I told her nothing more. She hasn't a clue who the man is." She put her hand on his arm, found it as rigid as steel beneath her fingers. "Alan, right from the start, when you first told me what you'd done, I've felt that the only hope you have—the only hope *we* have of any future together, lay in starting a new life in another country. I felt you must leave before there's any suspicion that your—that Maisie's missing. Once the police find out you'll be doomed, darling. *Surely* you can see that? But if you go *now*, and hide your tracks, we might have a chance. As soon as you're settled somewhere, and send for me, I'll come at once. I'll—"

His eyes blazed. "You bitch!"

She screamed as he hit her full in the face.

The blow was intentionally vicious, a back-handed one, catching her full across the nose and mouth and knocking her clean off her feet.

He reached down as she fell and caught her arm one-handed and jerked her savagely to her feet. "Which way did she go?" She was rocking, half dazed from pain and shock, staggering on her feet and would have fallen had he not been gripping her arm. Her lips were gashed and blood ran in a red stream from her nose, dripping down on to the front of her frock.

When she made no answer, he shook her as if she were a rag doll. "Which way did she go?"

She stared at him, mouth working, unable to speak.

He gave her an open-handed, full-blooded slap across the face.

"No!" she screamed, straining away, trying to protect her face with her free hand. "Oh God, don't hit me again! I can't stand any more!"

He caught her hand, wrenched it away from her face and twisted her wrist until she cried out, the lust to hurt and destroy hot within him. "This is only a taste of what's coming to you if you don't answer me." He balled his right hand into a fist, raised it to within an inch of her face. "Do you see this?"

She shrank back, staring at him with wild dilated eyes.

"This is what's coming to you next time, and by the time I've finished working on your face, your own mother wouldn't recognise you. *Now*, are you going to tell me?"

By now her whole body was shaking uncontrollably. She tried to speak but her trembling lips could not frame the words.

He tightened his fingers until they bit into her flesh. "If you don't answer me, I'll smash up your face."

She tried to speak, and then pointed with a shaking hand to the left.

His face tightened. "*That* way? You say she's run *away* from the tearoom? You're *lying*, you bitch!" He raised his fist threateningly.

"*No!* Don't hit me! I'm not lying. I'm *not*, I'm *not*." She began sobbing hysterically.

He stared at her steely-eyed, doubting, trying to read if she were speaking the truth.

"Oh God, can't you see I'm not lying! Can't you see I'm speaking the truth."

"By God, if you've lied to me—"

"I *haven't* lied to you! Why won't you believe me?" She was distraught with fear, and strained away from him, her free arm held up as a shield to protect her face.

"What is she wearing?"

She stared at him uncomprehending, too shocked and dazed to take the sudden switch.

"You heard me. What coloured dress is she wearing?"

"Red—a—red suit, with a white blouse . . . She took off her jacket—"

His eyes continued to bore into her, seeking to find out if she were speaking the truth.

"Don't look at me like that!" she cried hysterically. I'm *not* lying, I promise I'm not!"

He abruptly released her and thrust her from him with such violence that she staggered back, tripped over a stone and fell heavily.

She screamed, covering her face, curving her body inwards, expecting to be hurt.

After a time she took her hands from her face to look fearfully up at him, and found she was alone.

22

A WEEK back Ben du Toit had made a note of the number of Lorne Sellars' car and it was this act, done automatically without much thought, which enabled Karel Meyer to alert his men to patrol all the freeways leading from the city. He instructed them not only to watch out for Lorne Sellars' blue Volkswagen, but also to keep their eyes open for Mrs. Lincoln's white Triumph which could be parked off the road, in all probability somewhere in the country at the foot of a mountain . . . It was as vague as that and it was not possible for him to be more explicit. He knew that Alan Lincoln had left early that morning to climb a mountain, but he had no inkling which mountain it was, or in which district it lay. Their only hope lay either in spotting the white Triumph, or stopping the Volkswagen along the highway . . . He was convinced that Lisa Lombard was in mortal danger, and that her disappearance must be linked with Alan Lincoln. Just as he was equally certain that Lorne Sellars had been directed to lead Lisa Lombard to him.

He reproached himself bitterly that he hadn't telephoned Lisa the previous night to tell her that they had made a break-through and were almost certainly on the murderer's track; and to warn her once again that she must on no account go off on her own, or go anywhere with anyone, without informing them first; that he hadn't forewarned her that her friendship with Lorne Sellars might be highly dangerous . . . Yet to have done this, to have committed himself so deeply at that stage of their investigations, would have been contrary to all his training.

He could now make no decisive move, but must wait on the spot in case news came through that one or other of the cars had been seen.

Ben du Toit was the one to bear the full brunt of Karel Meyer's mounting tension. The young warrant officer was anxiously awaiting his arrival, and when the lieutenant came into the charge office at Caledon Square the boy was the first person he saw. He stopped and looked him over. If this incompetent young fool hadn't lost contact with Lisa Lombard, neither she nor they would be in the fearful predicament in which they now found themselves.

The boy wilted under his icy stare; and turned deathly pale by the time Karel Meyer had finished blasting and flaying him with his tongue. The duty sergeant and the four detectives present looked down in embarrassment until the tirade abruptly ceased and Karel Meyer turned on his heel and went into his office and slammed the door.

The telephone rang at that moment and the sergeant put out his hand and lifted the receiver. "Caledon Square . . . Yes, sir, he's here. If you'll hold on I'll ask him." He put the receiver on the counter, crossed the room and tapped on the door of Karel Meyer's office; waited until he answered and then opened the door and went in.

The lieutenant was standing in the centre of the room, drawing deeply at a newly lit cigarette. He was once more in command of himself, though the blood had not yet returned to his sallow face which still looked tight and hard. "Well, what is it?" he demanded.

The tone in which it was asked made the sergeant clear his throat before he spoke. "A call has just come through, sir. Mr. Standish said he would like to speak to you."

"Do you expect me to speak to him now? Tell him I'm busy," he said angrily.

"Yes, sir." He went out and shut the door.

The sudden thought flashed through Karel Meyer's mind that Mark knew Lisa, and there could be just a chance that he might give them a lead. A remote chance, admittedly, but he was prepared to clutch at straws.

He crossed the room and flung the door open. "Sergeant—"

The sergeant turned, with the receiver in his hand. "Yes, sir?"

"I've changed my mind," he said brusquely. "Put the call through, I'll speak to him."

He shut the door and went over to the desk and sank into the chair behind it, lifted the receiver. "Karel Meyer here. Is that you, Mark?"

"Yes, am I disturbing you?"

"I can spare you a minute or two," he

said grudgingly. "What can I do for you?" he asked without much warmth.

"I haven't heard from you for several days and thought I'd give you a ring to find out if you've made any further progress in Lisa's case."

"I haven't got time to talk about this now!" Stirred to unreasonable anger. "We're in the middle of one hell of a flap—"

"Oh, in that case—"

"Was this the only reason why you rang me?"

". . . Yes," Mark said slowly, as if he weren't quite sure.

"Have you seen her lately?" Clutching at straws again.

"Yes, I bumped into her this morning."

Karel Meyer leant forward, his hand tightening on the receiver. *"When?"*

"What's that?"

"*When* did you see her, man? What time was it?"

"I saw her about half an hour ago." The timbre of his voice had deepened slightly. "Why—"

"Where was she?" Karel Meyer interrupted.

"Why the sudden interest, Karel? What—"

"Christ, man, can't you understand English? I'm asking you a simple question. *Where* was she?"

"We met at the St. George's Street entrance to Stuttaford's."

"Was she with someone?"

"Yes, with another girl."

"Someone you knew?"

"No, but Lisa introduced us."

"Was her name Miss Lorne Sellars?"

". . . Yes—Look here, Karel—"

"Where were they going?"

"Just a minute. What are all these questions in aid of?"

"*Where* were they going, Mark? Did Lisa Lombard tell you?"

"Suppose you answer my question first. You said there's a flap on. Would it be connected with Lisa, by any chance?"

"*I'm* asking the bloody questions," Karel Meyer said angrily.

"I'd still like an answer."

"OK, Mark, if that's the way you want it, I'll give you an answer, and I'll give it to you straight. Your girl's in trouble, and every second you're wasting now in asking questions could spell the difference between life or death for her. *Now* are you satisfied?" When Mark didn't speak he said: "Answer me, for God's sake. Where did she say they were going?"

"They were going up the cableway to lunch on top of the mountain." Mark said hoarsely and cleared his throat.

"Up the *cableway*! . . . So it was Table Mountain . . ."

"That girl with her—something about her worried me. I suppose that was the real reason why I rang you. Karel, what trouble is Lisa in? Is this girl connected in any way with her case?"

Instead of replying Karel Meyer consulted his watch. They had just over ten minutes to make it if they wanted to reach the cableway station before the next cable-car went up. He'd get one of his men to ring them to hold up the car if necessary. "I can't talk about this now," he said abruptly. "We must get moving."

"You're going up the cableway?"

Something about the way it was asked made Karel Meyer say sharply: "Keep out of this, Mark. This is a matter for the police, and we don't want you butting in and chucking a spanner in the works. Understood?"

The telephone clicked as Mark put down the receiver and broke off the connection.

Karel Meyer muttered an oath, slammed down the receiver and leapt to his feet.

He was alway his best in a crisis. Cool-headed, well-organised, quick and decisive. His orders given in crisp succinct sentences, with no frills. He had the gift of leadership, and with it the added gift of inspiring confidence in the men who served under him. They might not all like him, but every one of them respected him.

The four detectives waiting in the charge office rose in a body as he came in. As briefly as possible he explained the position to them, adding that he would give them more details and clarify the picture when they were on their way.

He turned to the sergeant in charge and told him to telephone the cableway station at once to inform them that they were on the way, and to instruct them to hold back the cablecar if necessary until they arrived.

He knew they were cutting it fine, and there was always the chance there could be a hold-up in the traffic.

They would need reinforcements. This he could do by radio from the car. He instructed the sergeant to contact the dog unit and ask them to let him have two men, three if possible. Every second could count and they should make every effort to be in time for the next trip up.

The car was waiting and he abruptly hustled the four detectives out. At the last second he stopped and looked back. All this time Ben du Toit had been standing in the background staring at him, pale faced and tense.

"Well, what are you waiting for?" he barked. "Do you think we've got all day? Get moving!"

The boy flushed deeply, dived to reach for something under the counter and quickly followed him out.

The driver used the siren to disperse the traffic, and once they were through the city and he had turned into Kloof Road, he found he could safely drive at high speed. They reached the parking lot below the cableway station with three minutes to spare. While they were clambering out Ben du Toit spotted Lorne Sellars' blue

Volkswagen parked in the shade, and diffidently pointed it out to Karel Meyer.

The lieutenant turned his head to glance at the car, nodded, but made no comment.

They ran over to the building, and as they reached the foot of the steps a car drew up behind them with a screaming of tyres. Karel Meyer glanced over his shoulder and saw the driver leap out and slam the door before he sprinted over to them.

He stopped when he reached the head of the steps and said: "Venter, see about those tickets, I'll be with you in a second," and remained framed in the doorway and waited for Mark.

Mark came up the steps two at a time. When he reached the doorway Karel Meyer made no move to get out of his way.

"I thought I told you to keep out of this, Mark."

Mark was panting, black hair dishevelled, face thinned and dangerous. "Don't try and stop me, Karel. We both know you haven't the authority to do so."

Karel Meyer's lips tightened. They were both over-tense, and their mutual dislike of each other had got the better of them. They were like two snarling bristling dogs ready to fly at each other's throats. "I've got the authority to arrest you for exceeding the speed limit," he said grimly.

"I'd advise you not to try to enforce it, Karel. You'd make a fool of yourself if you did and you'd be wasting valuable time. *Get out of my way.*" He shouldered him roughly aside and went in.

The man operating the door, and Mark and the six detectives were the only passengers confined in the tiny windowed compartment. Only Mark looked out when they began to rise slowly and smoothly, and even he saw nothing of the unfolding panorama as he stood staring blindly ahead.

Karel Meyer began speaking in a low voice, and the detectives immediately gathered around while he explained the situation to them. They were all keyed up, and it showed by the tense expressions on their faces. Each nodded as he briefed them in turn on what must be done when they reached the top.

Mark was standing a little apart, his hands on the window-ledge as he listened with the same intensity as the others.

Karel Meyer finally half shrugged and

said: "Well, that's all for the time being" and put out a hand to finger the slender coiled rope slung across Ben du Toit's chest.

"Nylon?" he enquired with a smile.

"Yes, sir," he said with a heightened colour.

"How long is it?"

"A hundred and twenty feet, sir."

"So? And the breaking-strain?"

"Four thousand pounds, sir."

"Humph. D'you do much climbing?"

The boy blushed painfully. "I used to, sir. I c-climb now whenever I get the chance."

"Who taught you?"

"M-my father, sir."

"He's a keen mountaineer?"

"Yes, sir."

"It was a good bit of thinking on your part, bringing this along. We might yet find ourselves in a situation where we could need it. Good work!" He clapped the boy on the shoulder as he turned away.

He now regretted his outburst. The boy had deserved to be spoken told, but he knew he had been too harsh, and he felt ashamed that he had slated and humiliated the youngster so ruthlessly in front of the other detectives.

He glanced at Mark and saw how tightly his hands gripped the window-ledge and thought, God help him if he's still in love with her.

He moved over to him and said: "Mark—"

Mark turned his head to look at him. "Yes, Karel?"

"I take it you heard everything?"

He nodded and leaned back against the side of the cabin. "Yes, I heard."

"I know I told you that I'd keep you in the picture, but we only made a break-through yesterday morning, and spent the whole day following it up. We were pretty busy, to put it mildly, and even by late last night things weren't sufficiently clear to warrant my 'phoning you. If I had done so I would have failed in my duty as a police officer." They were nearing the top, and the formidable grey-rocked mountain face looked terrifyingly close, almost close enough to touch. "Look, Mark," he said quietly. "Let's forget our differences, and this animosity we seem to feel towards each other. What I'm saying now is for your own good . . . It would be better for you to keep out of this."

By way of reply, Mark lifted his chin and unknotted his tie, jerked it off, stuffed it into his pocket. His fingers fumbled at his collar and loosened it, and he undid the two top buttons of his shirt.

"Keep out of it, man. This is our job."

"You can't stop me from looking for her."

"No, but I can stop you from making a nuisance of yourself."

"D'you imagine I'd interfere or hamper you in any way?" Mark asked in sudden anger.

"Not intentionally, Mark—but you could do so unwittingly."

"Then look upon me as an extra pair of hands, an extra pair of eyes, extra ears. My God, what hope have a mere handful of you of finding her? Were these all the men you could muster?"

"No, Mark, we're the spearhead," he said smoothly. "We were the only ones geared to move at once. More of our men will be joining us: *many* more, and some of them with dogs. In another hour helicopters and a small army will be searching for her . . . Just promise me one thing. If things should get—tough, promise you'll keep out of it. That you won't try and butt in. This is where you could hamper us, and I would be sorry if I were forced into using my authority—"

"If things were to get—tough, as you put it, I've no more idea than you have how I might react, and I'm not prepared to make promises I may not keep."

They had now reached the top and when the door was opened Mark turned from him and was the first one out.

By the time the detectives had gathered in a knot outside the upper cableway station Mark was running in long easy strides, down the rocky path headed across the mountain.

Karel Meyer looked after him with a slight frown and then said sharply: "You've all got your orders. Spread out and try and find if anyone has seen the girls, to give us a lead which way they took. I'll repeat what Ben here has told us. Miss Lombard is wearing a red suit and Miss Sellars a yellow dress. And Venter, check if they've left anything at the tearoom."

"Yes, sir."

"And Ben—"

"Yes, sir?"

"I want you to follow Mr. Standish. Stick by him, but if the occasion demands, report back to me."

"Yes, sir."

He immediately set off with a peculiar long ungainly stride which made Karel Meyer smile grimly, having been put in mind of an ostrich.

Though Mark was well ahead, Ben du Toit was quietly confident that he would have no difficulty in catching up with him. Despite his gauche running style, he was a better than average middle-distance runner who took immense pride in keeping himself in tip-top training.

He was not to know that at his age Mark had been South African Universities 1500 and 5000 metre champion for three years, and recognised as one of the leading and most promising middle-distance runners in the Republic. He had dropped out of competitive athletics once he started practising at the Bar and found the strenuous training interfering with his work. Because of the sedentary nature of his work he had kept up the practice of rising early each morning, come sunshine or rain, and running several miles before breakfast. This had kept him in trim, and added to his natural talent still made him a formidable opponent. It was only Ben's youth and superb fitness which enabled him to gain on him very slowly.

Mark had made the mistake of pushing himself too hard at first, but he soon realised this and immediately slowed down, disciplining himself to run at his normal pace. He also deliberately emptied his mind, recognising that when he thought of Lisa's plight it affected his breathing and tensed his body; but he was unable to rid himself of the cold dread feeling in the pit of his stomach.

He had been running for close on seven minutes when some movement seen out of the corner of his eye made him glance to the left, and he stopped abruptly when he saw the figure of a girl etched against the skyline near the mountain's edge. She was wearing a yellow dress as brilliant as a buttercup against the clear pale blue sky. No one had been there a moment ago. It was as if she had materialised from nowhere.

He stood, staring at her, breathing hard,

remembering that Lorne Sellars had been wearing yellow; and though his eyes combed every inch of the grey landscape, he failed to find another figure in red. This could only mean that if the girl was Lorne Sellars, she was alone, and something must have happened to Lisa.

He plunged down a steep slope, up an embankment of solid rock and set off straight across the rocky terrain. Mounting tension had quickened his pulse and his chest had now tightened, making his breathing laboured and agonised. He could feel a numbness in his Achilles tendons as he drove himself to lengthen his stride. The rough uneven territory and the ungiving rock increased the strain on his legs.

As he drew nearer he saw that the girl was walking very slowly, her shoulders drooped and her head bent as if she were deep in unhappy thought.

She looked up and saw him when he was within fifty yards of her. She stopped dead and stood staring at him.

Even before he reached her, he saw the deep red stain down the front of her frock where blood had soaked into the yellow fabric. When he saw her tear-stained face, already swollen almost beyond recognition, an ice cold hand closed over his heart.

Her half dazed, almost vacant expression changed into sudden recognition. "*Mark Standish.* Oh, thank God you've come!" She put her hands to her face and burst into tears.

He didn't know what he had expected, but it certainly hadn't been this.

Wet hair clinging to his forehead, sweat running in rivulets down his face. Panting, chest heaving, he fought for breath before he could speak . . . "Where's Lisa?" He asked hoarsely.

"I told her to run away," she sobbed.

". . . When was this? . . . How long ago?" Still fighting for breath.

"A quarter of an hour—or twenty minutes maybe." Her speech slurred and indistinct through her cut swollen lips.

"Which way did she go?"

"She ran the wrong way," she said in a thin trembling voice. "I *screamed* to her to stop, but I don't think she heard."

"Which way did she go?" he repeated, the muscles tight in his cheeks.

"*That* way! Past the big square rock you can see over there."

He turned and looked in the direction she was pointing. "And she ran straight on?"

"Yes".

"Why didn't she run back to the cable-way station?"

"I've already *told* you why!" Voice too shrill. "She wouldn't listen to me when I screamed that she must run the other way."

"Why did you tell her to run the other way?"

She lifted an unsteady hand to push her tangled hair back from her face but didn't speak.

"Was—someone after her? Was that the reason?"

Tears welled into her eyes, spilled over, flowed down her cheeks. She brushed them away with the back of her hand. "Yes . . . *No*!" she contradicted herself wildly.

"What's happened to your face?"

She stared at him, breathing quickly.

"Did he hit you?"

Her hand went up in a quick instinctive protective gesture to hide her face, reminding him with a stab of Lisa. "Oh God, why do you stand there talking!" she cried hysterically. "Why don't you do something about *saving* her, instead of wasting time asking questions!''

"Was Lisa with you when he hit you?''

"*No*! . . . She had already—'' Her eyes went past him and she suddenly froze. "The *police*! You've brought the police, you bastard!'' Her reddened eyes blazed at him accusingly.

He looked round and saw one of the young detectives loping across the rocky terrain towards them. Lorne had recognised Ben du Toit immediately as the man who had followed her car from Dryads when she had driven Lisa back to her flat.

Mark turned back to her. "You were saying that Lisa had already run away. Is that correct?''

"I won't answer any more questions,'' she said high pitched.

"How much start did Lisa have, before she was followed?''

"I don't know what you're talking about! Leave me alone!''

"Look, Miss Sellars—''

"Leave me alone, do you hear! I won't answer any more of your bloody questions. Why don't you *go*!''

He knew it would be useless to question

her further. As it was, too many precious seconds had been wasted.

He waited for the boy to reach them and saw how the expression on his face changed to one of almost ludicrous consternation when he registered what had happened to the girl's face.

He said: "Go back and tell Lieutenant Meyer that Miss Lombard was last seen about twenty minutes ago, running in that direction." He pointed to the massive rock. "Take that square rock as your landmark. She ran to the right of it, and then straight on." He glanced at Lorne for confirmation, but she had turned her back on him, her body hunched, drawn in, as if she were in pain.

"Are you going on, sir?" Ben asked.

"Yes. I'll try to the best of my ability to keep contact with you people, but hurry, for God's sake. Every second could count."

Ben wheeled without a word and headed back, and within seconds Mark was running in the opposite direction.

Lorne sank down on to a rock and covered her face in her hands.

Once again Mark found that he had to exert an iron will not to drive himself too hard, when every instinct was urging him on to push himself to the limit. It took a little time before he got his usual even rhythm of running, and even then he was aware of strain because he was still too tense.

He ran well past the massive square rock until he reached the summit of a rocky koppie which commanded a longish unbroken view of the grey treeless rocky territory lying ahead. He lifted a hand to shade his eyes while he searched for some sign of her.

He lifted cupped hands to his mouth and called her name. "Lisa!"

A startled rock partridge rose with a frightened cry and a wild fluttering of wings from a bush above him.

Then on again until he reached the summit of the next rocky promontory. A shorter more desolate view this time.

"Lisa!"

Her name echoed eerily and chillingly across the lonely mountain top.

23

LISA stopped again and gave a smothered groan as she clapped a hand to her side. She bent over and tried to ease the agonising stitch which had now reduced her to a stumbling walk. She stood leaning over, gasping for breath, her legs jumping and trembling, her whole body shaking. She realised that she must have undermined her strength during those first five minutes of her wild flight.

She would not have fared as badly as this, nor would she have been so physically exhausted two years ago. She had never lacked stamina then, but since her accident and the subsequent operations she had found that she tired more easily.

She dragged a trembling arm across her streaming brow. She was *finished*. She knew that she could no more run the long distance across the mountain as far as Skeleton Gorge than fly. The path going down the gorge was safe, and she had once promised Mark that she would never go down the mountain any other way.

She remembered when he had elicited this promise from her. It was at the end of a day spent together on top of the mountain, and she had suggested on the way back that they should go down a different way for a change.

He had asked with a hint of sarcasm in the lift of his black brows: "Which path are you suggesting we should take?"

"What's wrong with the one straight ahead?"

"Have you ever been down that way?"

"No."

"Nor have I," he said drily. "And I have no intention of doing so now."

"Oh, Mark, why must you be so stuffy? Let's do it for fun."

"*For fun*! Good God. This thing you want us to do is the chief cause of at least half the fatalities on the mountain. If we did what you suggest we'd find ourselves in difficulties in no time, faced with a drop of hundreds of feet, and in all probability we'd be unable to turn back. Don't be an ass, Lisa. Leave these sort of antics to your real mountaineer who knows what he's up against."

"Why must you always be so emphatic and—domineering?"

"I'm emphatic all right when it comes to not risking my neck unnecessarily: and domineering, if you like, when it comes to stopping you from doing something irresponsible. Now promise me something—"

"What?"

"If you ever have to find your own way back—promise you'll only take the path down Skeleton Gorge."

. . . *Hide*. That's what she must do. Hide until the man went past. *No.* It stood to reason that it would have to be for far longer than that. He would guess that she was hiding somewhere and turn back, and if he saw her then, she would never escape. She must hide until dark. Stay there all night, in fact. It would be insanity to risk trying to find her way to the tearoom in the dark. She clasped her arms, shivering at the thought of the long, cold, lonely night.

An outcrop of rock lay to the left, close to the mountain's edge, the rocks almost entirely overgrown by a tall thicket of indigenous bush. It looked the ideal spot to hide, and she limped over to it, keeping a hand to her side. The tall olive green, leathery-leafed bushes looked vaguely familiar, and their curious pungent smell had some association with Mark which she could not quite place. If she could force her way in deeply enough, she would be completely hidden. Best of all, if she could push through until she came up against the rocks, this should provide her with some shelter during the night. She shuddered, thinking of scorpions, spiders and snakes, but quickly shut her mind to this and thrust a branch aside to make her way in. A last chance glance over her shoulder saved her.

The man was standing on a high shoulder of rock, not more than a hundred yards distant. He had a hand up shading his eyes, and he was staring straight across at her. She recognised him instantly by his ash blond hair gleaming as metallicly as silver in the sunlight.

Her breath caught in a frightened gasp and she wheeled and fled straight for the edge of the mountain and without a second's hesitation, dived down the path which lay ahead. She clawed and scrambled her way down, all promises to Mark forgotten, and if they had been remembered it was doubtful if she would have hesitated now.

It was soon no longer a matter of clawing and scrambling her way down. She found herself having to negotiate a precipitous wall of solid rock, with which she could have coped without much difficulty if she hadn't been hampered by her shoes. They were too light and loose and the smooth thin leather soles slipped whenever she sought a foothold.

She made a conscious effort not to panic or to allow herself to think of what might lie in store for her lower down. She forced herself to take things slowly and tried to damp down her quickened breathing.

Her foot slipped. For seconds she remained suspended by her arms, clinging desperately with both hands to a ledge before she lost her grip and began to slide and slither down. She managed to reach out and clutch at an out-jutting rock, hung on for a second before the weight of her body tore her hands free.

She continued to slide face down, gaining momentum with every second and knowing with certainty that she would plunge to her death if she could not stop herself. She felt her legs go over a horizontal drop, clawed desperately to find a hold to save herself. Screamed and shut her eyes as she went over.

Both feet jarred simultaneously against flat rock with such a shocking impact that her body was thrown off balance and she hurtled backwards to crash flat on to her back.

She was half stunned by the force with which she had fallen and lay for a full minute before she moved and slowly rolled over and staggered to her feet. She looked around in half dazed condition and it took several seconds before she realised that she was standing on a wide flat shelf of rock.

She could look way out to the east across the Cape Flats to the blue range of mountains in the distance. Immediately below there must be a sheer drop of hundreds of feet.

She was feeling dizzy and queer, and thought how aptly "Knees turning to water" described the curious lack of substance in her legs. She stumbled over to a flat rock, sank down and put her head between her knees and kept it there until the blood drumming in her ears quietened down.

When her head cleared she sat up and took stock of herself. Her tights were in shreds, and blood was streaming down both legs, scoured raw by the rocks. She found a deep gash above her right elbow where she must have cut it against a sharp edge. She flexed her shoulders and arms and found she could move them freely. She stood up to test her legs, took a step or two. They were still shaky, but no bones were broken, nor had she wrenched her back. Her head was aching dully. She gingerly explored the back of her skull and found a lump there, but no blood.

Satisfied that she had suffered no serious injury she now took stock of her surroundings. The shelf was as comfortably wide as a room. It was virtually the end of a cul-de-sac, skirted on both sides by vertical towering bulwarks of rock. A sloping wall of rock at the back, and a sheer drop of hundreds of feet in front. Despite this, there was all the evidence that people frequently came here. Cigarette butts, and an empty cigarette packet near the edge. Tin cans tossed into a corner, most of them rusted, but here and there one with the label peeling off. It was forbidden to light fires on the mountain, but a small circle of blackened stones, pieces of charred wood and ash were proof that someone had broken the law. She guessed this must be a place where the mountaineers picnicked and relaxed after a rock climb; or where they smoked a final cigarette before embarking on the climb down.

A stone came clattering down the wall of rock behind her. She swung round, her heart in her mouth, and ducked instinctively as a stone ricocheted off a rock, hurtled in her direction and bounced deafeningly three feet from her before it catapulted over the edge into space.

He must have dislodged it! He was on his way down.

She was trapped! It was as if she had unerringly led him to the one spot where he could safely finish her off. Not a soul would see him push her over the edge, nor would anyone hear her scream for help.

There must be a recognised way down which the mountaineers took. She ran to the edge and knelt to peer over. Heights held no fears for her, yet she recoiled now when she saw the sheer drop. From where she was crouched, the cliff appeared to be a vertical face of rock going straight down a depth of about two hundred feet . . . She swallowed, her mouth gone dry. It was either climbing down this, or certain death.

She crawled along the edge, peering down, seeking a way she could take. If he came now, one thrust of his foot would send her over. And then she spotted a steel piton driven into the rock two feet below the shelf. There was another a little lower down. She could now see the holds, and where one was missing, a piton driven in.

She drew in a deep shuddering breath and quickly pulled off her shoes, strangely calm now that she had made her decision. The dryness was still in her mouth, and there was a tight cold feeling in the pit of her stomach.

A thin shelf of rock at the edge gave her the leverage she needed and she took a firm grip with both hands before she let herself slide face down over the edge, very slowly, very cautiously. Stretched out a leg and sought with a bare foot for a hold lower down. Found it and let her weight slide down. With an effort of will she let go with one hand, took it down in slow motion and gripped the piton so firmly that her knuckles gleamed white. She waited, getting her nerves under control before she sought another foothold, brought her other hand down. She made all her movements deliberately slow and considered, shutting her mind to the man above, and to the terrifying drop below.

It took a little over five minutes before the strain began to tell. The muscles of thigh and calf tightened, and her legs began to quiver when called upon to support her full weight. Her fingers became numb, and she seemed to be losing the strength in her hands and arms. She realised that she was too taut, that she clutched too desperately to a hold; and though she rested more and more frequently, flexed her fingers to bring back circulation and tried with every ounce of will to make herself relax, her rigid body would not respond. She knew she would not be able to keep this up for any length of time.

When her bare foot came in contact with flat rock, her dulled senses were unable to take it in and grasp what this must mean. It was only when she looked down for the first time on her journey down, and peered sidelong undereath her arm, that she grasped the fact that she had reached a narrow ledge.

The relief was so great that she must have subconsciously let go when both her feet were planted firmly on the ledge, with the result that her legs gave way beneath her, and she slid down all of a heap and lay where she was, eyes closed, her breathing deep and painful.

Minutes passed before she stirred, opened her eyes and sat up.

The ledge was not much more than four feet wide, and less than twelve feet in length. It was overhung by a sloping ceiling of rock which would hide it from the shelf above. A yard from where she was sitting, the rock behind her shelved in to form a shallow cavity, verdant with moss, ferns and lush-leafed weeds, flourishing in the cool shelter provided. A slender mis-shapen pine sapling had thrust itself out and grew at right angles in search of light.

She was now perched on the very face of the mountain; and it was exactly as Mark had said it would be—she could go no further down. She knew that she was lucky to have got as far as this without mishap. To continue would be suicide. Nor did she have the will or strength left to turn back . . . If the man followed her down, she was trapped and there would be no escape for her this time.

She shifted inwards and leaned against the wall of rock and let her head fall back. She felt drained, apathetic, almost beyond caring what happened anymore.

And then the sound of a shoe scraping against rock jerked her upright.

The will to live was still there, and she scrambled quickly to her knees and crawled into the shallow cavity among the ferns and weeds. It was not a question of hiding from him. He must see her the second he set foot on the ledge. But it would at least mean that he would have to drag her bodily out before he could push her over. If she had remained sitting where she was, one brutal shove would have done it.

She waited tensely, her hands tightly clenched over the slender trunk of the pine, eyes riveted, unwinking, on the wall of rock above the end of the ledge where he must appear if he were coming down . . . When a bronzed, muscled leg eventually stretched down she felt her whole body jolt.

He was coming down every bit as slowly and painfully as she had. It seemed minutes passed before he brought his other leg down and his foot found purchase on the ledge. When this happened his reaction was the same as hers had been. He froze. She could see his body to chest height and saw how he stiffened and guessed he was peering down to make sure. When he finally got both feet on to the ledge, he did not turn, but slumped forward against the wall of rock and pressed his face to it. He clung with both hands to it, as if afraid he would fall if he let go. His shoulders heaved as he gulped in air with hoarse agonised gasps, as if he were in the last stages of exhaustion.

After a time he shuffled a little deeper into the ledge, still clinging to a hold. He visibly straightened and steeled himself before he turned to face the view which he must do if he wanted to sit down. When he was halfway round, he looked down and saw her crouched under the shelved-in rock, staring up at him.

She shrank back when their eyes met, but

for all the reaction he showed, he could have been blind. His eyes were glazed, unrecognising, and his taut white face, filmed with sweat, could have been carved from stone

Her eyes never left him, and it was with a sense of dull surprise that she realised he was in even worse shape than she had been. He was shuddering, and still gasping for breath . . . It took some time before it dawned on her that he was in a state of sheer sweating terror. She recognised all the symptoms, having seen them before in her brother, Robert. She had often used this horror he had for heights, as a weapon with which to scornfully taunt him when they were children. . .

He straightened and leaned back against the rock and stretched out his legs, but when he saw how close his feet came to the edge, quickly drew up his knees and let his head fall back and shut his eyes.

She stared at his profile, clear cut against the grey of rock. Lorne's description of her lover should have warned her . . . "He's fantastically handsome in a blond Nordic way. In fact, he's one of the handsomest men I've ever seen" . . . She would have known him anywhere.

She stiffened. She would have sworn that her imagination was playing her false, if he too hadn't straightened and cocked his head as if he were listening. And if it hadn't been for the way his face changed, his features tightening and becoming set.

The beat of her heart quickened, and against all reason hope was born that she might yet survive. She listened with painful intensity for the call to be repeated. But when the minutes ticked by and all she could hear was the soft soughing of the wind that had sprung up during the last half hour, hope died, and with it the fight went out of her.

Her fingers, rigidly clenched round the stem of the pine sapling, slackened, and she lay back and stretched out her cramped legs. That it would be easy now for him to seize her by the ankles and pull her out no longer mattered.

And then, unbelievably, the call came again. Closer this time, clear and quite unmistakable. "Lisa!"

"Mark!" she screamed, drawing up her legs, her back straightening, her head

smacking up against the low ceiling of rock.

His whole body jerked as if he had been struck. "Shut up, you bloody bitch! If you scream again I'll drag you out of there and chuck you over."

She shrank back until she was pressed against the rock, feeling its coldness through her blouse.

"I'm warning you. Open your mouth again, and you've had it!"

24

MARK's call came echoing down the mountain again. Though it sounded faint and distant, she could nonetheless recognise the urgency in his voice. "Lisa! Where are you?"

Each time he called it tore through her, and she half shut her eyes in something approaching anguish. The man had meant what he had said. It had shown in his cold blazing eyes. In his grim-set mouth. And in his athlete's body, poised and held in readiness to leap up if she screamed.

Mark's voice grew fainter as he moved further along the mountain's edge. She knew he was waiting for an answering call before making a decisive move down the mountain. Her wild scream spiralling up from below would have given him little indication from whence it came, and unless she answered him, he would have no idea which path he should take . . . One scream from her might do it . . .

The desperate resolve was only half

formed in her mind; something for which she must still steel herself, but she must have unconsciously parted her lips, or made some involuntary movement which warned him of her intention, because she saw his eyes suddenly harden and he gathered his body and put a hand on the ledge. Fear felt like a hand tightening round her throat, and instead of screaming, she swallowed and grasped a wedge of rock to lift her body and ease her cramped legs.

His eyes had never left her face since he had spoken. He had sat watching her as intently as a cat watching a mouse, his long, thickly-lashed, light grey eyes narrowed, holding a threat. His lashes were as pale as his silver blond hair.

They both heard the distant shout come across the mountain and Mark's quick call back. It was impossible to distinguish the words but the inference was there that he was not alone in searching for her.

Alan clenched his jaws. *Lorne*. If a search party was out looking for the girl, it could only mean the Lorne had given him away. *Betrayed* him. He should have known that once he hit her she would stop at nothing to get her own back on him. He ground his teeth and cursed her inwardly. He should have killed her. There had been a moment of hot engulfing rage when he had come close to doing it. If only he had paused to *think* before he ran off in pursuit of the girl, he would have known he must do it. And nothing could have been easier. The locality had been ideal with the drop below, and there would have been no chance of anyone seeing him. It would have been assumed that she had slipped and fallen to her death. He would have been compelled to do something about her sooner or later. Having been forced to confide in Lorne to get her co-operation, he had thereby placed himself in her hands, and being a woman, it would have been only a question of time before she used this as a weapon with which to bring pressure to bear and turn the screw on him . . . He was no longer looking at Lisa, but staring grimly ahead . . . *Women*. They were all the same, only out for what they could get. Except for Maisie. She had been different. She was the only one who had treated him with consideration, and who hadn't leaned on him and pushed him around. He had had a *companionship* with her . . . He leaned back, still staring unseeingly ahead . . . But she had proved to be no different to the others in the end. He would never forget the unforgivable, diminishing things she had said to him. She had been even worse than Linda. Bitching him, taunting and *driving* him into killing her . . . Hot tears stung his lids . . . Why had she so obdurantly refused to believe him, or to even *listen* to what he said? He had repeatedly told her that Lorne meant nothing to him. That it had been a temporary infatuation from which he was already freed. *Lorne*. It was she who was responsible for everything that had happened. She and this girl . . . He turned his head to look at Lisa again and saw how she shrank back when their eyes met . . . If Maisie had been prepared to give half a chance, he would have made things work. The five years he had lived with her at L'Horizon had been by far the happiest of his life. He had poured all his energy, enthusiasm, love, *everything* he had, into the farm, and it had been the most rewarding thing he had ever done. Given a few more years, he would have built up L'Horizon into being the finest farm in the district. He couldn't have done more to persuade Maisie to give him

EAD30

another chance. He had practically gone down on his knees to her, *abased* himself, and she had still spurned him, and would have thrown him out like a dog.

A sudden shout, infinitely closer than the last, jolted him back to the present.

His heart quickened its beat and he felt sweat break out on his forehead. Could the shout mean the someone had found his pullover? He had pulled it off and thrown it over a rock without even pausing to think before pursuing the girl down the path. If his jersey were found they might guess that this was the path down. And once they reached the shelf they couldn't fail to see her red shoes lying at the edge where she had discarded them before climbing down . . . To think he was the one who had said to Lorne: "That's how most people get caught: by omitting to take precautions which should have been obvious at the time." *He* had erred by omitting to take one precaution after another. He had allowed himself to be blinded by his desperate need to catch the girl before she got away. If he had paused to think, he would have killed Lorne, and he would also have had the sense to hide his jersey, and throw the girl's shoes over the cliff.

When Karel Meyer and the other detectives caught up with Mark, he could only tell them that Lisa's scream had come from somewhere down the mountain. Echoing as it did, it had been impossible for him to tell from which direction it came, and though he had called her repeatedly since, she had not replied.

Karel Meyer wasted no time but abruptly told the detectives to spread out and try to find a clue indicating which path she might have taken down. If one of them found anything, he was to shout and let the others know.

It was Ben du Toit who found the long-sleeved dark green pullover where it had been tossed on to a rock at the head of a rough footpath with which he was familiar. He had often taken this precipitous rocky way down the mountain to reach the shelf of rock above one of his favourite rock climbs.

It was his shout that Alan heard ring across the mountain. And it was the shout which brought the scattered detectives at a run to join him.

Karel Meyer was the second there. He nodded briefly when Ben showed him the jersey and then dived down the path without saying a word.

Mark was the furthest away when Ben shouted, and though he immediately doubled back, he nearly missed seeing which path they took. He reached the crest of an outcrop of rock and was just in time to see the last detective disappearing down the path.

Karel Meyer jumped down on to the wide shelf of rock and paused for a second to scan it with practised eyes. His heart turned over when he saw Lisa's discarded red shoes lying close to the edge. It could only mean that she had assayed to climb down the sheer drop. He went over and stared down at her badly scuffed shoes covered in dust, and felt a tightness in his throat. He knelt to look over the edge, anticipating his stomach hollowing, and the wave of vertigo which would assail him once he looked down from this height. Jannie Barnard was the only one who had known of this weakness of his. When he had overcome the initial onslaught of dizziness he let his eyes slowly traverse every inch of the sheer cliff.

It took nearly five minutes before he was finally convinced she was nowhere there. When he got to his feet he found he was trembling slightly. He fumbled clumsily for his handkerchief and wiped his face before he turned to the detectives grouped silently behind him.

"There's no sign of her," he said heavily. "She must have fallen."

Ben du Toit cleared his throat. "Sir—" he said hesitantly.

His brows drew together. "Yes, what is it?" he asked harshly.

"There's a l-ledge about thirty feet down. She might have reached it."

"If she's on a ledge thirty feet down, do you imagine for one second that I would have failed to see her?" he said angrily. "There's no sign of her, I tell you."

Ben reddened. "There's a sloping ceiling of rock above the l-ledge, sir. If she were on it, you wouldn't be able to see her from here."

His eyes sharpened . . . "So? . . . Would it be possible for someone who was not a mountaineer to climb down this—wall of rock unassisted, and reach the ledge?''

"Yes sir, I think so. The climb as far as the ledge is quite straightforward. It's only later that there are fissures and a couple of awkward bulges of rock.''

"I take it you know what you're talking about? Are you familiar with this climb?''

He flushed slightly. "Yes, sir. I've done it many times.''

"Roped, of course?''

"Yes, sir, we would never have dreamt of—'' He broke off.

Karel Meyer lifted a hand to stroke his cheek as he felt himself starting to sweat. There was a uncomfortable queasiness in his stomach, now that he had made up his mind what he must do.

Ben du Toit's flush deepened unbecomingly . . . "I've brought a rope, sir. I could easily show someone how to h-hold it and brace himself while I go down. Then I could find out if she's on the—''

"Are you trying to run this show?''

The boy paled under his icy stare.

"You'll do what you're told to do, and nothing else! Now give me that rope—'' He looked round as Mark leapt down on to the ledge.

He came over to them, checked fractionally when he looked past Karel Meyer and saw the red shoes lying at the very edge, but the expression on his face did not alter and his voice was quite calm when he asked: "Has she climbed down the drop?"

"It looks like it," Karel Meyer said. "Though there's no sign of her: but it seems there's a chance she could be on a ledge lower down, which we can't see from here . . . Show me approximately where it is," he said to Ben du Toit.

The boy came to kneel at the edge and the other two crouched down at each side of him. He pointed with a hand which was not quite steady. "It's there, sir. Just to the l-left of that green—"

"Lisa!" Mark shouted. "Are you there?"

"Yes!" she screamed.

The impact of her unexpected scream was as shattering as an electric shock, and evoked in each one of them the conflicting sensations of sweating relief and escalating tension.

Mark leapt to his feet and went over to

the spot where Lisa's shoes were lying.

Karel Meyer rose quickly. *"Mark,"* he said sharply.

He stopped, looked at him. "Yes, Karel?"

"Where do you think you're going?"

"Where the hell do you think I'm going?" It was said with a sort of angry contempt. "I'm going to her, of course."

Karel Meyer's mouth tightened into a thin line. "I warned you to keep out of this."

"And I told you that there's nothing you can do to stop me from looking for her."

His sallow face blanched to the colour of old ivory. "Take one more step and you're under arrest!" He swung round. "Venter, did you hear what I said? If Mr. Standish moves another foot, he's under arrest."

"Yes, sir."

"If you don't want me to go down to her, then what do you propose doing about it?" What are you waiting for? Reinforcements? Helicopters? How much longer are you going to stand there before you do something about helping her?"

"Shut you bloody mouth and get back from there! By God, if I have any more trouble from you I'll have handcuffed. You heard what I said, *move back*, or you're under arrest!"

Mark pushed past Ben du Toit and went over to a flat rock at the back of the shelf and sat down.

Karel Meyer found that rage had constricted his chest and quickened his breathing. He cleared his throat two or three times, drew in a deep breath and exhaled slowly before he knelt again and looked over the edge.

"Miss Lombard!" he shouted.

Miss Lombard! Miss Lombard! Miss Lombard!

Flung back at him from the towering bastions of rock. The strengthening wind was cold against his damp forehead and he could feel it ruffling through his hair.

"Miss Lombard!" he shouted again. "This is Lieutenant Meyer. Is anyone with you?"

Her hands closed over the pine sapling. She gripped it tightly and continued to stare at the man who had not moved since her scream. He was slumped forward with his face buried in his hands, but some instinct warned her that if she screamed again it would galvanise him into violence.

"Mr. Lincoln!"

His body jolted, and he pressed his face deeper into his hands.

"Mr. Lincoln, we know you're with Miss Lombard. We don't want her to come to any harm, so I'm coming down to fetch her."

The man lifted his head. Was the moisture on his face tears or sweat?

"If you come down here," he shouted hoarsely, "I'll take her over the edge with me."

Karel Meyer shrugged off his jacket, pulled off his tie and undid his collar. He ran a hand over his holster, and eased out the revolver. Then he slid it back. He nodded at Ben du Toit. "OK . . . Tie that rope round my waist and let's see how you do it."

He watched the boy narrowly. "A bowline, hey?"

"Yes, sir."

He unfastened the rope, reknotted it. "That right?"

"Yes, sir."

"You say the climb's quite straightforward? Are there any snags I should look out for?"

"No, sir, the footholds and handholds are all there."

"The ledge, how wide is it?"

"About five feet, sir."

"Quite level? I could drop on to it in an emergency?"

". . . Ye-es, sir, but it would take practice."

He grinned grimly. "There certainly won't be any time for that . . . OK, get yourself settled, I want to get moving." Feeling a sickening lurch in his stomach as he said it.

The boy took the short length of rope and tied himself expertly to a rock near the edge. The long length he slid round his back, then braced both feet firmly against a rock and looked up. "Right, sir."

Karel Meyer bent to finger the slender rope lightly clasped in big raw-boned hands. "Four thousand pound breaking-strain, eh? Aren't you going to wrap it round your wrists?"

He gave a slight strained smile. "No, sir.

A friend of my father's once did that—and lost his hand."

"So?" He straightened, cocked his head and listened intently. His hearing was exceptionally acute and it was only he who caught the distant phut-phut of the helicopter's engine.

He glanced at Detective Sergeant Venter who was operating the walkie-talkie. "Venter," he said sharply. "Get in touch with that helicopter and tell them I don't want them reconnoitring and buzzing around here. Say I'll contact them when I need them."

"Yes, sir."

His reason was two-fold. The helicopter hovering in close proximity could panic Alan Lincoln into some desperate action. And he himself wanted no distractions. There must be nothing to undermine his concentration or to blunt his single-minded purpose.

He slid carefully over the edge, his smooth face giving no indication of his sweating fear.

He thanked God for his shoes. Handmade, worth every penny he had paid for them. Fitted his feet like gloves. Thin ridged rubber soles. Grip anything. He'd given a pair to Jannie Barnard. If he got out of this alive he'd give a pair to Ben du Toit. The footholds and handholds were fairly evenly spaced and he tested each one as he went slowly and steadily down. Sweat pouring off him. An awful sick feeling in the pit of his stomach. But his mind cold, clear, keeping an estimate of his decreasing distance from the ledge.

The two on the ledge had not moved or spoken since Alan's shouted threat. For a time muted voices had come from above, but now there was a heavy waiting silence.

Alan was leaning back against the rock, staring straight ahead, his face haggard and very pale . . . And this was how his life was to end. Hunted. Trapped on a ledge like a stag at bay. It *was* the end. He had no illusions left that there could be any escape for him now. They knew his name, which could only mean that Lorne had told them, and she would never have stopped at that, but would have told them everything else . . . To have to die the way he feared most. To fall from a great height as he had done time and time again in the nightmares which had haunted him all his life. It was as if there had been a premonition that this would be the way he would die . . . The alternative he could never face. Life imprisonment, or death by hanging. This girl as the chief witness against him would see to that. She and Lorne. If it was the last thing he ever did, he would take her with him when he threw himself over. He felt his stomach muscles knot. It *would* be the last thing he ever did. Could he do it? Would he find the courage?

They both tensed as a chip of rock came rattling down. It hit the ledge and shot at a sharp angle over the edge.

It acted as a spur, and gave him the impetus he needed to overcome his fear. He leapt up and Lisa screamed as he bent and caught her arm. She tried to cling to the pine sapling but he seized both wrists and wrenched her hands free and dragged her brutally out by the arms. She got a hand free as he pulled her up against his braced body and clawed his face, drew blood. He swore, caught her arm and twisted it behind her back. Got an arm like a vice round her and swung her around. She gave a desperate scream, and in that last second, when she thought all was lost, the earsplitting, shattering sound of a shot smote her eardrums. And with it his whole body jolted violently. His arms were torn from her and he reeled back as if he had been dealt a tremendous blow. She saw his mouth and eyes widen in shock and disbelief. For seconds he teetered on the edge. Then he heeled over backwards and gave a hoarse scream as he felt himself go over.

A great roaring filled her ears and everything went black. She swayed as her knees buckled and then she fell like a log.

Karel Meyer froze as she collapsed full length, less than six inches from the edge. If she so much as stirred, half rolled, she would plummet over the edge. The time it took him to cross the ledge, crouch quickly and pull her up into his arms, were the longest seconds of his life. He dragged her to the back of the ledge and half collapsed himself to lean against the wall of rock and hold her crushed to him, his eyes shut and his ashen face pressed into her hair.

A shout came from above. They would have heard the shot, would be wondering what had happened, but for the life of him he could not shout back . . . He had so nearly been too late. Everything had happened so quickly. He had been eight feet above the ledge when the girl screamed, and he had immediately let go and dropped. He must have automatically whipped out his revolver as he landed on his feet and in a split second had shot Lincoln in the left shoulder. It had been as quick as that, and it now brought him out in a cold sweat to think how easily he might have shot the girl in error. Her back had been to him, her body acting as a shield, and it had been a miracle that he had been able to shoot the man at all . . . And a further miracle, God knew, that they hadn't pitched over the edge together.

He loosened his arms and let her head fall back. "Miss Lombard—"

She was very pale, her lashes dark against her cheeks.

He stared at her, feeling a sudden tightness in his throat. He could not remember ever having experienced such tenderness as he was feeling now.

He bent over her. *"Lisa—"*

Saw her lashes flutter, lift, green eyes look up at him without recognition.

"Are you all right?" he asked gently.

". . . It's you—" Half shut her eyes. "Oh God, I thought—"

His arms tightened and he very nearly kissed her. "He's gone. There's nothing to be frightened of."

". . . Did you shoot him?"

". . . Yes."

"*Karel!* Are you there? Is Lisa all right?" It was Mark.

He looked down at her and smiled, unable to stop himself from brushing a strand of hair from her forehead. "Yes, Mark," he shouted back. "She's OK . . . Give her a little time, and she'll be coming up." Felt her stiffen in his arms.

"No," she said hoarsely.

"You can do it."

"I *can't.*"

"There'll be a rope round you this time. You'll be quite safe. The boy at the other end is an experienced mountaineer and the worst that could happen if you slipped would be to swing a moment or so."

She shuddered. *"No."*

"Lisa—Miss Lombard. We can call out the Mountain Club to get you off here, but it will take time, possibly hours. If you could bring yourself to climb up now, it shouldn't take you more than ten minutes, and then the whole nightmare would be behind you." When she didn't speak he added: "Mark's up there waiting for you. It was all I could do to stop him from coming down."

Her eyes were down. She stared at her hands, flexed her fingers and drew in a deep breath. "All right. I'll do it."

"Your hands are cold?"

He found they were like ice. Slim fingered, small-boned hands. He took them between his and massaged them briskly until they felt warm. "Now get on to your feet and move around a bit." He helped her up and supported her while she took the first few steps.

"How did you hurt your legs?"

"It happened before I climbed down . . . I slid down the rocks—and fell."

He unfastened the rope and tied it round her waist. "You're a brave girl. I admired your courage right from the start."

". . . You didn't believe me—"

He tested the knot, didn't look up. "I did, you know. I was mixed up at the time . . . I didn't realise just how much . . . You OK now? Ready to go up?"

She nodded.

He shouted: "Ben!"

"Yes, sir?"

"Miss Lombard's coming up."

She looked white, tense and frightened.

He said: "I could be demoted for this" and put his arms about her. "And Mark would probably knock my block off." He kissed her.

When he loosened his arms she didn't speak, and he led her across the ledge. He stood and watched her climb up until she was hidden by the ceiling of rock.

Mark was crouched at the edge of the shelf thirty feet above and saw her the moment she appeared. He had been staring down, tense as a tightly coiled spring, ever since they had heard her scream, and the sound of a shot. He watched with bated breath as she came up foot by foot, and each time she paused to rest and gather her strength he groaned inwardly, angrily frustrated that there was nothing he could do to help her. He daren't call out a word of encouragement. In the end he even moved back in case she looked up and was startled at seeing him. It seemed that time stood still while he waited for her hand to come up and grip the edge of the shelf. When her other hand reached up he quickly leant down and caught her arms. Green eyes flicked up to his in sudden alarm. Face dead white, the curved scars deep purple. Then he pulled her up and she came into his arms, and clung to him like a drowning woman.

Ben du Toit watched them, then flushed slightly and looked away, wondering why he felt as if he'd been peeping through a key hole. It wasn't as if they were even kissing, or anything like that.

A shout came up from below. "Is Miss Lombard up yet?"

"Yes, sir."

"Then what are you waiting for? Let that bloody rope down. Do you think I want to stay here all day?"

Ben undid himself, got up and went over to them, cleared his throat, flushed furiously before he spoke. "Excuse me, Miss Lombard—"

She stirred and Mark immediately loosened his arms.

"Could I have the rope? Lieutenant Meyer—"

"Oh."

Mark undid it, and one of the detectives hovering round held up her shoes. "Are these yours, Miss?"

"Yes." She took them. "I'd better put them on."

She went over to the flat rock, sank down and tried to pull on her shoe but found her hands were too unsteady.

Mark said: "I'll do that," knelt and slipped them on her feet.

They were the first words he had spoken. He took off his jacket. "Put this on."

She said: "What about you? I'm not cold really, it's just that I'm still a bit tensed up—"

"Put it on, and don't argue."

She blinked and suddenly wanted to cry. She thrust her arms into the sleeves and wrapped the jacket about her, and after a moment he sat down beside her and felt in his pocket for his cigarettes.

No one spoke until Karel Meyer appeared. His face looked pale, and his features somewhat set as he pulled himself up on to the shelf. When he was on his feet he went over to Ben du Toit and flopped down next to him, as if the strength had suddenly left his legs. He fumbled for his handkerchief and mopped his streaming face with a shaking hand. He looked up and grinned wryly at the boy as he stuffed the handkerchief back into his pocket. "And you tell me you do this sort of thing for fun! Look at me, I'm shaking like a drug addict."

The boy flushed and smiled shyly. "Some people can't take heights, sir."

"You can say that again!" he said grimly. "Hand me my cigarettes. You'll find them in the pocket of my jacket."

When his cigarette was alight he inhaled deeply and then leaned back and closed his eyes. He sat like that until he stopped sweating and trembling. Then he levered himself up and went over to Lisa and Mark, who were sitting on a stone at the back of the shelf.

"You feeling OK now, Miss Lombard?"

She still looked very pale. "Yes, thank you."

"There are quite a few questions I'll want to ask you," and was about to add, "But I won't bother you about this now. I think we should get moving and take you home."

When Mark said: "Any questions you want to ask her, can wait."

"I was about to add that," he said smoothly, but with a glint in his eyes.

She said quickly: "Karel, I haven't thanked you—" and felt Mark look at her.

"You have nothing to thank me for."

"My life? What more could I possibly thank you for than that?"

"I was doing my job," he said rather stiffly. "The same as any other police officer would have done."

"Was that all?" She smiled at him with sudden brilliance.

He coloured, dropped his cigarette on the shelf and ground it out beneath his heel. "Well, I think we should get moving." He glanced up as someone shouted from above and a dog barked. "Christ, the reinforcements," he muttered. "Too late, as usual."

25

KAREL MEYER had sent one of the detectives to apprehend Lorne Sellars and take her down to the police station at Caledon Square for questioning. When he arrived there several hours later, he was met by the news that they had been unsuccessful in getting any information out of her. She had apparently denied all knowledge of what they were talking about, and she had flatly refused to answer any questions put to her. He gathered that she had also been aggressive and abusive.

He tapped on the door before he went into the room where the two detectives were still closeted with her. She turned her head to look at him as he came in. Mark had mentioned that her face had been injured, and he should have been prepared. Nonetheless he stiffened when he saw her. He remembered Ben du Toit saying she was a pretty girl, but there was no trace of beauty left in her swollen, bruised face. Her mouth was puffy and badly gashed, and it looked to him that her nose had been smashed to a pulp. The same blow had also half closed her eyes, which had been reduced to bloodshot slits. It was obvious that she was in considerable pain. It showed in her ashen, drawn look, her tightly clenched hands and by the sweat beading her brow. She was sitting slightly hunched, staring at him with the frightened hostile eyes of a cornered animal.

The detectives had both risen when he came in, and he said: "Has a doctor been called in to have a look at Miss Sellars?"

The man he addressed looked slightly uncomfortable. "No, sir."

"Why not? Surely you could see that she's been badly hurt?" It enraged him that no one had had the humanity to call in a doctor.

The man flushed slightly. "I didn't occur to us, sir."

This lack of compassion and "savvy", as he called it, was something he found he frequently came up against. "Couldn't you see for yourselves that something should be done about her? Did you have to wait and be told?"

"I don't want to see a doctor," she said harshly, her speech nasal and indistinct.

He turned to her. "Miss Sellars, I think it would be advisable for a doctor to see you."

She glared at him like a tigress. "You heard me. I don't want to see a doctor."

"Your nose could be broken."

Her mouth quivered and she pushed her tangled hair back with a shaking hand. "And if it is—what bloody business is it of yours! If I want to see a doctor, I'll see one when I choose."

He nodded at the two detectives and indicated that they should leave. As they reached the door, he said: "One of you give Dr. de Wet a ring, and tell him that I'd like him to come round at once."

"I won't see him if he comes!" she cried shrilly. "You can't force me to see a doctor if I don't want to. Who the hell do you think you are? . . . I *won't* see him, and what's more I demand that you let me go home. You have no bloody right to keep me here!"

He waited for the door to close before he sat down rather wearily. "Miss Sellars, you know as well as I do that we've every right," he said quietly.

"I don't know what you're talking about! If you've come, like the others, to ask a lot of questions, I can tell you now, you're wasting your time."

He lifted a hand to stroke his cheek. "I'm not here to ask questions."

The way he said it made her stiffen slightly and search his face. "Then why are you here?"

"Miss Sellars, the first thing you must accept is the fact that we know of your relationship with Mr. Lincoln."

She spat a four letter word at him.

"We have proof that he spent four hours with you last night. He entered your flat just after one, and left at ten past five this morning."

"So what? If he chose to spend four hours in my flat, it's also no bloody business of yours . . . Is this why you're here? to tell me that you've been—snooping around?" she asked contemptuously.

"No. There's something else I have to tell you."

She stared at him tensely. "What have you come to tell me?"

This was what he dreaded most in his job, and he was silent while he sought for the right words.

"*What* have you come to tell me?" she repeated in a high quavering voice, as if she already knew.

"I'm afraid I have bad news for you."

"No!" she cried out. "Oh God, you're not trying to tell me that something's happened to him! It isn't that, is it?"

". . . I'm afraid it is."

"Has he been hurt?"

". . . No."

She swallowed as if something had stuck in her throat . . . "Is he—dead?"

She read the confirmation in his face, and burst into tears before he could speak. He could not remember ever having witnessed such unrestrained grief. She twisted and writhed as if she were being torn apart. And she didn't cover her face in her hands, as was usually the case, but cried openly, as he had seen small children do. Her wounded mouth open, tears streaming unchecked down her cheeks. He watched helplessly, and tensed when she half rose, as if she intended dashing from the room.

A knock on the door brought him to his

feet, and he went over to open it and breathed an inward sigh of relief when he saw it was Dr. de Wet.

He said softly: "I wanted you to have a look at her face. But she's rather upset just now—"

The doctor looked past him at the weeping girl. "Leave us alone for ten minutes and I'll call you once I've had a look at her and calmed her down."

Karel Meyer nodded and left him and went down the passage to his office. As soon as he shut the door he lit the cigarette his system had been craving for, and crossed over to the chair behind his desk and sank into it with a tired grunt . . . He didn't find it particularly uplifting that he knew from past experience, that the girl would now talk.

He would have to telephone Bessie van Tonder to let her know that he would no longer be able to dine with her and Suzanna . . . Alan Lincoln's body was presenting a problem even for the experienced climbers of the Mountain Club. It had fallen over a second precipice into a particularly inaccessible spot, and it had been decided that no attempt would be made to bring the body up until the morning . . . Meanwhile he must write a full report on the case.

He consulted his watch. If he waited ten more minutes Suzanna should be back and might answer the telephone. He frowned slightly. When the opportunity arose he must suggest that she call him by his Christian name. Each time she addressed him as Lieutenant Meyer, it jarred him almost physically.

His mind switched automatically to Lisa . . . *Lisa.* The kiss had by no means been one-sided. It was strange how a thing like that could suddenly flare up between two people who were not remotely in love. He remembered someone telling him how this same thing had happened to him, and that it had been responsible for wrecking his marriage. The episode had evolved from a set of circumstances, and their situation had been such that it had been easy for them to go to bed. His wife had found out, and had packed her bags and left him. He loved her, but was unable to convince her of this, and nor would she believe that the woman meant nothing to him. He had, in fact, never been near her again . . . He recognised that in the case of Lisa and himself it must have been partly due to the sudden release of mutual tension, and to their complete isolation on the ledge. From his side it had undoubtedly been sparked off by holding her in his arms and looking down on her pale haunted face, which could have been Suzanna's. It was Suzanna whom he had kissed, *she* whom he had clasped in his arms, and *she* whom he had wanted to make love to on the ledge . . . He was in love with her—a girl young enough to be his daughter. He was too old for her. Too set in his ways. Too wedded to his job. Marriage with her could wreck his career. There would be talk, scandal, speculation. His mother always had an ear close to the ground, and Knysna was a small place. She would be among the first to hear the rumours about the baby, and the last woman in the world to accept Suzanna as a daughter-in-law. Viewed from every angle, the marriage must prove disastrous.

He took a final draw on his cigarette and then stubbed it out . . . Suzanna evoked feelings within him which he hadn't known existed. Tenderness, gentleness, protectiveness. He knew that if she should ever come to care for him, he would marry her without hesitation.

He looked up at a knock on the door and called: "Come in," levered himself to his feet when he saw it was Dr. de Wet.

"How is she?" he asked.

"She's better now. I've given her a shot to deaden the pain and calm her down. She'll have to go to hospital. Her nose is broken and her upper lip may have to be stitched. I'd like to call in a plastic surgeon."

"Have you told her this?"

"Yes."

"How did she take it?"

"Apathetically. Almost as if she didn't care. There's a deeper emotional involvement somewhere."

"I had to tell her that her lover's dead . . . It was he who smashed up her face."

The doctor ran a hand over his silver grey hair and puckered up his face in a moue of distaste. "Thank God I'm a doctor and not a policeman . . . She tells me she has no relatives, nor any close friend whom she'd like me to contact. It seems the poor kid is completely alone . . . Is she in any sort of trouble?"

Karel Meyer hunched his shoulders. "Ja, she's in plenty of trouble. But the main thing now is to get her into hospital. Can you fix it right away?"

"Yes."

"OK. You'd better come with me while I have a word with her."

He opened the door, waved a hand for him to go ahead, and followed him out.

Mark drove Lisa home.

He had been silent, slightly withdrawn and had hardly spoken to her. The ordeal Lisa had undergone, terrifying though it had been for her, had in the end affected him the more drastically of the two. He had been compelled to play the role of onlooker. One of scarifying anxiety and alarm, culminating in her scream and the sound of a shot, when he had thought all must be lost. It was an experience from which he must still stage some sort of spiritual recovery.

It was she who broke the silence when they were halfway home. "Mark, I overheard you saying something to Karel about

Lorne's face. Did she fall and hurt herself?"

"I doubt it," he said shortly.

She looked at him searchingly. "If she didn't fall, then how did she get hurt?"

"I'd say her boyfriend beat her up," and immediately regretted having put it so bluntly when she drew in her breath. "I wouldn't let it upset you. When she got in tow with a man of his type, and connived with him to commit murder, she asked for it. As she has asked for everything else that's coming to her."

". . . She loved him," she said in a low voice. "She told me she was madly in love with him. He made her do it."

"That still won't get her out of trouble . . . I suppose he turned on her when he found she had upset his plans. Dealing with the man she was, she can consider herself lucky to be alive."

"You say she deserves everything that's coming to her. What could happen to her?"

"She'll go to prison," he said with characteristic bluntness.

"*Prison!*" she cried out in dismay.

He flickered her a look. "Don't shed any tears on her behalf. Have you forgotten that she was involved in a plot to take your life?''

"I haven't forgotten: but I also remember that she *saved* my live . . . She *did*, Mark,'' she added emotionally when he didn't speak. "She saved my life when she told me to run away, and *he's* dead.'' A sudden thought struck her. "She doesn't know he's dead. Imagine what she'll go through when someone tells her. She'll feel as if she's killed him.''

"For God's sake, don't get involved with her feelings. She doesn't warrant it.''

She said: "The man sat on the ledge staring in front of him . . . I noticed his cheeks were wet . . . I—think he was crying—''

"If he was, then you can be certain they were tears of self-pity. Look, Lisa—''

"If Lorne was responsible for saving my life,'' she interrupted, "surely it must count in her favour?''

"It will, without question. The defence will obviously make the most of it. Her youth will help. And the fact that he was much older, and had already committed two murders. The judge will take all this into consideration. But the fact still remains that she's been guilty of a very serious crime, and the law demands that she must pay for this."

". . . For how long could she be sent to prison?"

He fingered his jaw while he thought it over . . . "Five years, possibly," he said eventually. "But the judge—"

"Five years!"

"You didn't let me finish," he said quietly, hoping to calm her down. "As I said, she could be sentenced to five years, but the judge will almost certainly suspend most of her sentence. She may get away with two years' imprisonment: even one, if she's lucky. This could easily happen if she appeared before Hanley, for instance. He's well known to be compassionate and lenient if the case warrants it." And added with a dry smile: "Particularly if the accused is as young and presentable as she is."

She turned her face away and stared out of the window, thinking of Lorne . . . Her life would be in ruins. Her lover dead. Her reputation gone. A term of imprisonment would spell the end of all her hopes of entering high society . . . What about her face? How badly had he hurt her?

"Did he hurt her badly?" she asked.

"He hurt her all right," he said grimly. "She was hardly recognisable. It wouldn't surprise me if he broke her nose." And wanted to kick himself when she gave a smothered moan. "I shouldn't have told you this. Lisa, try not to let it upset you so much."

"Would you do me a favour?" she asked in a stifled voice.

"Gladly."

"When she stands trial—will you defend her?"

"Yes," he said simply. "If she'll let me."

He swung the car through the gateway to the flats and parked near the entrance. They both got out, and were as silent as before when they climbed the flight of stairs. But this time she handed him the key when they reached the door and he unlocked it, pushed it open and followed her in.

Their proximity now made her feel shy and a little flustered. "Shall I make tea?"

He shut the door. "I wouldn't bother about tea just now. The first thing you should do is to wash all that blood and dirt off your legs, and fix that cut on your arm."

She opened his jacket which she had kept wrapped about her all this time and looked down at her grimy, sweat-stained blouse, her torn skirt, her shredded, blood-soaked tights, as if she had noticed them for the first time. She saw that her nails were chipped and her hands ingrained with dirt. "I'm filthy!"

"Why don't you have a hot bath and get into bed?"

"I'll have the hot bath, if you wouldn't mind waiting. But I won't go to bed yet. I'll think about it after you've gone."

He tossed the keys on to the mahogany table by the door. "I'm not going."

She turned somewhat abruptly and went into the bedroom and shut the door.

Her exit had closely approached flight and made him smile. And the tight cold core in the centre of his being seemed to melt. He prowled round her room not unlike a friendly dog, getting the feel and scent of it. He gazed at her pictures. Scanned the titles of the books on the shelves: eased out *The Prophet* which he had given her before they became engaged and opened it at the fly leaf. "For Lisa, from Mark." Lifted the lid off the cobalt blue toilet-box, turned it over and stared down at it thoughtfully.

He was leaning back in one of the armchairs, eyes closed, smoking a cigarette, when she called that she had finished her bath, and that she had left a towel in the bathroom in case he would like a wash.

When he went into the steamy and scented small pink and white bathroom, he found that she had left not only a towel, but also one of his shirts, neatly folded and placed on the stool. He remembered that she had borrowed it once, and he had told her she could keep it. His jacket was draped over the back of the chair.

He quickly stripped and showered.

He felt a new man when he went back into the livingroom. She had made tea, and the tray stood on the low table in front of the settee, and she was standing in front of the fireplace waiting for him.

She put a hand up to the mantelshelf as he came over to join her. "I've made tea."

"So I see." Looking her over.

She had that clean, scrubbed look. She had brushed her hair until it shone, and it fell in a pale, smooth wing across her left cheek. Her eyes were brighter, and the colour was back in her face, heightening now as he looked at her. She was wearing a patterned deep green and blue midi with little buttons up the front.

"Since when have you and Karel Meyer been on first name terms?" he asked.

She dropped her eyes and smoothed her skirt. "Since we were on the ledge together."

"Did he kiss you, by any chance?"

She stirred uneasily at his perception. "Yes." Looked at him a shade defiantly. "And I kissed him back."

"I suspected as much. I wondered why he had that sheepish air, and why he was so goddamned friendly all of a sudden."

"The kiss meant nothing. It was something to do with the *relief*—and in some way it gave me extra courage to climb up."

"If anyone was entitled to kiss you, he was. I don't begrudge him a kiss provided he doesn't make a habit of it." His eyes went over her. "I like your dress. It suits you, but there are too many buttons to undo." He bent to bring his face closer to hers. "You still smell the same. Didn't you tell me once its called Arpége?"

"No," she said hoarsely, cleared her throat. "You're confusing me with someone else."

"That would hardly be likely." He put out a hand and brushed the wing of hair back from her face. "Let me look at you."

For a second she drew back, stiffened. Then she stood quite still, looking past him.

He traced the scars curving across her cheeks with cool fingertips. "These will fade in time. Didn't the surgeon tell you this?"

She nodded but didn't look at him.

"Now that I know what your face looks like, you can stop hiding it from me. Did you really believe that a few scars across your cheek would stop me loving you?"

She turned to look at him fully, her eyes bright with unshed tears. "I thought it was going to be far worse—you don't know what happened."

"Tell me," he said gently.

"I don't remember the car hitting me. But I must have regained consciousness shortly after it happened . . . It was like waking up, to find myself lying on the ground surrounded by a crowd of people. They were all staring down at me." She drew a deep uneven breath. "A young couple were in front. I remember they both had fair hair, and his was almost as long as hers. She was staring at me with an expression of—horror, as if she couldn't tear her eyes away. I heard her say, "Oh God, look at her face!" and she quickly turned and hid her face against the boy's shoulder, and he—put his arm around her." Her face had become pale and strained . . . "I realised she was talking about me, and put my hand up to feel my face. I—" She stopped and swallowed. "I could feel teeth, and something below my left eye which felt like splintered b-bone . . . I could feel no *flesh*. . . I—I—"

He gave a sort of groan and caught her to him. "God in heaven, why didn't you tell me? Had I failed to convince you that I loved you?"

"I was so sure that I would be dreadfully disfigured. I wouldn't believe Robert or the surgeon. I believed them even less after the first plastic operation. My face was hideous—*grotesque*."

He kissed her.

After a time he loosened his arms. "You've been coming between me and my work and my sleep. And God knows, I can't afford it. I can't possibly go on like this. I'm giving you one of two choices. Either we get married at once, or I move in with you. Take your pick."

"Mark, your mother doesn't like me," she said with seeming irrelevance.

"My mother has allowed her maternal instincts to get the better of her judgment. She has always liked you. And once she knows your reason for breaking off our engagement, I have no doubt that she'll be far more sympathetic and understanding than I could ever be." The anger still within him that she could have doubted his love for her. Thinking too of what she must have suffered. Not only the physical pain, but the mental anguish as well. The loneliness she had chosen to inflict upon herself. He tightened his arms. "Well, what are we going to do? Get married at once, or live in sin?"

". . . You've always said that your mother has a Victorian outlook. I don't think she'd approve if you moved in with me—"

"Agreed. So you have, in fact, no choice at all. We'll get married at once. There'll be no honeymoon, I'm afraid. I'm snowed under until the end of the year. We'll have one then."

"Mark, I don't think your mother would approve of a hurried marriage either. She might think—"

"I'll see about a special licence tomorrow, and I'll give Karel a ring in the morning. I'd like him to be there if he can make it."

"Darling, don't you think we should wait just—"

"No."

"But—"

"Don't argue." He kissed her again.

She said a little breathlessly when she got her mouth free: "Do you always make up your mind in such a hurry?"

He suddenly smiled "Yes," he said "When I know what I want."

THE END

This book is published under the
auspices of the
ULVERSCROFT FOUNDATION,
a registered charity, whose primary object is to assist those who experience difficulty in reading print of normal size.

In response to approaches from the medical world, the Foundation is also helping to purchase the latest, most sophisticated medical equipment desperately needed by major eye hospitals for the diagnosis and treatment of eye diseases.

If you would like to know more about the
ULVERSCROFT FOUNDATION,
and how you can help to further its work,
please write for details to:

THE ULVERSCROFT FOUNDATION
The Green, Bradgate Road
Anstey
Leicestershire
England

GUIDE
TO THE COLOUR CODING
OF
ULVERSCROFT BOOKS

Many of our readers have written to us expressing their appreciation for the way in which our colour coding has assisted them in selecting the Ulverscroft books of their choice.

To remind everyone of our colour coding—
this is as follows:

BLACK COVERS
Mysteries

★

BLUE COVERS
Romances

★

RED COVERS
Adventure Suspense and General Fiction

★

ORANGE COVERS
Westerns

★

GREEN COVERS
Non-Fiction

We hope this Large Print edition gives you the pleasure and enjoyment we ourselves experienced in its publication.

There are now more than 1,600 titles available in this ULVERSCROFT Large Print Series. Ask to see a Selection at your nearest library.

The Publisher will be delighted to send you, free of charge, upon request a complete and up-to-date list of all titles available.

Ulverscroft Large Print Books Ltd.
The Green, Bradgate Road
Anstey
Leicestershire
England